About e Series

Can fiction become fact?

Advanced technology threatens to control every aspect of our lives—from elections to wars, cars to societal safety—the Max Revenge series plunges readers into the dark underworld of hacking, misinformation, and cybercrime. Thoroughly researched and chillingly realistic, these technothrillers explore what's possible today and, more alarmingly, what could unfold tomorrow.

Reading a Max Revenge book is like getting a glimpse of tomorrow's headlines—Anthony Silman's gripping tales of technological warfare, AI manipulation, and state-sponsored cyberattacks expose the cracks in Western society's digital defences. His stories reveal a future where social media becomes a weapon, AI dictates reality, and chaos reigns as international fake news overwhelms the truth.

With sharp wit and electrifying prose, Max Revenge delivers both thrills and terror, as readers from around the globe can confirm. Each novel is as gripping as it is prophetic, weaving a narrative that is as fascinating as it is frighteningly plausible.

This is the sixth Max story and as before it is imagined but based on known facts and occurrences.

Max Deepfake Revenge

Max Bomber Revenge

Max Crypto Revenge

Max AI Chatbot Revenge

Max Cyber Terror Revenge

Max Russian Revenge

MAX RUSSIAN REVENGE

ANTHONY SILMAN

This edition first published in paperback by
Michael Terence Publishing in 2024
www.mtp.agency

Disclaimer:
This story is fiction. It contains information and ideas which some readers may find unsettling. Please be aware that all names, characters, circumstances, discussions and incidents portrayed in this technothriller novel are fictitious. No identification or opinion about or with actual persons (living or deceased), places, buildings, beliefs, ideologies and products is intended or should be inferred.

ISBN 9781800949027

Front cover image (AI)
by Michael Terence Publishing

Michael Terence
Publishing

1

Max's eyes scanned the road as he rounded a long bend. To his left and some five metres below him lay a concrete car park at the foot of a vertical grassy bank. To his right, some beautiful, old and very solid trees bordered the oncoming carriageway, oaks he thought. Further ahead, coming towards him in the middle distance, travelled a dark blue family saloon car; a man driving, a woman in the passenger seat and, he was sure, two children in the back.

It took him under fifteen milli-seconds to absorb this visual information before his eyes pin-pointed, his muscles tensed, and his right foot stamped on the brake with a strength only available to those about to die. A surreal slow motion engulfed his car, and his world imploded in a violent crescendo.

Between him and the family saloon, had raced a sports car, roof down, the driver's head just visible above the steering wheel which, to Max's careening mind, appeared on the wrong side of the car. Oh God, the car was on the wrong side of the road, his side of the road and speeding directly at him. His subconscious decisions clashed, to crash dive into the car park below meant instant death, likewise, the unyielding oaks to his right. Swerving to avoid the sports car would slaughter an entire family.

No time for fear or mortal panic for what was it, a nano-second? One, two? Reality ceased as Max's car shuddered under its heavy anti-lock braking and smashed head-on into the hurtling sports car.

All Max could remember was the percussive, explosive, deafening cacophony of the crash, the tearing metal and his multiple airbags detonating. On impact, he felt no pain, nothing but intense, invasive sound. He couldn't say for sure if he had stayed conscious, or if time had stopped or accelerated. He didn't know if his mental stock-take of limbs and movement was accurate or if one of his legs deceived him about its well-being or his ribs were fibbing about remaining safe and intact in their usual location. He remembered hearing the sirens; feeling uncomfortable and oddly positioned in his car. He had vague recollections of what seemed like pillows in his face, by his ears and even on his knees. Very odd.

A face appeared. Not the face of an angel, Max thought, feeling somehow short-changed. It peered at him, looking concerned and friendly. The face's lips moved but Max could hear only a constant, consuming reverberating ringing. The face smiled at him. Hands moved his arms and legs. He felt affronted by this manipulation. Away from the acrid stench of fuel and burnt rubber and the acute discomfort of his driver's seat, Max felt relief as lying flat on a stretcher, he relished fresh air and the surging, comforting, drug-induced warmth which invaded his mind and body. Tranquillity followed, a soft, gentle peace as he believed he was in transition from the earthly world to what? Where? Who cared…

The next thing he remembered was not wanting to open his eyes; he didn't want reality to return. He yearned for that comforting morphine-induced nirvana. He didn't want his ears to hear, he had grown used to the isolation created by constant echoing, jarring noise.

"Come on Max, time to wake up now. Max? Max, time to wake up, come on now."

Gradually, unwillingly, he felt his senses seeping back. Everything hurt, some parts more than others. His inventory started at his toes, and he intended to work his way upwards. Yes, toes ok, now knees. Uh-oh.

"Here you are Max, a nice cup of tea."

Tea? A nice cup of tea? His disorientated mind struggled. What the fuck? I've been trampled by several elephants, I'm in agony and all I get is a nice cup of tea. You think I'm waking up for that?

Then he felt more hands easing him upwards, adjusting his body's odd position, one leg out straight, the other hanging in mid-air, numb and unmoving. His eyes slowly focussed on the cup being offered to him. Cup and a straw? He tried to lick his lips but felt only a rough, dry, unfamiliar texture. A hand inserted the straw between the bandages and into his sore lips. As he sipped, slowly at first and then thirstily, his mind began to make sense of what had happened.

Car crash? Yes. The left-hand drive Mazda sports car had smashed into the right of his Audi. Front, side and knee airbags deployed; the car's crumple zone kept his driving position intact but the pressure waves of such a ferocious impact caused unavoidable injury. His brain had been flung against his cranium, and forced under enormous pressure into the seatbelts, several of his ribs had cracked and broken. His right femur, tensed and rigid against the brake pedal, stood no chance and snapped halfway along its shaft as the shockwave stresses hit it.

He could see bandaging all over his body and felt the dressing around his face and over his head. Tubes radiated from him; he had a cannula on the back of his left hand and one on the inside of his elbow joint, a small nozzle in each nostril. Max was too nervous to move any further from the semi-reclining position he had been given.

More tests, blood pressure, pulse, and oxygen saturation, all noted by jolly, smiling intensive care nurses whose confident demeanour did more for Max in those frightening early moments of recovery than any drug could achieve.

"How're ya feelin' Max?" enquired a nurse who would have looked more at home on a rugby pitch.

"Well," answered Max feeling that he should be as positive as possible, "I think I'm probably a damn site better than I might look?"

"Ah now, isn't that the truth." Her slight Irish lilt sounded oddly reassuring. "By any measure, you should be with your maker…"

Reassuring?

"But then you got lucky and had Mr Barrington do the job on ya, so you'll be just marvellous now, sure you will."

"Mr Barrington?"

"Oh yes, we like him here, a proper job doc he is, none of your flouncy prima donna acts with him and as an orthopaedic surgeon, well, his work is nothing short of spectacular. You done good when you came in and got him to put you back together again. You've all your bits back in their right places, looks like that anyway."

Max smiled, wondering how much of his smile was visible through the bandages.

After an hour or so, interspersed by short, light-heart interchanges with the nurses doing his frequent observations, Max felt almost alive again and slightly excitable which, he concluded, might be the after-effect of the fentanyl or some other component of his anaesthesia. From post-operative intensive care, they wheeled him to Olderbury General Hospital's high-dependency ward where they told him he would stay for a day or two before being transferred to a longer-term ward.

His heart palpitated with pleasure. Amanda, his Mrs Golby, wife of all wives, had been allowed into this usually visitor-free zone. He saw the shock on her face, the face he loved, he felt her fear at seeing him in such a broken and dependent state.

"I don't care how much you plead and beg, I'm not dancing," he said, realising again how sore a smile could be.

"You silly bugger, you frightened the shit out of me, out of all of us! What do you think you're doing, crashing into cars? It's not a video game you know!"

"Wasn't me, Miss, 'onest, wasn't my fault, it was the other bugger, 'onest."

"I know, the traffic boys told me all about it. You had witnesses, so you're completely in the clear, just in case you were wondering."

"I wasn't actually, my brain aches so much and I can still hear that ringing sound so I'm not thinking about anything much."

"I'm not surprised, you've got a mild concussion. Why it's only mild I don't know. By the state of your car, you're bloomin' lucky to have any mind at all."

"So, I gather. Look, have you spoken to anyone, you know, like what's happened to me? I've only spoken to the recovery nurses - utterly wonderful but not very forthcoming."

"I've had a quick chat with a young chap called Adrian who, I think, assisted the surgeon who operated on you. He described your condition as, and I quote, 'a bit second hand', that you have, as you know, concussion. They will scan but they don't think it's anything too serious."

"That's good news, I suppose. What else did he say?"

"Well, headline news and it comes with a clue, you know, like your leg being hoisted aloft like that, is that you've broken a femur which, Adrian said, went back together pretty much ok. They have had to put a metal rod down the centre of the bone to keep it straight while it knits together again which, he says, will happen over the next six weeks or so of traction. It will take a bit longer than that before you'll be able to walk on it again, three months I'd say, with the help of some physio and all that."

"Ok, I see, could have been worse, I suppose. What else? I mean is there anything else I should know about?"

"Max, as far as I know, they are mainly concerned about your head and leg. You've got some broken ribs which they tell me will hurt like stink but not for too long and you've got all manner of cuts, abrasions and bruising all over you, especially on your head and face which is why you are wrapped up like an Egyptian mummy."

"Don't you worry now," said a senior nurse, appearing beside Amanda. "We've got him safe and sound and he'll be just fine in no time at all. Mr Barrington will be along soon, so, now I need Max, just a check to see if have you passed urine? Have you managed a wee do you think?"

"Time for me to go," grinned Amanda.

"Bloody hell, Mand, I've even got a tube stuck up the old fella. I mean, how embarrassing."

Two hours later, Ben Barrington got around to Max, who by then felt off-colour and tired; the good spirits he enjoyed with Amanda, replaced with aches, pains and a malaise of body and mood. The surgeon explained at some length the nature of his injuries and the anticipated schedule of recovery. Max replied with his customary good humour, although it took a great deal of effort to maintain the illusion.

Just as he looked as though he was about to leave, Ben Barrington paused and added, "I remember you; you know. One of my colleagues treated you after some madman blasted you with, if I remember correctly, a motorbike-mounted blunderbuss shotgun."

Max smiled in confirmation, feeling so tired now that even that was an effort.

"And I see from your records that we treated you for bomb blast injuries too when some gang or other tried to blow up the Onetelcall offices."

Max made one more effort, but the smile was thin.

"Interesting life you lead," laughed Barrington as he walked away, half turning to add, "I need to talk to you about something I'm worried about, not you, I didn't mean that, no, not about you but about our hospital and why someone is trying to sabotage our IT systems."

Is there no fuckin' rest? thought Max as he drifted into a deep, restorative sleep.

2

John and Pauline Harrison were a popular couple in their village. As smaller-scale farmers, they worked long, hard hours to make a living and were forced to find new enterprises, at least to make their books balance or, even better, make an acceptable profit from all their invested labour and capital. With just under two hundred acres and a herd of sixty, high-yielding Holstein milking cattle, they were fortunate to be close to a dairy and benefit from an affordable bulk collection service. They had also developed a direct delivery round and an on-farm and in-store refillable bottle milk dispensary.

John, a stubbly, square-jawed, solid farmer, strong in arm and resolve, loved his cows almost as much as he loved his wife and children. His dream was to create a predictable, secure livelihood from his farm, just as his father, grandfather and great-grandfather had dreamed of. More than half of his farm fell within the county council's regional plan. Nobody quite knew what the regional plan might be, but they were told quite emphatically where it would be. John had tried to find out more, but the planning department officials were practised and skilled in dodging questions. They were even more adept at side-stepping any attempts by residents to quiz them face to face, to talk by phone, or to be contacted by email or be held to account by anyone, anywhere at any time. The elected councillors had, long ago, given up attempts to persuade the paid officials to be more helpful to the public, or customers as county residents were sometimes ironically described. Officials stridently defined their defence with many factors in the not-my-responsibility vein, eventually overwhelming all the councillors' efforts.

John knew this first hand. He wished he had a job without accountability which carried a generous pension package, but he was a farmer and couldn't aspire to such benefits. He knew his job was all about responsibility and liability and would never carry any pension packages paid by the public purse, the same purse which swallowed a significant percentage of any profit he might make. His county councillor, Tim Turner, shared John's frustration about the fate of a large chunk of his land but could do no more than sympathise.

"The deal is this, John," he said, "the council is deeply divided about almost everything except about what little power we actually have and how little control we can command over those who are supposed to deliver the decisions we make. They are buggers, John. If they like it, they do it, if they don't, well, they don't and won't, nothing we can do."

"Good job you're not an MP," laughed John. "If you can't manage at a local level, how would you get on at a national level with all those departments and factional interests?"

"Same as the current MPs; can't be done. The cogs drive the engine these days mate and that's a fact."

"I shouldn't complain, well, I'm not really. I have this beautiful farm, my cows, my family and a life I would never change for anything, not even money but I just wish I could do some future planning with a little more certainty, not only about the regional plan but, you know, generally; but I expect most people who aren't in government pay feel like me."

"You still thinking about expanding the herd then, John?"

"Yeah, it crosses my mind and if I could be sure that John Junior wants to be a dairy farmer when he grows up, I'd do so without hesitation. But, on the other hand, I've got over a hundred and twenty acres or so of tip-top grazing, more than enough for my herd as it is, which means I've got quite a bit of land, goodish land certainly, but not quite the best, to use for something else or even, if circumstances dictate as the children get older, to sell, see what I mean?"

"So, let me see. I'll bet the land you'd sell is the land that falls within our regional development plan, yeah?"

"Yeah."

"And that's why you want to know more detail about this plan, yeah?

"Yeah."

"Well, I wish I could tell you."

"Thanks."

The two men laughed as John, always pleased to have some company after a typically lonely farmer's day, opened a bottle of scotch.

"You must have an idea what this wretched regional plan is about, Tim, for heaven's sake. It is the product of your council and your fellow members' combined wisdom."

"All I can say is that we discussed and agreed on outline limits for areas which could be used for development, some for residential and some for light industrial or retail. I know some councillors, those with pound signs in their eyes, would like to see a retail park on the outskirts of Olderbury but I don't see that happening, too much opposition, and too much competition. The Green Valley Park does impressively well anyway, so there isn't really a need."

"Thank God for that. We get lots of residents' traffic from Olderbury coming through here to go to Green Valley and it's great that we do, some of them stop off to buy real, fresh milk and other stuff, you know, cottage cheese, ice cream, farm-churned butter and all that and we'd lose a lot of that if another retail outlet came along."

"Would you consider renting a bit of land out to someone who, I don't know, wants to start some countryside endeavour, a livery or run a riding school or whatever?"

"I would, Tim, yes, I would. I've thought about it before. I even thought about creating some sort of light usage units over by Parkside where I could easily run in some power, water, drainage and all that but I've never done anything about it because, and you'll love this, I don't think I can bear all the hoops I'd have to go through to get planning and usage permissions."

"Ha, I can understand that. It's a bloody minefield and you'd have so many officers to deal with, you know, planning, commercial, environment, infrastructure, services, countryside, agricultural, highways, oh, a whole bloody posse of them."

"Nothing you could do to help an old mate?"

"You're a good chap, John, handy with the scotch bottle too," he offered his glass for a refill, "but I've made it a rule not to help friends unless their request is one I could support, even if they weren't friends if you see what I'm saying."

"I do, Tim, I do and I think all the more of you for it, but if my request was just what I've described, some light usage units, a bit of an entrance and driveway, yard and weight-limited truck areas and so on, with all the bells and whistles for broadband, security and so on, what would you say?"

"I'd say I'd back you all the way. I can't see anyone objecting except, perhaps the folk in the Parkview cottages and the people who live on the road from the top of your farm to Olderbury and, to be honest, I don't think any of them would object unless you wanted to build a damn great factory or distribution warehouse, which you don't. What I do know, John, as you do, is that a few of the Parkside people would love to have a crack at any part-time work your units might bring with them."

"Hmm, I agree, and the thing about factories or warehouses is why I suggested a truck size and weight limit. I reckon that would remove at least one reason to object and the prospect of creating a few jobs would easily outweigh any others I can foresee."

"Any man who thinks he can foresee objections is either Nostra-bloody-damus or a complete fucking idiot. Oh, sorry Pauline, I didn't hear you come in, so sorry about the language."

"I've heard worse, Tim. I heard worse from the kids the moment they started school." Pauline laughed happily. She liked the honest and efficient councillor, he was a refreshing change from the walking egos and opportunists who made up so much of most councils, she thought.

"I heard the bit about John's ideas for creating some units up by Parkside and, I didn't tell you John did I, when I was delivering to Mary's Café, she was talking to a man who was asking about somewhere to house his new business. So, naturally, I jumped in and asked him what he was looking for and he described almost exactly the sort of unit you've been rattling on about."

"Get his name, did you?"

"Duh, poor little Pauline, silly little girl, shouldn't be allowed out on her own…"

"Sorry love, let me put it another way, did you get his name?"

"Yes, John, yes, I did. Not only that, I offered to help him in his new venture. He seemed like the sort of man who would appreciate my contribution, instead of continually taking the mickey like others I could mention."

"Good looking is he, this new captain of industry?"

"John, in comparison my love, let's face it, so many men are…"

"Yeah, yeah, see what I have to put up with Tim?" grinned John, his arm lovingly wrapped around his wife's waist, "nothing but insults and constant condemnation, I don't know how I tolerate it."

"You're a lucky man, John."

"I know it, chap."

"Tell me, Pauline, did your new friend tell you what sort of business he is starting?"

"He did actually Tim, yes, because I was delivering foody type stuff, well butter and soft cheese, he immediately piped up about how people should be offered more natural foods which are good for them rather than the ultra-processed high fat, sugar, salt and noxious chemicals that the food industry chucks at us all the time."

"Good man, well said."

"I thought you'd think that John, that's why I said we'd help him if we can. He's not ready to get going yet so his timing and ours, if we go ahead with any units, might work well and he could, I thought, have an opportunity to be in on our early plans so he gets exactly what he wants and needs. What do you think?"

"I'd say we should have a bit of supper with him and, if you would Tim, with you too, so we could scribble down some early thoughts which would work for your man, us and for the council too. What do you think?"

"Ok by me, John, I'd enjoy that, and Pauline is such a brilliant cook, I'm always game on for supper with you two."

"You always manage to say the right thing, Tim, no wonder you are a politician and, look, bring Estelle with you and I'll invite Adam and whoever might be his significant other."

Farmer John + Wife Pauline asking for developing some land for small unit

3

Melor looked in the mirror and chuckled to himself. According to popular belief, he didn't exist. Could he be some sort of avatar, or perhaps a bot, or the creation of some extraordinarily talented hacking group? Melor was Bogdan Belov's creation, his alter ego and he was amazed that it had caused so much speculation.

Bogdan's history was confined to the suburbs of Moscow, an area of its hinterland known for high-priced comfortable houses, glamourous Mosfilm studios and the famous Moscow State University. He had been educated at Moscow's School 57 and won a place at the city's State University, also known as Lomonosov University, just a couple of kilometres from his home. Professionally, he aspired to be the world's most revered hacker. To do this, Bogdan preferred an alias, and he had chosen a name which reflected his commitment to communism and his admiration for the old Soviet rule. He chose 'Melor', a boy's acronymic name commemorating the former soviet state, derived from Marx, Engels, Lenin and the October Revolution.

As Melor, he had no past because he had no present, just a mystical, mythological power over any cyber target that took his fancy. As Bogdan, he attained multiple degrees and qualifications in computer sciences, IT infrastructures, networking security, digital engineering, artificial intelligence studies and quantum technologies. He went on to work in an exclusive wing of Moscow's Central Clinical Hospital as a central systems programmer.

In retrospect, Bogdan might have agreed that he had an inflated sense of self-worth, not just for remuneration but for approbation too. He wasn't getting enough of either. It was then that the Melor persona started to take over from Bogdan. He'd show them, he'd prove his value and he was, he thought, in the perfect place to do it. Also known as the Kremlin Hospital and set in beautiful woodland just fourteen miles from the Kremlin, the facility was heavily guarded and, surprisingly for a communist state, extremely expensive. It catered privately for politicians, high-ranking diplomats, state officials and wealthy individuals who could afford it. For those in the know, it was also a place to be avoided if people in power had taken against you. A critic of the regime unexpectedly died after falling from the sixth floor of the hospital. Nobody asked how, everyone knew why.

There could be no doubt that the Central Clinical Hospital of the Administrative Directorate of the Russian Federation had a high profile, and those whose jobs and lives depended on its unsurpassable reputation knew no limits in maintaining its elevated image. Melor's myth started there. He could and would insert a small bug, just a line or two of malignant code, into the recently built fifty-million-dollar Kremlin wing's communication system, a system reserved for exclusive service of the president, prime minister and senior government personnel. In what he believed to be an example of cunning-in-action, Melor would wait for the system fault to be discovered and, heroically, step in to put in an immediate fix. They'd know his true worth then.

Melor's malignant bug, intended to cause arbitrary stoppages in the VIP pharmaceuticals order system for medical and recreational products, remained frustratingly undiscovered for too long and Melor began to worry. Could it be that his code would be responsible for the incorrect medication of one of his country's leaders? Still young and callow, Melor could feel his feet cooling like a Siberian escapee in prison socks; he could stand the strain no longer.

Vasily Vassiliev, Bogdan's boss's boss was not answerable to the hospital management committee, he was a major in Russia's FSB, the Federal Security Service and an important, influential man in the country's computer intelligence network, including, unusually, being an adviser to both the SVR and MVR, the foreign intelligence and internal affairs agencies. Bogdan had admitted what he'd done to his immediate boss who immediately reported the incident to Vasily Vassiliev, confidently expecting Bogdan to be detained for questioning and punishment.

"This young man has endangered our magnificent leaders and interfered with the security of our vital systems," explained Bogdan's boss in what Vasily thought was a snivelly, sanctimonious way.

Vasily, not that he could admit it, was vaguely amused by the audacity of the young programmer's attempt at stardom and summoned him to his office. Bogdan, hollow, cold and shaking, anxiously anticipated his meeting with the impressive Major. Fearing for his future and then, with an inner resolve he didn't know he possessed, Bogdan faced his inquisitor.

"Major Vassiliev, you now know what I did but permit me, please, to tell you why I did it before you pass judgment on me. I am honoured to work in such a prestigious location and I take my work very seriously. Despite my abilities and my knowledge, my prowess is subdued by oppressive management, so much so that I knew I had to make a statement by action, a statement which would show those superior to my immediate managers that I, Bogdan Belov can offer so much more. Major Vassiliev, my country is all to me, I can serve my country so much better, but my abilities will never be available for higher purposes for as long as my work is buried here. I plead with you to give me an opportunity to show you, show my country, how much I can do for our greater good."

A tough climb up the ranks of the Federation's more secret services had taught Vasily Vassiliev to be hard and pragmatic. He was habitually immune to appeals to his better nature; he no longer had one. He walked around Bogdan closely, to be intimidating, emulating scenes he'd seen in old spy movies.

He stood behind Bogdan and whispered in his ear, "I hear your juvenile plea, I hear that you want to serve Russia but what I know is different, what I know is that you jeopardised the safety of this important hospital, the hospital which might, one day be needed by our president. Do you, Bogdan Belov, think that your pathetic ego is more important than the good health of our leader?" Vasily stopped speaking abruptly and moved to be face to face with Bogdan, very closely face to face.

"Major, please understand, it was never my intention to risk anybody's well-being. I expected my demonstration to be noticed in minutes and I would have fixed it in an instant; nobody was ever at any risk, I promise you and if our leader, the President himself, had been a patient you must know, you have to know, I could never, ever do anything to endanger him or the country I love so much."

"You are an ill-disciplined whelp with an ego which far exceeds your relevance. If everyone who believes that they are better than others were to sabotage their workplaces there would be chaos and disaster. And you stand here now, expecting me to be impressed by your display of ingenuity and bravado? Well, you cocky little whelp, I am not impressed by you or your stunt, in fact, quite the reverse. Do you understand what that means? It means that life as you know it has just ended. I am not sending you to Black Dolphin or White Swan, prisons where I don't think you would survive. This, I must tell you, is a great concession from me, because a corrective colony is where you ought to be. But then, would a general prison be the appropriate justice for you? The FKU Corrective Colony number 6, you know of this I expect, it is where the traitor Navalny was kept for some considerable time, is certainly where you should live and almost certainly die. I shall decide."

Bogdan was about to protest at this description of Navalny who, like many Russians who favoured free speech, he regarded as a brave voice of opposition where opposition was harshly, brutally, even lethally discouraged. His better judgement told him to say nothing; he was in dire danger, and he knew it.

The Major continued, "You could insist on a hearing at district court but this would be foolhardy, as I can assure you a prison sentence would be handed to you with no appeal and Siberia would be your home for many years to come, do you understand me? I hope you do, I hope you see the wisdom of accepting my decision, if I make such a choice, to allow you to serve your punishment in a general prison and not a Corrective Colony. What is your view Belov, do you have anything to say?"

"Major Vassiliev, I concede that I am, what did you say, yes, cocky and a whelp. I do accept that my belief in what I can offer my country led me to actions which were ill-advised at best, not dangerous, not risky, honestly not that, never that but stupid nonetheless."

"Is that it, whelp? You say nothing to make me decide?"

"I fully understand that I am in no position to negotiate, Major, but may I make a suggestion, please? May I suggest that you extract reparation from me, whether whilst I'm incarcerated or not, by way of my developing something of real value for my country, something which will add extra power or new techniques to the Federation in its glorious battle against the West and all the evil that the West delivers to our doorstep? I mean, why lock me up and get nothing when you could use me and let me astonish you with what I know I can do."

It was then that Vasily's pragmatism kicked in. Deep in thought, he paced around the small, windowless interview room, brushing his fingertips along the sheen of the old grey paint flaking off the walls.

At last, he spoke again. "There was a time when you would have been shot for such impudent insurrection. There was a later time when you would have been imprisoned without appeal for a very long time, perhaps for life, in one of our penal colonies. Now, I fear Russia is softening like the decadent West you hate so much, as do I. I regret the march of liberalism and the fistless glove but, for once, I can see an advantage in allowing you to prove your point. So Belov, I have made a decision, and I say this, I say you will be held under a restrictive order to return to the computer science laboratory of the Moscow Institute of Physics and Technology, where our research into Artificial Intelligence, as you know I expect, is currently proceeding. There you will have three months to prove your worth. If you succeed, you will be absolved of all charges and allowed to continue with your work. If you fail, well, just don't fail Belov, you won't live long in prison, if the TB doesn't get you, the other inmates will."

Bogdan Belov's creation Melor.

(Marx, Engels Lenin October Revolution)

A small bug in the Hospital system.

4

Adam Huddard had no time for pretence. Business Development Manager? Customer Services Executive? Not Adam, "I'm a rep, nothing more, nothing less, just a salesman."

At school, his careers officer had suggested retail or hotel management, but Adam wasn't interested. He liked parties, girls, drinks, football and laughing. He liked lots of things, but he didn't like the thought of work, not real work. Reluctantly, he took a job with his hometown's largest office supplies company where, for three surprisingly happy years, he learned a lot about business equipment, from copiers to small and medium enterprise-level computers, printers and peripherals. He learned even more about the art and psychology of selling.

When a wealthy entrepreneur started a new higher-level computing sales and support business in the area, Adam jumped at its opportunities. The company offered him a sales job with a good salary and high commission which he executed with energy, creativity and increasingly advanced knowledge. He became known as RiteByte's Mr Right and enjoyed a long and stable relationship with the founder, and everyone involved with the company.

Eventually, RiteByte was sold for multi-millions to a US capital fund. They assured Adam his job would continue or, alternatively, offered him a redundancy option with a generous, life-enhancing lump sum. Adam walked away with a bulging bank account and a mind brimming with ideas.

Over the years, Adam, once married and now divorced, had become comfortable in his bachelor lifestyle. His freedom meant he could travel as he wished, drive the car he wanted, buy the home he desired and answer to nobody. But there was a snag; age had crept upon him and all the things he thought he'd always wanted to do or own no longer seemed so irresistible. He preferred the easier access of SUVs to squatting and squeezing into low sports cars. He had lost his travel lust, finding that flying had become a tawdry affair in comparison with the halcyon days of expenses-paid business class. He was so settled and rested in his flat that the thought of moving into somewhere grander filled him with dread.

Adam had, however, become an ardent advocate for healthy eating and the effect of what we feed into our gut has on our daily well-being and performance abilities. Ah ha, his fertile and agile mind said to him, let's do this. Let's make a business bringing healthy foods into the UK from their places of origin, Japan, Malaysia, Indonesia, India and wherever delicious, healthy produce might be found.

He was as excited again now as he had been when he first started selling photocopiers. Adam had enjoyed those days and found he had a knack for getting past buyers' gatekeepers, such as receptionists and personal assistants, enabling him to bring in some of the biggest sales in those early, formative years. During that time, he had also learned all about effective, effortless lines of least resistance from his more indolent but surprisingly successful colleagues.

His new enterprise would, he decided, be as streamlined as possible, sacrificing a little profit for outsourcing some of the more onerous tasks to specialists. He would source the goods personally, oversee the branding and marketing and identify the various routes to market and strategic partnerships necessary to reach the niche customers he sought. The import, packing, order-taking and deliveries would be expedited by one of the online shopping giants which excelled at such services.

Of course, he would need premises. He knew that if he tried to start up at home, he'd give in to passing temptations and indulgencies before working as hard as he knew he needed to. Meeting Pauline Harrison was, he thought, divine intervention, or fortuitous at least. He could use a sensible, dependable assistant and the redoubtable farmer's wife appealed to him on all practical and commercial levels. He had explained his simple needs from a business unit to her. He'd need about two hundred square meters of warehousing with decent access, loading and parking for deliveries and, of course, sufficient office space and facilities, including high-speed fibre optic broadband connection. He'd need a kitchen and a cook too, if she might be interested.

Pauline had agreed that his wish list would be a common specification; his requirements were something she and John could describe to architects and the various planning officials in their bid to progress the development. As she had offered to help Adam in his new adventure, so Adam offered to do all he could to help her and John get their plans off the ground. More than that, Adam caught that unmistakable whiff of opportunity and offered to become a co-funder of the project.

The prospect of having a healthy upfront cash injection appealed to the permanently cash-strapped and generally risk-averse Pauline who, making it clear that she would need her husband's acquiescence, intimated that some equity deal, balancing the value of the land against the amount of Adam's investment could, no doubt, be agreed. Adam understood Pauline's willingness. Land values had increased dramatically over the last two years and now, if she and her husband earmarked some twenty acres for the new units and essential services, Adam would need to throw in an amount around two hundred thousand pounds if a fifty-fifty deal were to be struck.

Even so, it appealed to Adam. What, he asked himself, could he get for that sort of money? One good-ish classic Ferrari? A handful of luxurious cruises? No, this deal had a lot to recommend, including a useful, reassuring secondary income, just in case.

"Adam," he answered his phone to a distantly familiar voice.

"It's Pauline, you know Pauline Harrison, we met at Mary's Café, yes?"

"Yes, of course I remember. How could I not? How lovely to hear from you."

"Good, well, look, John and I wondered if you'd like to come to the farm for dinner? It would be you, me and John, a chap called Tim Turner, that's Councillor Tim Turner and his wife Estelle and, oh, your, er, wife or whoever, you know, if there's someone, you'd like to bring with you. I do hope you can make it, say Thursday evening? Nothing posh, just my simple supper, I'm afraid."

"I already know it will be delicious and I'd love to come and, in answer to your unasked question, I'm no longer married so I'll just come along on my own if that's ok, doesn't unbalance the table too much?"

"I've never had a balanced table, Adam, never even thought about it. We aren't that sophisto down on the farm you know."

Adam could hear the slight mickey-taking tone in her voice and chuckled in reply.

Adam Huddard
Sales exec - retired
buying into Pauline
o. John's farm project

5

Max had endured two days in the high-dependency unit before being transferred to an orthopaedic ward where he spent his first night in an observation bed before being wheeled into a room of his own where he would stay for the weeks ahead. The first week passed in a semi-stupor induced by pain management drugs, muscle relaxants and antibiotics. His ribs hurt no matter which way he turned, although, with one leg suspended in traction, any turning was restricted.

The usually active Max reflected on how quickly he was becoming institutionalised. His days, every day, began at five-thirty with morning observations and, soon after settling in and becoming friendly with the rota of nurses, he was then presented with a considerate pre-breakfast cup of tea. A cheery 'hello dear', irritatingly cheery sometimes, came next from either Pru or Evelyn who chattered away happily while taking Max's daily menu selections. Max was in two minds about whether to eat anything. On the positive side, the hospital food was quite tasty, on the downside came the resultant embarrassment and ignominy of the bedpan.

The standard early morning ward round by Ben, Adrian or another of the orthopaedic team, which, to Max, demanded that he bed-washed and shaved, it seemed important to him somehow, was the zenith of the hospital morning regime, after which Max had an opportunity to snooze and make up for the early start. Apart from the very occasional excitement of being wheeled to an MRI scan or x-ray, Max's days became tediously repetitive, until visiting time. Initially, only Amanda was allowed to visit him and then, as his strength grew, many of his Onetelcall colleagues took it in turns to do the grape run, as it became known, not that many took grapes to him.

Max was a director of Onetelcall, a foremost IT security company which provided its global customers with a range of services ensuring computing and networking safety and continuance of service against an increasing number of cyber threats. The company had been started by a genius who proved to be a psychopathic criminal too. Spray Wilson had developed a suite of IT security products, from impregnable exclusive chipsets through to hardware and networking items which quickly won worldwide approbation from big companies and became a grand challenge to the most talented industry miscreants. Throughout the dark world of state-sponsored malware, ransomware, phishing and denial of service and the myriad evil attacks that have propagated from Russia, China, Iran and all the other major suspects, Onetelcall had become a hated beacon of Western resistance and fortitude.

Max had first met Spray at a conference in Amsterdam where, after much 'Jonge Geneva' and not much less 'Paddo', the Dutch coffee shop menu listing for magic mushroom, he had been captivated by the charismatic IT virtuoso and easily duped into working for Onetelcall in Olderbury where Spray used him as a conduit for handling imported drugs. Filled with remorse at his innocent but guilty actions at his new boss's behest, Max subsequently spent many years making restitution and supporting rehab facilities and as Onetelcall's digital snoopers uncovered cybercrime, he had fought the good fight against eastern European drug smugglers, as well as crypto fraudsters from Hong Kong and all digital devilment wherever it might occur.

It was in the burns care unit, after a bomb attack at Onetelcall's HQ, that he had become close to Amanda, now his wife, then a DCI in Olderbury's police station. She had tried to gather evidence from the local hero, but Max was a poor witness when he had romance on his mind.

Now, forced to stay in bed and in traction, Max felt bored and restless. After the flurry of early morning activity, the rest of the day took on a dreary lethargy and he watched the seconds click by until one of his afternoon visitors made it to his bedside.

"Hey, Dug, mon-old-ami, Christ it's so good to see you. I'm going crispy crackers lying here looking at my low-flying ankle. Tell me something happy for fuck's sake," Max greeted his friend and colleague.

"Something happy, eh? Well now, yeah, this'll cheer you up. I've brought you your laptop so you can do a bit of streaming or whatever. I've had a word with my mate here, he works in the hospital's technical support you know, and he says if you log in to the network, he'll route you to their high-speed feed. It's more secure too, just in case."

Max looked at his buddy and smiled. "Duggie Miller, you are the worst fucking liar I've ever met. Now start again with the real story."

"Really?" Duggie looked hurt. "Am I really that obvious, I thought I'd been well sneaky."

"You did? Mate, you're as sneaky as an arthritic cat burglar."

"Who'd steal an arthritic cat?"

"Prat, anyway, what's going on? You've fixed me a secure connection and you wouldn't do that so I can watch bloody box sets all day now would you?"

"No, I s'pose I wouldn't at that. So, Max, well, the thing is this, you see my mate, the one who's fixed your broadband here, he is called Perry by the way, short for Pericles, his dad was a classics prof-"

"The point Dug, get to the point!"

"Yeah, yeah, you going somewhere?"

"Dug!"

"Ok, you remember Killnet and Rhysida, the Russian hacker groups? Yeah, of course you do, sorry. Well, we all know that they have been hitting UK central services with denial of service and ransom attacks for some time but, just recently, we've noticed increased activity coming in from Moscow. No doubt about that, but not from the usual sources, this is new, clever and dangerous and it is hitting, mainly, the NHS."

"I'm not surprised," replied Max. "A lot of NHS stuff has leaky old firmware, runs all sorts of downloadable updates and, I've got to say, isn't spending its huge budgets very wisely on any of its IT."

"You mean they are not Onetelcall clients."

"Ha, spot on mate. Let's get stuck into whatever is bugging them and perhaps we can change their minds about using us."

"Did you really say bugging them?"

"Sorry, can't resist a little quip you know. So, tell me Dug, who is behind you delivering my laptop and what are my orders?"

"Hmm, well, I'll give you two guesses and here's a clue, she's the boss's wife."

"Didn't need the guess or the clue. I suppose she's got her teeth into this now and we are all going to be involved, yeah?"

"That's about it, mate. I know she's got Kath on it. Sue and Indira too and Graham and his team."

"The goonhillies, eh?"

"He hates you calling them that you know."

"Yep, I know, better than the hill goonies though, eh?"

"Here, Max," Duggie pulled a crumpled A4 sheet from his pocket, "sorry about the hi-tech notetaking, this secure document here has a videoconference link URL on it and another link to a secure vault where you'll find all the briefing information so far. Seems that Jo has been on the case for some time, certainly before you got all bashed up so there's plenty to read and catch up on."

"I'll say this mate, when I asked for something to do, I didn't expect this. I'm actually well made up you know; it makes being tied down here less of a resentment."

"Resentment, eh? Here you are being pampered and coo-ed over by angelic nurses while, back in the real world, it's the usual non-stop whirlwind. Orders are way up for kit and consultancy; the waves of hacking and cyber-attacks are driving new business like you wouldn't believe, so, as Dan would say, our core business is booming and yet, and yet, there is still time for our favourite foreign powers to reveal all sorts of plots for world domination, like bloody James Bond sometimes."

"Well, all I know is that even on my bed of pain I am allowed no peace. And bloody good news it is too. Ok, bud, you know, I think I'll have fun wading through all of Jo's stuff, might as well get going soon as."

"No Amanda today?"

"Not until tonight, she's still being run ragged chasing down organised violent pro and anti-Hamas activities and another outbreak of gang-driven mass shop-lifting attacks, so precious little time for her poor old, injured hubby."

"Oh, there, there and diddums. So now you can get on with your homework."

"Sod off Dug."

"Ok, I'm gone."

As Max began to read, he suddenly felt very vulnerable and unsafe.

Max in hospital has had a laptop delivered in has work to do!

6

Luka chewed noisily; his Dirol gum filling the Moskvich 3 government staff car with a whiff of liquorice. As Vasily Vassiliev's appointed driver, Luka saw himself as a secret service special support agent working for his high-level intelligence officer boss. He didn't need to be briefed, he knew instinctively what his boss was thinking and what he was required to do, often before even Vasily Vassiliev knew himself. Luka would have been devastated to learn that Vasily found him presumptuous and irritating. He knew that his passenger had, for reasons yet to be extracted, been the subject of some reprieve from his boss. Nobody other than his boss could have such an effect on others, grant them a stay of execution and yet make them feel so utterly dejected.

Luka was to drive Melor to one of the SVR's retained flats near Moscow's State University where he would blend in with the hundreds of students who lived close by. What, wondered Luka, had this young man done to achieve such a concession?

"You know where you are going comrade?" asked Luka, still a child of the old Soviet.

"Only what the Major told me," answered Melor tersely. After his morning's ordeal, he didn't feel too chatty.

Luka was not so easily deterred, "What do you know of the Ramenki District?"

"I know it pretty well, I suppose. It's a good area with beautiful spires and ugly towering blocks of flats. Why?"

Luka was at his happiest when he knew something that others didn't.

"Oh, the Major didn't tell you everything then, eh? That's not unusual. Don't be worried, he frequently tells me what he doesn't want others to know. I am his confidante and, sometimes, his sounding board. I think he sees us as a team, actually."

Melor smiled to himself for the first time that day. At school, the young Bogdan had noticed character traits in the sneaks, the tell-tales and the obsequious; in many cases, they showed a compulsion to imply an importance far greater than their real status. He recognised this attribute in Luka.

"I can tell you are a man of insight and dependability," said Melor, masking his disingenuity with a friendly smile. "I hope that one day, I too will be able to profit from your support."

Luka warmed to his new acquaintance, "I'm sure you will find me to be a benefit."

Melor, he decided, would now put Bogdan behind him for good and build the brand Melor, a hacking hero in the world of cyber manipulation. He settled in the back of the comparatively modern Moskvich and allowed his mind to review some of Russia's magnificent malware moments, a history which he would soon dominate. He thought about malware like Cyclops Blink, affecting more than one per cent of all firewalls in the entire world; like the groups known as Sandworm, Black Energy, Electrum or Voodoo Bear, creating cyber havoc against any government leaders or institutions around the world that might be enemies of Russia.

He reflected on the successes, often unpublicised, of groups like Killnet which had achieved cognoscenti notoriety by hacking critical medical equipment in the UK, a technique close to Melor's heart. And then, of course, there was Evil Corp, venal, vicious and immensely profitable. Money was a loud, commanding conversationalist in Moscow, as Melor knew.

Vasily Vassiliev placed him on a form of open prison-cum-bail. He would be free to do as he wished but would be watched constantly, have to report daily and fulfil his promises, giving the Major sufficiently detailed updates for him to be assured any progress Melor claimed was real and verifiable. His new home was a studio apartment close to the university where computing and internet facilities would be made available for his work. They positioned him as pursuing his Doctorate, following on from the Masters' degrees achieved as Bogdan. He would commute between the university and the Moscow Institute of Physics and Technology where they would check the more arcane aspects of his skills. The Nobel laureate-funded MIPT was ranked as one of the top three hundred universities in the world and he certainly wouldn't jib at having his early work inspected by such luminaries as the facility's top cyber specialists.

Luka interrupted his happy musing, "Let me tell you more about your new home."

"Please, don't let me distract you from your driving."

"I am good Russian, a son of Soviet USSR and like all our brave men, I can do more than one thing at one time. I can drive, talk, think, observe and record my thoughts all at one time, so no, my young *muzhchina,* you do not distract me when I am about to enlighten you."

"In that case, I shall be delighted to listen carefully to all that you have to say," Melor replied, with his finest false sycophancy.

"Well judged, I shall tell now of something that many people do not know. I know because of my position of extreme trust and value but people of lesser worth are unaware or know only the rumours, so you are privileged that I tell you now about the hidden development that exists under the streets, parks and buildings of Ramenki district."

"Now I really am fascinated," said Melor, encouragingly.

"Indeed, let me tell you that under Ramenki, under the very street where you will be living and all around you, there is a subterranean city, much of it some two hundred metres down and some two kilometres square and spacious enough to house fifteen thousand people."

"That's amazing, how come nobody knows about it?"

"It was created a long time ago, more than fifty years at least and was kept very secret throughout its development. It had many, many kilometres of underground tunnels and connected to some of the Metro to link it to the Kremlin you see, so secrecy was crucial."

"Was it in case of war?"

"I cannot comment but its depth tells its own story and, of course, our army and security officers have never admitted its existence, nor has anyone ever commented in public on what happens down there now. We can all make informed speculation though, can't we?"

"You may be able to do that, Luka, but I am not informed enough to make any guesses."

Again, Luka looked in his mirror with a satisfied smile. "I am informed, the Major is informed; we know, and you can speculate but I cannot comment any more now."

"I'm grateful for you telling me so much, thank you."

Melor had reached the end of his indulgence and made a fuss of extracting a newspaper from his bag, hoping Luka would now leave him in peace. As he looked at the papers, his mind meandered; an underground city that had existed for so long but remained so secret, it seemed unlikely, impossible even but, as Melor knew, previous and present presidents had been very capable of great concealment and dissimulation. The semblance of an idea grew, a secret city, a cyber ghost; it had the stuff of drama, mystique and mythological heroism.

His mind returned to his newspaper where he read yet another denunciation of the UK, its duplicity in all matters and its constant support of Russia's enemies. For the second time in one journey, Melor's mind drifted into the what-might-be territory. Starting his new career by targeting the UK made political sense and Melor was not so naïve as to believe he could succeed without accepting that some political posturing would be essential. He knew that the previous WannaCry cyber-attacks on the UK's NHS, promoted and supported by North Korea, had cost its victim over ninety million British pounds by disrupting operations and appointments and by the massive costs of data and system recovery, in nearly fifty separate NHS trusts and health services.

Melor knew that his country's policy was to use cyber insurgence as a weapon to add to the military and political arsenals, all to push up its enemies' costs and expenses in any way possible. His plan fitted these demands perfectly. It would humble the UK; it would cost a vast amount of money, and he knew that the highly protected NHS would be given all the money it needed when a cyberattack hit.

As Luka delivered him to his new home, Melor knew what he would do, he also knew how he would do it, the name 'Melor' would soon strike fear into every health system in the world, especially the UK.

7

"You look lovely, and something smells delicious, or is that the other way round?"

"Come in Adam, anyone who appears on my doorstep with two compliments in one sentence is always welcome here."

Adam followed Pauline into the farmhouse's kitchen where the aroma of roasting meat and vegetables just beginning to bubble made him hungry. He gazed around the kitchen and knew immediately that his new acquaintance was no ordinary, typical farmer's wife cook. Of course, there was an Aga but the sharp-eyed Adam noted that all the cooking accoutrements were purposeful, not the gimmicky gadget automated pasta-plaiter novelty of Christmas present ilk, but everything he'd expect to see at a professional chef's station.

"You enjoy cooking, I can see."

"Yes, Adam, very much. I was taught to cook by my grandma, then my mum and also at school, in the days when cooking was part of the general curriculum."

"No, surely, you're far too young!"

"If you're going to start being oily, you can sling your hook right now. I struggle enough to get any flattery in this house, but false flattery is just so ick."

"Whoa, it was supposed to be one of the entre-nous friendly leg-pulls, like friends do, you know, take the proverbial pee?"

"You can say piss, Adam. I'm married to a farmer and have kids."

"Says it all Pauline, says it all. My wife, when I had one a long time ago, used to say a similar thing about being married to a rep and when my son first went to school, I started learning things I never knew, some of them physically impossible."

Pauline laughed, as she efficiently juggled saucepans.

John greeted Tim and Estelle as their taxi pulled up in the yard. "Come in this way, you two. Pauline is already entertaining our new friend in the kitchen so we can sneak straight into the sitting room and get a couple of scotches in before we have to start behaving."

Estelle giggled, "Are you planning some sort of misbehaving then John?"

"Every time I see you Estelle, but, sadly, you've brought Tim with you again."

Over dinner, they enjoyed an immediate meeting of minds. Adam rekindled his how-to-charm-new-clients skills, Estelle relished the attention of a newcomer and Pauline was pleased that her lopsided dinner party was passing so amicably. Adam was surprised how long the social chit-chat lasted in what, he'd assumed, would be a business meeting. Unusually, he didn't mind the chit-chat, he was enjoying the company and satisfying himself that he was dealing with people he could trust, as far as he ever trusted anyone.

It was Estelle who inadvertently kicked off the main topic for the evening. "I've started making my own kimchi," she announced for no obvious reason. "I've been tinkering with it for ages, you know, how much fish sauce, how much garlic and that sort of thing. Poor old Tim, well, he got fed up with it, so I've been testing my last batch on my park-running friends, and they all love it. I must give you a jar, Pauline, oh, and you too if you'd like to try it, Adam?"

"Actually, I'd love to, I'm very interested in…"

"Tell them, Adam. I haven't said much about your ideas, so now would be a good time for you to outline your plans."

"Yes, thanks Pauline, I'll be brief."

"That'll make a pleasant change from a council meeting," chuckled Tim with an encouraging wink at Adam.

It took all of thirty minutes for Adam to describe his plans for importing niche health food products. He was frequently interrupted with questions about the whats, hows, and whys of his project. Tim, a thwarted entrepreneur, grasped the potential of Adam's creation immediately. Excited by the proposition, he was eager to assure that he would support any application Adam might make and do what he could to enable the development John had in mind.

"My boss at RiteByte used to describe me as a bigger-picture player. What he meant was that I wasn't too hot on details and often made decisions on the fly. As I expect you'll have guessed by now, he was quite right and I'm going to do it again, so, look, I've just decided that we should include a development kitchen in the plans for my unit."

"Don't see an issue. You'll have Health and Safety and the environmental folk all over you of course, but, done right, I can't see any real pitfalls or objections," Tim said, helpfully. "But what will you develop and who will do the developing? Are you a chef too, Adam? Yet another skill you've kept quiet about?"

"No, Tim, not me, I'm no cook but I do know someone who is, possibly two people and, well, you'll never guess, they are both at this table right now."

"Oh no, Adam," smiled Pauline, "I said I'd help in any way I can, and I will but I'm nowhere near good enough to do anything close to food development. I mean, I can cook ok but I am no chemist and I don't know a jot about regs and rules and all that sort of stuff."

"Am I to assume that the second person might be me?" asked Estelle.

"Well, yes actually, you are already refining your kimchi-making prowess and next you'll be thinking about recipes which include it won't you?"

"Well, yes, of course, but like Pauline, I'm not in the league you'll need. Tinkering with a bit of fermented cabbage doesn't make me a qualified home economist or whatever they are called these days."

"So, I'll take that as a 'yes' from you both then," grinned Adam, knowing that it would take only seconds to talk them into being willing accomplices.

It took until later that night before the subject of joint development could be raised, over another generous scotch.

"Don't worry, Adam, I've booked a taxi for you," said John.

Adam looked meaningfully at his host. "John, tonight isn't the time to talk in detail but in principle - and I know Pauline has mentioned this to you - but would you consider a joint development for your units? You know, you put up the land and I'll put up the money, or at least an equal share in value, hoping that it won't cost more than that?"

"I'd quite like a share too," said Tim, "but as a councillor, I don't think I'm allowed."

"I expect we can work something out," replied Adam jovially and conspiratorially.

"I hadn't seen a partner in my original thinking," said John, "but I'm not a wealthy man, or couple should I say really. You see the farm is doing just ok at the moment, but it is a variable business and, I must say, a risk shared, or even better, a risk halved would make good, prudent sense for me. Less so for you though, Adam. I mean if, for any reason, it all went wrong, I'd still have the land, but you wouldn't still have your money."

"Hmm, well, not necessarily but I take your point. I never look at the possibility of anything going wrong; there's only upside for me so I don't see risk, I see an opportunity to make some money and have a lot of fun doing it."

As the taxis disappeared down the farm track, John put his arm around Pauline and said, "You know, I've got a good feeling about all this. Well done my girl, brilliant dinner and an even better bit of fishing when you caught our Adam."

"Yeah, he seems like a good man, the real deal, and I have to say I'll look forward to being involved in something that doesn't include being up to my armpits in the hidden bits of an animal's body or wading through piles of shit."

"We'll see how much new shit you get into in a couple of years."

John's estimate of timing was a long way out. Tim, as good as his word, rushed the planning permissions and building regulations through in record time and the contractors were ready to go as soon as the approvals formally came through. John had the groundwork, car park, delivery splay pads and roadways done and most of the services laid in anticipation of the green light. In just ten months, the development of the Parkside Enterprise Park was ready for its first occupant.

In the meantime, Adam had completed his first exploration and educational tour, sourcing, testing and selecting amazing products in Japan, Korea, Indonesia and India, taking in as many foods, food growers and manufacturers as he could on the way. By the time the units were operative, he had a list of the products and foods he intended to prepare for market. He had brought back sufficient samples of each product for Pauline and Estelle to read about, trial, play with and understand.

In their home kitchens to start with, strange and oriental fragrances, some less fragrant than others, filled the air as recipes were drafted, rejected and reworked. They both loved this work and produced some special 'Adam Superfoods' including a clever, complex Konnyaku in a sauce of wasabi and soy which would make the flavourless, rubbery miraculous superfood a tasty, healthy treat.

When Adam Superfoods was launched, it had a range of fifteen healthy gut and microbiome-friendly, pre and probiotic products available to sell as Adam Superfoods products or without a label within the food and health shop sectors. He ensured that press and social media launch items showed off his premises, creating publicity for the remaining units which saw them all occupied within three months of the development's completion. In this new, vibrant Parkside Enterprise Park environment, Adam's food range took off and flew. Adam worked to develop his range and services, confident that the business could only grow, and that the future looked wonderful. Surely nothing surely could go wrong now.

8

Ben Barrington did not look as ebullient as usual. He took Max and Amanda by their hands and appeared more serious than either of them had seen him. He hoped Max would soon be released from his hospital ward. He'd have to walk on crutches, but he'd be free again. Now, they looked at the surgeon's face and worried.

"What's up doc?" Max couldn't resist it, but Ben failed to grin at this tired quip.

"Oh, don't look so worried, there's nothing wrong with you now, you are healing very well and you should be fully mobile and limp-free very soon."

Amanda giggled.

"Limp-free isn't a joke young lady," smiled the sombre Ben, "and if you think it is, you've been spending too long in the police changing rooms."

"Oh, come on you two, please, let's get to the point here," insisted Max. "There's something on your mind, Ben, and it involves us, so please, spit it out."

"Ok, I'm sorry to talk about what is work to you, Max whilst you are still recovering but this is serious otherwise I wouldn't..."

"Look, Ben, I've been working for ages, on my laptop here and on a brief that is pretty challenging, so whatever you have to say won't set me back or spoil my recuperation, quite the opposite actually." Max had already decided that he'd keep Jo's briefing about cyber threats to the NHS away from any external awareness, even the evidently trustworthy Ben.

"Yes, I've been told about the hours you've been putting in on your screen. Anyway, what I have to say is, well, maybe, for both of you," continued Ben, "because it combines computer security and a possible crime. The thing is, this hospital and we are not alone by any means, is facing increasingly frequent IT attacks. We are being targeted, we think, by hackers but we haven't had any demands, so it isn't ransomware attacking, that's what you call it isn't it? This seems to be just wilful intrusion to create chaos in our systems and daily running."

"I see," said Max. "I know the NHS has been vulnerable for years and we all know why. My company, Onetelcall, has danced around handbags with various trusts management and the NHS at a central level many a time but without success. They stick to all sorts of old arrangements with manufacturers who won't admit their mistakes, even less do anything about fixing them, even if they knew how to which I don't think they do."

"Are you saying you can't do anything to help us here the Max?"

"Absolutely not, Ben, no, not at all. None of us in Onetelcall ever walks away from computer crime whether it is perpetrated on a client or not. I promise you now that we will do all we can to discover who is targeting you and what needs to be done to protect you from these attacks. What I can't do is put your systems right or stop any more attacks."

"Yes, of course, I can see that. I know, believe me, I know, how difficult our layers on layers of managers and non-medical bureaucrats can be. We ask for money for equipment to save lives and are told we can't have it because of, well, because of all sorts of crap that we don't need. I won't go into all that now, let's just concentrate on finding out who is doing this if we can," Ben looked glum.

"I can tell you that now," replied Max. "It will be a Russian hacking group. We already know most of them and you are not alone in the Western health industry, if I can call it that, to be hit for six by these cyber maniacs. Since Ukraine, every country which gave Zelensky any support has been targeted, not just in the health area but every vulnerable public service. The idea is to create havoc which is as costly to fix as possible and to undermine the political structure of those countries. That's partly why you are seeing so much public unrest throughout Europe and in the States too."

"From the UK police perspective Ben," Amanda joined in, "we are limited in what we can do. We can't take a patrol car to Moscow and arrest a few bad-guy cyber-crims, so we can only act if we find some UK collusion or local activity which breaks the law. Can't tell you how frustrating it is for our IT section, let alone the specialist security agencies, some known about and some kept secret, but we all keep on fighting and working with those agencies and companies like Onetelcall."

"Understood, Amanda, understood and that's why I asked you to be here too. You see Perry, our IT sage, tells me in words I don't understand that there could well be a UK involvement in our intrusion, not sure of course, but there is that suspicion."

Amanda was always cynical, always on guard with even the most innocent and prestigious of contacts. "Ben, I have to say this, if you and your IT people are creating some UK suspect to lure us - Olderbury police and our colleagues - into investigating on your behalf a cybercrime which may well not have any UK origination or involvement, then we would treat that harshly indeed. I'm sure you are not but it is my duty to warn your IT colleagues, through you if I may, that we are not so easily entrapped."

"Oh, my word. Well, that's told me."

"Please don't get huffy, Ben. You know that I think the world of you, we both do, and you've looked after Max better than anyone could hope for. What I just said is the same as you having to pass on bad news to a stricken patient. Some things need to be said and then never mentioned again."

"Of course, Amanda, yes, that's right and I fully understand. I would never knowingly mislead anyone or waste police time. I know you know that, but I will pass on your warning to all the relevant people."

"Oh God, enough, enough!" interjected Max. "We are all on the same side. Gawd knows, Amanda, I have seen enough attempts to hoodwink, not only the police but some of the international agencies too, but not usually by eminent surgeons!"

"So Max, you have a good idea who is doing this, what is the next course of action?" asked Ben.

"To say I know where would be more accurate than who. The who is a much bigger question. Even if we trace the origins, we will probably never know who they are. Some of them won't exist at all as human beings, they will be bots or spiders or some AI confection, but we do know, pretty much, how they do it and can advise you on countermeasures. Don't know about you Mand, but I think we should start by having a good chat with all your IT team here and regionally or centrally or however, it all works in your trusts, and the NHS as a body. Also, I think we should put some of our super-snoopers on your case to see what we can find. Believe me, Ben, if it is there, they will find it, no matter how convoluted and masked the offenders and their techniques might be."

"Tell you what I find strange," added Ben as he nodded in agreement with Max's suggestions, "is what sort of stuff these bastards go for. You'd expect it would be our new, big health-critical systems they would hit, but it isn't, they are attacking the older small stuff, the peripheral gadgets. They do annoying things like causing ambulances to be rerouted and interfere with our building control systems like central heating and air conditioning, they interrupt the drugs ordering process. You see, they disrupt all sorts of non-critical and mainly non-essential, non-life-threatening stuff and petty though it seems, it throws us into complete disarray and costs huge chunks of our limited budgets to cope with it."

"Yeah, that's the plan alright, that's what they want to achieve, and, in a way, it is good that their strategy stays as it is. If they started getting at the critical systems, if they started causing deaths and harm, it would be too awful and so difficult and expensive to counter. It is a major worry though. If you ask me, it is just a matter of time before the Russians up the ante in their cyber-warfare and you can be sure that when they do, it will be the UK that gets hit hard. Putin hates us and if he does, so do his minions."

Ben nodded again. "In a country where free and fair elections are a mockery, where opposition is banned or falls from roofs or whatever, what else can you expect? I know some of my colleagues in Russia are in despair, but I also know some zealots will do anything to rise in Putin's ranks and fight for whatever he tells them to fight for."

"You are uncharacteristically quiet Amanda," said Max. "What are you thinking?"

Amanda looked at her husband, "There must be a home component here. I mean all this little stuff, the gadgets as Ben described the target kit, well if it is a firmware weakness, it won't always be a common fault or a standard open door for hackers. Or would it? That's my question because I'm thinking someone local, in each hospital being affected by these outrages must be supplying some spec or info about all the easily hit bits of kit in each hospital, see what I mean?"

"I do, Mand, I do indeed."

"Ah ha," grinned Ben looking lighter and less depressed now that at least some action would be taken. "See, told you. Me, wasting police time? As if!"

"Alright, alright, no need to rub it in," smiled Amanda. "I'll never say anything the slightest bit horrid to you ever again, ok?"

"Dearest Amanda, there is nothing you could do or say that would ever make me think any the less of you. Max is a supremely lucky man to have you."

Amanda giggled again.

"Have you been on the nitrous oxide, Mand?" Max asked.

"I haven't been on anything for ages!"

"I think the sooner we send Max home, the better," laughed Ben.

Ben - Consultant
& Max & Amanda
discuss how & what
would be affecting
the NHS

9

"When the President hears that your protegee, your discovery, has forced the United Kingdom to its knees, you, Major Vasily Vassiliev will be hailed as a national hero." As instructed, Melor was sending his daily email to his captor, a daily explanation of his actions and his intentions.

He continued, "I am now creating my weapon of destruction. It will be as our President bids, a technique which will undermine the UK's national health system. It will cost their economy billions and demand so much attention that any thoughts of arms or support for any of Russia's opponents will be driven from their minds and become beyond their economic capabilities."

Melor hit the send button. He had been careful not to mention how he would achieve his great ambition. He had yet to finalise the details and deployment of his cyber-Armageddon and was certainly not ready to be quizzed about it. To delay further scrutiny, he would requisition development time in the Moscow Institute AI laboratory, time which he would spend developing and automating his grand plan to plant breeding bugs wherever he could access networks and standalone equipment via auto-downloads, firmware updates and even emails.

His new student-style accommodation suited him well. His needs were austere, the only important requirement was a high-speed internet connection which he was delighted to note, had been made available to him in his flat. As a reminder of his servitude to his homeland's secret services, Melor could see the sloping roofline of the Federal Security Services campus from his twelfth-floor window. He needed no reminder that the president had been the director of the FSB for a year at the end of the nineties and had served in its predecessor, the KGB. Suddenly, a cold chill ran through him. The thought of failure in his grand quest was too terrifying to contemplate. The Putin regime didn't tolerate failure and wasn't famed for overlooking mistakes with a happy, forgiving joke.

Flopped on the palliasse that passed as a bed, Melor read again about the precarious state of the UK's NHS IT infrastructure. He'd already read about the chaotic British Post Office computer disaster which caused political upheaval when its systems falsely showed miscounting for which hundreds of sub-post office operators were charged with fraud and theft. Some committed suicide for being so cruelly victimised. Fingers had been pointed at the computer manufacturer for the disastrous errors, others had suspected a more remote, malevolent external cause.

The same manufacturer had been involved in a consortium for the National Programme for IT, an attempt to provide centralised integrated patient records and services computing. It was the largest public sector IT investment ever made in the UK. It didn't work well; it didn't even work badly. It cost the NHS, or the taxpayers, some ten billion pounds.

To Melor's joy, he understood the fundamental flaws of the project were founded on a lack of knowledge of the technologies involved. Such ignorance, he thought, would only aid his purpose. It had also failed because of uncoordinated, unmanaged and inadequately briefed multi-sourcing of suppliers. Again, Melor rejoiced, the workarounds created to hammer the ill-fitting jigsaw pieces into place left several weaknesses in the resultant legacy systems, weaknesses which Melor could exploit.

Melor could fulfil his ambition to be the world's most infamous hacker if his project succeeded, but he had competition, a lot of competition. All the cyber-aggressive states had their hacker heroes. India, China, Iran, and the list of state-sponsored hacking ingenuity was long, but it was an independent genius who threatened Melor's status the most. Subconsciously, Melor had paid tribute to his greatest competitor, the one-word name, the man famous for creating and deploying stuttering chatbots. He had styled himself on a universally acclaimed hacker, Pal.

Like everyone, he knew little about Pal other than he had once worked for an Albanian gang and had been the architect of a brilliantly conceived and executed AI Chatbot attack in which thousands of AI chatbots were infected, creating international cyber mayhem and making, so rumour said, many millions of dollars on the way. Then it stopped. Pal's wraith-like presence evaporated, and nobody knew where he now lived or what he was doing. Perhaps, mused Melor, one day I will find him and we might work together. Until then, he had a lot of work to do. It would have been impossible without AI intelligent processing power and, unexpectedly some significant assistance from Major Vasily, a helping hand which had resulted from one of their weekly meetings.

"Our search and report functions have identified all the larger items of equipment commonly used throughout the NHS, but we are struggling to find the makes and models of the extensive range of peripheral items of technology used in hospitals and health centres, like what controls their heating, their various smaller monitoring items, their internal ordering and stock systems and so on. It is a minor setback for me as it is those minor items which are the most open to my approaches," explained Melor.

Vasily smiled, "Your approaches, you make it sound like seduction."

"In a way, it is, Major. My little bugs knock on the door, smile sweetly and make coo-cooing noises and the host lets them in and shows them their private parts which my little lovers wrap their arms around. So, yes, Major, I like the seduction analogy."

"I understand your requirements, whelp. Leave it with me, it is in my interests too to help you succeed and score a victory over those imperialist Russia-hating swine. I will acquire all the information you need, by the next time we meet."

"I am even more in your debt, Major. Thank you, this will make a major- a most important difference to my effectiveness and speed of strike, thank you."

"Don't grovel, boy. Go now and work hard, be here at this time next week and I will give you all you need."

He was as good as his word. The following week, Vasily gave Melor a memory stick. "Here you have the technical equipment inventories for about twelve hundred UK hospitals. You will have manufacturer, model type and number for everything from small calculators to the largest processors and networked computers, including all the facilities equipment, management and organisational equipment and all the medical and laboratory specialist machines too. Is that what you need, boy?"

"That's fantastic, Major, just fantastic. May I ask how you can get such comprehensive information so quickly? I am most impressed Major, and I am inquisitive to know how you can achieve such a feat."

"It is no secret that the British Medical Association, a UK trades union, has political activists amongst its members and some of those activists are known to our SVR foreign intelligence service. Some of those activists may support the British government, some may support its opposition parties, some may fight for more pay and better conditions, and others believe that there is a greater battle to be fought and are enlightened enough to be of assistance to us as and when we ask them."

"I see, Major, at least, I think I see. It is interesting to know that we have friends installed in such organisations. I don't suppose any of them would be available to me at any time, would they?"

"I don't suppose they would be, impertinent whelp that you are. However, if you were to make a case for some additional local involvement, I may consider your request and, if I approve, I may be able to expedite such activity."

"Thank you again, Major. I can see I owe you more each time I see you."

"Go now, your words and your presence are emetic to me."

Melor stood and grinned cheekily. He was almost sure that he saw a glimmer of amusement in the Major's eyes.

As expected, the data from the UK was supplied in a standard spreadsheet format which the Institute's powerful machines analysed in no time, giving Melor all the information he needed to launch assaults according to the weakness of all vulnerable machines in each machine in every location. He would start slowly with his trusty slow burn interference bug, fed into non-critical machines in hospitals' ward drug ordering systems. He would explain to the Major how he had identified a simple system to exploit flash memory updates and BIOS adjustments via automated downloads to implant a random activity which would interrupt normal function on an unpredictable but significant basis.

In more advanced locations, where all the normally isolated functions such as freezers and fridges, air purification, water temperature and other control systems were controlled via Wi-fi, Melor's task was made easier and installing irritant malware in the network appealed to his infrequently exercised sense of humour.

Another silent tribute to Pal, the AI chatbot stuttering creator, thought Melor. A hacker with humour was a worthwhile aspiration, he said to himself. He knew too that Pal had been able to plant a reverse data stream in some of his hacks and was able to steal millions of dollars' worth of data and information. Melor had worked on this technique and believed he'd found a way of incorporating such a feature in his ward drug ordering bug. He hadn't yet figured out how to profit from this feature, not that he would say that to the Major.

"Your initial work seems satisfactory," announced the Major after Melor's next presentation. "And the laboratory supervisor confirms that your work is sound and so, you worm, you may proceed with your first phase."

"Thank you, Major, I shall commence without delay."

"Good, it is a start, but it is a piddling little start, a bit of confusion here, a little misguidance there but it doesn't all add up to the cataclysmic humbling of the once grand NHS you promised me, does it?"

"The NHS is already humbling itself without any help from me," observed Melor. "But, believe me, Major, this piddling start is just that. They will get rattled and start delving into where this interference is coming from. When they delve, we jump in with yet more piddling bits of confusion in more machines and at more critical levels. Bit by bit, we will occupy and control all their systems until their surgeons won't be able to operate on a single haemorrhoid without our permission."

Major Vasily looked pleased and Melor took a risk. "Do you think, Major, that any of the friends of our heroic SVR might be willing recipients of some rerouted hospital drugs?"

Major Vasily looked more pleased.

10

Max had swapped his hospital-issue crutches for the traditional old-style under-arm variety on which he could swing around happily and still be able to stand while he held a glass in one hand and something to nibble in the other. He had been restricted to working from home, not because of a lack of mobility but because of corporate insurance regulations. He was beginning to feel cooped up and frustrated, even though he was still working on Jo's NHS investigations. He was planning to make his way back to the Onetelcall campus very soon but, for now, if couldn't go to his office, then his office could come to him, and he smiled happily as he welcomed Jo and Kathy to his home.

Amanda had moved into Max's apartment after their marriage. It was a conversion created from a beautiful stone and brick farm building. She had sold her flat and invested the proceeds, claiming it to be the first fiscally prudent act of her life.

"I love your place, Max," announced Kathy as she perched on a kitchen worksurface. "And I must say, Amanda's flair brings a refreshing touch of civilisation, so lacking before."

"That's because before Amanda emasculated my place, it was a bachelor pad of some repute."

"And the downfall of many a girl's reputation," laughed Kathy.

Kathy Viggers, now Kathy Miller, was Onetelcall's emerging technologies specialist. She had married Duggie Miller, the company's logistics manager, troubleshooter and Max's friend and sidekick.

"Whoa, that's enough," said Jo, putting her hand over her wine glass. "I might not be driving but I still want to be able to speak."

"Damn," said Max, "I was hoping you might have given up on wanting to talk."

"Tough, Maximillian, 'cos I've got a lot to say."

Jo Rackham was married to Dan, the CEO of Onetelcall. They had been lovers from a time when Jo ran her own events consultancy, specialising in enabling high-level meetings between her clients and senior figures in national security.

"Jo, when do you not have a lot to say? And usually what you do say ends up with me and Duggie getting beaten up, shot at or blown up by all sorts of lethal types. As our company's chief cybercrime terrier, you certainly know how to dig out the world's nastiest criminals."

"I know Max. It's becoming an obsession, mainly because so much of what appears online is a con, a crime or worse. It drives me potty and if I can do anything to stomp on the bastards, I'll do it."

"You mean you'll get your two mugs to do it, don't you?"

"Yep, that's about right, Max and I know you love it, and Duggie does too. In fact, the entire team loves it, not only because we enjoy catching the shits but, as Dan keeps telling us, it's very good for Onetelcall to be seen as the rigorous champion of cyber rectitude."

"When that mad Albanian let loose a blunderbuss at me, it was more like rigour bloody mortis."

"Stop moaning, you sympathy-seeking con-artist, and tell me what progress you've made whilst you've been living the life of the idle rich in your bed?"

"No, really, I'm much better now, thanks for asking," Max answered. "But since you've chosen to ignore my recovery in favour of talking about your brief, I'll tell you what I've found so far about Russian hacking and NHS vulnerability."

Kathy nodded, "Yeah, Duggie mentioned that Amanda and you had been briefed - is that the right word? - by your surgeon and I had a word with Graham about it. He says that his listening stations linked to our Deepmatters AI analysis facility have been watching the NHS intrusions recently and he's building a dossier on the problem. Graham says it is a big problem getting bigger."

"He's not wrong, quite terrifyingly not wrong. I was beginning to feel like a sitting duck in Olderbury hospital which, I believe may well be suffering its own attack of malicious interference in some of the networked systems and peripheral processors."

"Why do you say that?" asked Jo.

"My scalpel-wielding sawbones, a splendid chap called Ben Barrington, told me and Mand that Olderbury is suffering all sorts of random cyber-attacks hitting, largely, non-critical functions but affecting stuff like ambulance routing, ward drug ordering and distribution, as Jo said, peripheral activities but annoying, time-consuming and expensive to manage and correct."

"I suppose the question is, how widespread is this interference?" asked Jo. "Did you find out anything about the scale of the problem?"

"Yep, some info, like the NHS has upped its act a bit since the infamous Wannacry 'Windows' outbreak which hit so many companies around the world and about eighty NHS trusts. Why? Because they were all running old and unpatched versions of Microsoft operating systems. So, mainly, that has been addressed now but the health trusts are all still open to attack on old-fashioned kit, automatic update services and, of course, over its networks, especially its N3 broadband network which links all the England NHS sites. And that's not all…"

"May I butt in?" said Jo. "I'd like to add to what you've discovered, Max, with some gen I've gathered from my contacts at the National Cyber Security Centre. Apparently, it isn't only the NHS directly that's being targeted by our Russian mateys, suppliers to the trusts too are getting hit."

"Which ones? Do we know?" asked Kathy.

"I now know more than most," said Jo, "but even my usually candid security consultants are strangely quiet about some aspect of these more widespread and unpredictable hits. They did tell me that NHS external suppliers of a variety of functions, from patient notes and records through to care plans, admin-type applications and software for managing 111 calls have been affected by a ransomware-style bug that locks the application until a ransom is paid. Naturally, I asked all the questions, but my contact clammed up."

"That's interesting," said Max, "as I haven't found any standing policy from the NHS about whether it pays ransoms or not and if it doesn't, I can't find out from research just how it gets over the denial-of-service. What I did find is that some trusts have failed cyber security vulnerability tests, mainly because they relied on dodgy updates. They claim lack of money, of course, but when you consider the forty million or so quid they wrote off on that IT system that just didn't work, GP Extraction System I think it was, lack of funding seems to be a go-to excuse for rampant inefficiency."

"Hold on, Max," said Kathy, "that's a bit hard. The NHS was screwed over by suppliers who promised everything and delivered nothing. Shameful, and some of them still get government contracts, amazing."

"I know, I know," nodded Jo, "but NHS efficiency or otherwise and the quality of their suppliers, all of which we know and often have to dig out of various piles of dung, isn't really our concern right now. We need to figure out more about the attacks and what we can do about it all."

"Tell you what, folks, with an extra six billion quid in their coffers, if we succeed in knocking out the Russian hacker, I'll be on their doorstep with a Onetelcall contract," grinned Max. "But, for now, what I do know - some of this is guesswork - but I believe we are dealing with a small hacking unit, not one of the big Cozy Bear or Revil Sodinokibi activities, or any of the other big groups. I suspect it is a newcomer, a hacker or a hacker team with a point to prove and probably overly ambitious. I reckon what we've seen so far is just a scouting exercise. I am sure the NHS is being set up and measured, ready for a major onslaught."

"Why do you say that, Max?" asked Kathy.

"I'll tell you, look at the ransomware used against the NHS that we know about, yeah? I mean, it is an impressively stylised bug in itself and delivered in such a way as to be highly scalable, that is to say, the bug as an entity could carry more functionality than it does now. I think it is a clever toe in the water and, what's more, its core ransomware is a version of Lockbit Black. It carries a silly tag, something like, 'MelorLock' but we don't know yet what that means. I believe that the NHS has a deal with a Lockbit ransomware specialist who can get into the old malware servers and neutralise the ransom but, well, this time I don't think they are being successful."

"So," said Kathy, "I assume we need to monitor Olderbury hospital to see if we can spot a Russian hacker, is that right?"

Max chuckled again, "You've got the gist perfectly, Kath. Interestingly, Ben believes there's a local angle to this hacking, so Mand was at pains to point out that the feds have no powers over Russia or its multiple teams of cyber-criminals and that she could only take any action if there was suspicion of a UK component. That's why Ben mentioned it and I, for one, believe him. Someone in that hospital is a mole."

"Now that really is interesting," said Kathy, "because that implies two-way traffic and usually, that means we can spot it over whatever network or digital method the covert messages are being sent. We'll get 'em as long as they don't talk by posted letter."

"Still up there moving with the times…"

"I have no idea why Duggie and I even tolerate you, Max Golby, you are a child and a walking disaster area."

"Oh, Kath, what can I say? If there is a mole, you'll be the one to cut it out."

"I give up!" Kathy laughed as she received a huge hug from the man she knew had put his life on the line to save her husband in the past and had proven to be a valued friend.

"When you two have finished playing, how about we agree on a plan?" Jo looked serious. "I'll crack on with Sue and Indira looking at mobile traffic and external communication run over the network and, Kathy, I'm going to ask you and Graham's listening teams, to look out for more covert messaging moving in or out of the hospital and, perhaps, some of it by a more obvious supplier. I've got a list ready."

Kathy couldn't resist, "If it's fishy, we'll catch it."

Everyone chuckled but deep inside, Max knew that they were setting out on a perilous path.

11

"No more for me, thanks, that was absolutely delicious," said Adam. He was sitting in John and Pauline's kitchen where, along with his cup of tea, Pauline had provided a huge slice of creamy, chocolatey, icing-slathered sponge cake.

"I know you are all about gut health and biomes and all that but, be honest now, you just can't beat a bloomin' good cake, can you?"

"Can't argue with that, Pauline," smiled Adam, "but it's when I taste food like this, cooked here on your old Aga, I wonder why I spent so much money for you and Estelle to have a development kitchen in the unit."

"I don't think what I cook on the old girl here," said Pauline, patting her Aga affectionately, "would go down too well with our health-conscious clients and certainly not with our new restaurant customers. Although it seems to me the pendulum is swinging back from delicate and complex dishes to good old favourites. I see the Lion d'Or is putting steak and kidney pie back on its menu after about thirty years."

"Really? Good for them. I know the business I've selected mightn't suggest it, but I'm a big fan of traditional British foods. I mean, the French may call us the rosbifs in a derogatory kind of way but, for me, a Sunday roast is one of the finest dishes in all creation."

"Then on Sunday, Adam, you shall have the best roast beef you've ever eaten."

"You are so kind, Pauline. I'll bring the wine, and I promise, no shop talk."

"Up to you of course, but I love talking about the business. It's so interesting and I keep learning things I'd never have known without doing all this with you."

"Yeah, I know, it is fascinating, isn't it? I keep on learning too."

"What's on the agenda next then, eh? We've got a good range going now and the most popular lines, you know, Estelle's favourite Kimchis, all the miso products, the Tempeh, the unpasteurised Sauerkrauts and, of course, the Kombuchas are all selling hugely well online. And the Adam Superfood Club memberships, a good idea that was, is growing every day. The recipes with ingredients packs we sell direct from here are on the up too, so, well, from what I see, I think we should look at the fish sector next, what do you say?"

"I say I agree entirely, and I've been thinking about a fishing expedition, quite literally, to source some really good lines. Oh, the puns keep coming, sorry!"

"It's a bit of a minefield though, so I understand," said Pauline. "I was talking to Derek, he's a sous chef at Le Gastronomique, got a Michelin Bib Gourmand appropriately enough, and he was saying that they must be on their guard against fish which is mislabelled, misrepresented and altogether… er… fishy. It's a real problem."

"He's not wrong, as you'd expect from someone of his standing. I've been doing some research, and I can hardly believe the extent of fish fraud, it's massive and worldwide and most prevalent in the higher-priced produce, but then I suppose you'd expect that."

"Do you mean caviar? I mean, would we add caviar to our range?"

"Apart from the fact that I love, it, I think we would add it, Pauline, if you and Estelle agree?"

"Boy, I love it too, but, well, is it healthy enough for our brand profile?"

"Oh yeah, it's super good for you, bang full of EPA and DHA omega-3, strong in B12 and a great source of choline which helps us with brain health, cell signalling and muscle mobility. I understand choline is good for pregnant women and breastfeeding mothers, so that might be a new niche to explore, especially as it is a great source of calcium too."

"Sounds ideal for us, doesn't it, so what's the problem?"

"Well, I think if we stock it, we should stock the real, good-quality Russian stuff but, I'm told, we must be wary about overly attractive price offers. Some of it isn't caviar at all, it's sturgeon offal. Some of it comes originally from Italy and is sent to Russia. The Italian caviar comes from a whitefish and is mild, much milder than, say, Beluga and some, believe it or not, come from the USA, the people who scream most about being ripped off; ironic isn't it? They produce a sort of caviar from, oh you know, salmon roe or hackleback, mind you, some of it is genuinely nice to eat, it just isn't the real thing and shouldn't be the price of the real thing which is what is going on."

"That's a lot to look out for."

"Well, that's not the half of it, the biggest headache is caviar being sold in underweight packs or tins or adulterated caviar, bulked out with excessive salt and other additives, some of which are artificial and not that good to eat. I'll tell you this though, we won't be dealing in cod, sole or haddock imports 'cos some of the fraudsters are substituting the real, expensive thing for cheapo lookalikes such as catfish and pangasius, even pufferfish for heaven's sake, and that can be deadly, or so I believe."

"So, we steer clear or go for it?" asked Pauline.

"To be honest with you, Pauline, I've already ordered some samples. Had to pay for them upfront mind, direct from a Russian supplier who looks like the real thing, an honest broker, or so I've been told by a local import company. It's on its way and comes in as part of a consolidated consignment of other Russian products, foods I assume, to the importer's clearing depot right here in town, so I should be able to collect it in a couple of days."

"Oooh, by Sunday do you think?"

Rushian Import Export's warehouse was older and smaller than Adam had expected, not much larger than his own unit at Parkside. A brick and prefabricated sectional building, it had a single office entrance door and the usual large goods roller door at the front, where there was a car park area and a larger splay for vans and small lorries to turn and park for loading.

Adam rang the visitors' bell and, following instruction signs, climbed the slip-resistant steel staircase, past a toilet door and an open kitchenette area to a desk with a 'reception' sign stuck to it.

"Yeah, hello, what d'ya want luv?" Rushian's receptionist smiled helpfully.

"Adam Superfoods, I believe you have a parcel from Ekskluzzivnyy Export for me. It is a consignment of caviar," Adam smiled back.

"Oh, is it luv, you lucky man, I'm partial to a spoonful myself," said the girl to Adam's amusement. "Yeah, right you are luv, it came in a day ago as it happens, yeah, Wednesday, came in with a load of other gear, well, you know, when I say gear, I don't mean, you know, gear and that, at all." The girl blushed slightly; Adam wanted to suggest she shouldn't play cards.

While she wandered off, clutching a consignment note, Adam wondered if she had meant what he had inferred. Surely nobody would be so indiscreet as to let a crime like importing drugs slip out so easily. He dismissed his suspicions as being too ridiculous to be true.

The girl came back to the reception desk. "You're alright luv," she said, "all clear, just got these forms for you to sign please and you can collect your box downstairs. I'll open the roller for you."

"That's a lot of forms," said Adam looking at the sheaf contained by a plastic paper clip.

"Yeah, tell me about it, bloody government, it's all bloody forms and I have to file them all and then I have to put them on the computer, it's a mare I tell you, a mare,"

Adam looked at the papers, most of which were straightforward declarations and confirmation of identity.

"Driving licence, ok?"

"Course it is luv, I'll photocopy it, ok?"

"How do I know how heavy my consignment is?"

"Dunno luv, hang on, I'll look on the docket." She ruffled some more papers. "Yeah, here you are luv, here it is, yeah, looks like it is five kilograms to me, look here." She showed Adam a packing form which listed multiple items with an accumulative weight figure for the entire consignment, although it wasn't obvious to Adam whether this included packaging or was a mean contents weight.

"Does it normally look like this, you know, the weight declaration?"

"Oh yes, luv, it's on the docket, see, that's what we always take as being gospel. I mean, we don't weigh anything when it comes in, we just follow the docket and enter the details straight from it."

"Well, that's fine with me then," smiled Adam as he signed and dated the various forms.

She gathered them back and attached the photocopied driving licence image. "There you go luv, all done. If you'd like to make your way downstairs, I'll open the doors."

In the car park, carrying a larger box than he had expected, Adam said, "Thank you, er… what's your name?"

"Anna, luv, I'm Anna."

"Well Anna, thank you so much for all your help."

"No worries luv, see you again I hope."

Through the open roller doors, Adam could see the open space, the walls of which were fitted with heavy-duty racking. A small forklift truck trundled back towards the rear of the unit where Adam noted, with some surprise, a large and sophisticated-looking cabinet safe-cum-deepfreeze, about three times the size of a large domestic double upright freezer, fixed to the ground with industrial-level security bolts. It was an incongruous image that fixed itself in Adam's mind.

Instead of travelling directly back to the unit, Adam called Pauline and Estelle and asked them to meet him in Pauline's kitchen, a room that was quickly becoming the de facto Adam Superfoods boardroom. On his way, he stopped off at his apartment to collect a couple of packs of blinis and a bottle of superior vodka he had been keeping in the fridge for this occasion.

"Howdy pardner," chuckled John as he greeted Adam in the farm's home driveway.

"John, great to see you. Not riding the range on your tractor today then?"

"Not bloody likely when there's some caviar to be tasted. At least that's why you are here, so I've been told. I've even put a bottle of our driest champagne in the cooler especially."

"Good man yourself," smiled Adam. "I've brought a bottle of super-chilled vodka. It's what the Russians drink with their best caviar, so I'm told. We can open both and see if the Russians or the French are right."

"Got yer taxi booked again then, Adam," laughed John, "or are you planning on sleeping with the cows until Sunday lunch is ready?"

"Can you guarantee a pretty one?"

Estelle gave a little squeal as she sipped her vodka, so cold it was almost oily. "Oh, that's amazing!" she said, reaching for a caviar-laden blini and giving another little squeal of delight.

"I think she likes it," grinned Adam.

"Bet Tim's never heard her squeak like that," laughed John.

Estelle blushed and sipped more vodka.

"How much did you buy, Adam?" asked John.

"Well, I went direct to an outfit called Ekskluzzivnyy, and they did me a sample deal for six 150-gram tins of Ossetra Royal for about three hundred quid a pop, and then another six 125-gram tins of Royal Beluga at eight hundred pounds each. Expensive I think, but they do good discounts for proper trade orders, and I've got twenty per cent off my next order."

"Wow, not cheap, this healthy eating. Is the idea that we taste all the samples and vote for our favourite, or do we just lunge in and savour the moment?"

"Oh, John, really," said Pauline in mock scold, "this is business not a shindig."

John, who had two plates of caviar blinis, a glass of champagne and a glass of vodka in front of him, replied, "Feels like a party to me, girl."

Adam knew from the outset that nothing objective would be gained from the afternoon's tasting session, but he wanted to share the moment with the people who had become his friends and colleagues, as an unspoken thank you. He enjoyed the discussion, serious at first and progressively sillier and funnier as the champagne and vodka hit home.

The usually demure and self-disciplined Estelle announced, "I've given the matter a great deal of thought and my decision is," she paused to toss back another shot of vodka, "that I prefer a vodka, followed by a blini, followed by a glass of champagne, a sort of slurp-nibble-glug rolling process, love it, I say, love it and, you know something, do you, well you don't 'cos I'm going to tell you, I'm telling this man here, this Adam, well he's not a hard-headed, hard-hearted businessman, he an old softie with a kind mind and he's giving us caviar and getting pissed 'cos he likes us and we like him, well, we do, don't we, we do Adam, we like you a lot, I like you so much I could slurp, nibble and sip…"

"Whoa, Estelle, steady on there girl, a coffee perhaps?"

"Good idea, Pauline, I think I'm getting the tiniest bit tiddly you know."

John and Adam smiled as Pauline and Estelle stood and headed unsteadily for the kettle.

"Pissed perhaps, but she's right, isn't she?" said John, "This is a very thoughtful thank you from you, isn't it. You're alright Adam, I'll say, that for you, and you are always welcome here and you make a damn good partner to be in business with. Is this caviar going to be a profitable sideline do you think, or is it too expensive and too much of a pain to import?"

"First off, John, I know how lucky I've been since I met Pauline by chance in Mary's Cafe and went into business with you on the Parkside development. It's been a good deal and a great pleasure too. I now have friends who I really value. Secondly, well, caviar, I don't know, I think we'll test it in a sort of luxury superfood niche and see how the market reacts. It is quite easy to import, I just order it from Ekskluzzivnyy and they send it to Rushian here in Olderbury for me to collect, couldn't be easier."

"Rushian, did you say Rushian?"

"Yeah, they are an import and export shipper in town, one of the old light industrial small warehouses near the river."

"Oh, Adam, believe me, I know Rushian. Let me tell you," John drew closer to share his confidential story. "Ten years ago, I was a special constable with the Olderbury nick. A few of us from the rugby club joined up to add a bit of muscle, mainly for the footie weekends when some of the louts thought they could come here all hard and cause trouble, know what I mean?"

Adam nodded.

"So, as it goes, me and my mates enjoyed a bit of a bundle back then and the proper noddies, well they kind of liked how we handled crowd policing, so, well, some big bust was going down and we were pulled in to beef up the thin blue line, see what I mean?"

"I do, John, I can see you being a bodyguard for some young PC. I bet they depended on you."

"You know, I think they did, especially when they were setting out to nick a local gang of drug pushers. There was a scumbag called Sniff Taylor who had the local drugs market, mostly coke, tied up around here. He and his cruddy henchmen ruled the roost to the extent that this Sniff character believed he could get away with anything. You know, he even attacked a young girl on her doorstep. Jo her name was. She's married to the boss at Onetelcall now, you know, that big IT security place on its campus-type development on the edge of town?"

"Yes, I do know it. I met one of their chaps at one of those business club meetings at the hotel in town. Max, yeah, a bloke called Max, seemed ok to me, very likeable and clearly very clever."

"Clever? Oh, yes, I expect so, that company is known everywhere for fighting those computer criminal gangs and the assholes who do- what is it? You know, all the hacking and spreading lies and shit, more shit than I can spread, that's for sure."

Adam laughed and topped up John's vodka glass.

"So, back to the story, and it turned out the Sniff character done a runner, and his half-witted musclemen were eventually caught somewhere in Brum and everyone thought that Olderbury would be less coke-infested with the supply cut off."

"And was it? And for how long?" asked Adam, guessing the answer.

"The thing is, it was for a while. Street violence and yobbism died down and I suppose those who needed coke were getting it elsewhere, but that didn't last long."

"No, really?"

"You may take the piss, but when drugs came back to town, they came back in a much bigger and better way, complete with a new division of organised crime living in broad daylight in our poshest gated housing, right under plod's noses. Well, the gang bringing all the stuff in was, I believe, Albanian and they imported most of the stuff along with the people they boated in to be soldiers. I mean foreign soldiers in our country, for God's sake, but that's not the point. The point is that what they didn't bring in via their own various channels and routes came in via make-believe imports and, yes, I can see you are ahead of me…"

"The Albanians were hand in glove with the Russians who sent their coke and other drugs into the UK, through importers like Rushian, yeah?"

"In one, old man, in one. So, see, the Olderbury police, along with some other dudes - that Max bloke seemed to be involved with it - had a real go. The Max bloke nearly got his bollocks shot off, the Albanian boss died soon after in hospital and we, me and my mates and few other PCs, got a real fun day busting all the houses, warehouses, garages and, yes, suppliers and importers known to be associated with the gang. I got to leap about the Rushian building but, and here's the thing, they were as clean as a fucking police whistle. They had a massive safe fridge in their warehouse which the police were sure was filled with white powder, pills and moody drugs but, let me tell you, oh dear…" John had to pause to laugh uproariously, "It was filled with industrial detergent powder, bloody boxes and boxes of fucking washing powder! Talk about a whitewash, oh dear, laugh…"

"John, do you know what the detergent powder was for?"

"No mate, no idea, I just remember the cops wetting their truncheons when they saw all that powder only to be well and truly washed up when they tested it for narcotics and found loads of chemicals, like mainly sodium sulphate which is good in washing powder but rubbish at getting you high, makes you shit a lot though, so I believe."

"I believe cheap sodium sulphate is just one of the cutting agents used by drug dealers to mix with coke to reduce the purity and make it go a lot further, more powder, more profit. I suspect your police colleagues found a smoking gun without knowing it had been fired. Tell me, what happened after the bust?"

"Bugger all, that I know of anyway. There were no arrests and, last I saw, it was business as usual at the Rushian warehouse. I know the cops kept a close eye on it, but nothing more ever happened as far as I know and, anyway, I quit soon after that 'cos I was needed on the farm. My old dad was beginning to fade by then and my muscles were needed for better purposes than smacking the occasional pratt."

"Hmm," said Adam, thinking back to the safe and Anna's suspicious slip of the tongue, "I wonder…"

12

Melor's campaign of infecting all the machines identified by the UK friends of the SVR was more successful than he dreamed. NHS trusts throughout the UK were reporting alarming increases in the amount of downtime suffered by non-critical processors in a range of monitoring, control and management systems.

To add to the effectiveness of his first attack wave, Melor created an AI-driven social media initiative which took newsfeeds from respected international news agencies and cited them in rabblerousing messages attacking the NHS, the government, civil servants and any other populist targets, so emphasising the effects of his hacking handiwork.

Because of the haphazard nature of Melor's hacking stratagem, he created a monitoring system based on the technical identity information he'd been given by the British collaborators. His monitors followed his system's distributed bugs and noted where they had hit home and where they had not landed. This gave him the analysis he needed to direct his attacks more accurately. He also developed a more advanced code which, once installed in a simple device such as a patient observation monitor, would emit random and, where the devices were networked, on-command instruction-set changes. Absurd blood pressure readings of three hundred over eight became common.

Melor noted that he had also been successful in installing his malicious code into several of the internal pharmaceutical request systems and could now control both the order and its destination. This, he knew, with some work could be valuable to his longevity and eventual freedom from the domineering Major. He was proud of his work and issued several blogs on dark web cybercrime platforms to crow about his achievement. The more he blogged, the more the myth of Melor became established.

Meanwhile, in a remote hillside villa above the Italian coastal town of Mattinata, Pal, the self-acclaimed greatest hacker ever, read of Melor's activities and snarled in fury and derision.

"Have you seen this shit?" Pal yelled at his friend, housemate and fellow in cyber chaos, Agron.

"Is that the UK NHS hit? Some Russian arse who thinks he's big stuff, making a big deal out of a silly little prank if you ask me."

"You are right, Agron. As always, you are spot on. Wankers like this fucking hackovitch give people like you and me a bad name. I feel like his bollocks should hang from our Christmas tree."

Agron laughed. It was an infrequent treat to hear something amusing from his dour genius friend.

Agron, a wordsmith and social media manipulator without peer and Pal, most probably even better than his proud self-assessment, had been a secret weapon in an Albanian mafia-style organisation and had achieved worldwide acclamation. When the gang imploded, the pair fled to Italy where they had lived happily without any upset. However, they were then coerced into joining forces with Max at Onetelcall - an anathema to both these psychotically misanthropic firebrands - to defeat a zealot fundamentalist's synchronised onslaught of riots and violence throughout Europe.

"The thing is Pal, what he's doing is effective," warned Agron. "It isn't pretty or elegant, but it is working. His backup social media is whipping up even more UK anti-government rhetoric and is as good as it needs to be, I suppose. Nothing like our work but, it must be said, for a Russian, it is less crappy than the usual attempts."

"Whatever, Agron, whatever, it has made me angry and if I learned anything from our old boss, Lorik, anger should be acted on. Now, I don't know whether to stamp on the jumped-up little turd from here or think of something clever and sneaky for over there in his world but which keeps us away from any suspicion."

"I know what you are saying, I know what you are thinking. We are getting to be the archetypal 'odd couple', do you know that?"

"Just think about it, yeah, and we'll talk again about this Melor, the Moscow moron."

Major Vassiliev had also heard rumours from the Moscow Institute about Melor's dark web preening. He was not amused and sent Luka to deliver Melor to his office.

Luka knocked on Melor's door. "You in trouble my friend?"

Luka's matey enquiry, as intended, made Melor feel even more anxious.

"You tell me, Luka. You know what is in the Major's mind, don't you?"

"I do my friend, I do, and I don't think he is at all happy with you but I shall leave it to him to explain why."

"Of course you will."

Vassiliev wasted no time in explaining, "You miserable, crawling worm, you dog's excrement, I should have sent you to prison but, no, I was lenient and that was a mistake, I think. You wouldn't be telling the world how clever you are with a broom handle up your arse and a murderer's cock in your toothless mouth, would you?"

Melor knew the Major wasn't exaggerating. Tales of depraved barbarity in Russian prisons were common and he knew he wouldn't survive incarceration in any of them.

"I am guilty of hubris, Major. I am and I admit it, but I was eager for the world to know how you, Major Vasily Vassiliev, allowed me, a humble code writer, such a magnificent opportunity to serve his state, and his country and to strike, with great ingenuity, at his country's enemy. I meant no personal glorification; I was only over-enthusiastic in praising the munificence of this great Russia of ours."

"Unmitigated little creep, oily spawn of a slithering viviparous reptile, you think your dissembling will save you from my harshest judgement, do you?"

"But Major, I have achieved what I promised and great appreciation of the initiative you enabled is already being spoken of in the offices of the Kremlin. I know this from my colleagues at the university and at MIPT. However, Major, I know you to be a perfectionist who always looks for more, for better, for the best and now, Major, I think you will be pleased to hear that I feel I can make even more glorious the reputation of Major Vasily Vassiliev."

"I am yet to be convinced that you have delivered all you should have achieved. If you have further developments, now is the time to tell me, before I remove your liberty, before you brag to the world again, and, indeed, while you still have a tongue!"

"Last time we talked, I asked you if some of our friends, your contacts who lurk in the contemptible British hospitals, would be happy to receive some, ah, what- well pharmaceutical windfalls perhaps for their own consumption or, perhaps to send on to their colleagues here in Russia, remember?"

"I do."

"I can now tell you, Major, that I am able to develop a new electronic agent of Mother Russia to insert into the lax British systems. My code, written and created by me alone, Major, will divert drugs - including the popular opiates and street favourites the Chinese distribute to America so successfully through Mexico - to any destination we dictate. Our friends can click and collect, ha! Better than any shop, and I will ensure supply. This can make millions if commercialised and will drain essential stocks from the NHS. I can disrupt their daily activity and cost them a large fortune at the same time, so providing exactly as our leader has described as a desirable endeavour."

Major Vasily paced slowly and thoughtfully around his office. His silence was a practised intimidation, and it worked on Melor who, knowing this could be a pivotal moment, felt sick and shaky.

"I will say this, worm. I had intended this day to transport you to Omsk, to the IK-6 prison colony, a gulag where I can promise sub-zero temperatures, regular beatings and liberal amounts of electrocution from enthusiastic guards and inmates who would see torturing you as a privilege." Vasily stopped talking and let Melor mull over this information.

Melor felt his stomach contract and his bowels shudder, a coldness engulfed him. He held onto that precious word 'had.'

"I understand you have the power to do this, Major. I can do nothing but reinforce my determination to make you even more powerful and, one day, perhaps, see me with a little less condemnation. I can do what I say, Major. It is a scheme so clever it hits many targets in one manoeuvre. Who could not be impressed, even the army generals would approve of such a multi-pronged attack, and you know how much influence the army generals have these days."

"While they deliver, while they nod in sycophantic agreement and while they are allowed to live," observed the major grimly. "There are still many windows and many rooftops for those who fall from favour, quite literally. I hope you fully understand what I am saying."

Melor had an insight into the Major's mind. For Vassiliev to succeed in his career, he must excel and delicately navigate political deceit; to fail at any level would mean death. For a man like him, placing trust in anyone was a risk far greater than it might seem.

"Major," said Melor with a strange sense of fellowship, "my life is in your hands, I know this. I also know that while success brings glory, failure brings death and to that extent, your life is in my hands. You have allowed me to live and to prove my worth to my country. I could never endanger any of that by not fulfilling my promises to you, never. My death would be an insignificance, but yours would be a national tragedy and my love for my country would never allow that to happen, never."

"You read the situation correctly, so correctly in fact that my decision is simplified. To remove you now would raise eyebrows in some unimportant areas, that is true, but I would be safe. On the other hand, to continue with this strategy could bring with it future accolade and approbation in more important sectors, if it succeeds as you say it will. You are not correct, however, in thinking that there is any equivalence in our positions. I shall always have fallbacks, always a plan upon a plan, that is how I am in the position I enjoy now and that is how I shall continue to be more and more powerful."

"I fully understand, Major. Am I to finish my development and transfer the British drugs to Russian ownership?"

Vasily Vassiliev paced again. "You have one week from today. You will return in one week with a working proposition and then I shall tell you how it will work, where the drugs are to be sent and how. Is that understood?"

"It is understood, Major, and at the risk of resorting again to hubris, I promise to make your success, your power a byword for brilliance in the offices of the Kremlin."

"Get out, worm."

"Good day, Major."

13

"Well, I'll be damned!" said Max, loudly.

"I hate it when you do that. You make a great exclamation and then don't say what or why."

"Oh, sorry Mand, just a bit in shock. You see, I've just had a surprise, a most unexpected email from an old foe who now, after that murdering Iranian mullah, Boss Dick and the cyber terror affair, appears to be a friend."

"Who's that then?"

"It's that little Agron dude, remember? The Albanian Shakespeare, the fella who worked with the man known only as Pal and what a brilliant hacker he was. I wish we could employ him; he'd do more to stop cybercrime than most of Onetelcall combined."

"But you caught him, didn't you?"

"Well, in a manner of speaking, I suppose we did. But Mand, he is bloody clever, it's just that he hates everyone, well just about everyone except Agron and perhaps me and Duggie."

"So, what's he want then, this super-hacker Pal's pal? Why is he contacting you?"

"I'll read what he says, listen: A feeble Russian hacker is attacking your NHS using a bad copy of one of Pal's techniques. Are you investigating this? I am sure you are. Know this, we will help you again. He is angry. I am angry. Agron."

Amanda laughed. "Surprisingly few words, that's unlike Agron. Remember how he and Jo formed a real bond, even though he was working for such a hoodlum?"

"Yes, I do. I remember Dan and the thug bossman, Lorik, being almost matey in their biggest-willie showdown too."

"Hmm, just before he blasted you in the nethers. Yes, what fun memories."

"Anyway Mand, coming in straight after everything that Ben had to say and after all the investigation I've done and what Jo and the team already know, it seems this NHS onslaught is growing into a very big deal indeed. You have to think that if Pal has noticed it, then I am even more convinced that whatever techniques they are using must be capable of a far bigger attack than the intrusions and hacks we have seen so far."

"You aren't alone in thinking that," agreed Amanda. "After our chat with Ben, I had a word with the cybercrime unit at the Met and their chums at the National Crime Agency Cyber Specialists. They all agree with what you said that what we are seeing may well be an array of testers, fishing expeditions, perhaps trials, you know, to see how successful they can be, to assess the firewalls and anti-hacking precautions they need to overcome."

"That's probably true. Hackers learn a lot from how their attempts are fought off. They analyse, tweak and try again until they can penetrate the impenetrable. You know, Mand, I'm getting an odd feeling about all this. I can sense trouble ahead and the more we push, the more I think we'll find. I assume you are Ok to follow up on Ben's suspicions as an official police enquiry? I'll go back to work and begin to put some direction and purpose into our research."

"Are you going to mention Agron and Pal?"

"No Mand, I think I'll keep quiet about them for now, don't want to confuse things with who is a good guy and who isn't."

Increasingly mobile, Max could get about, swinging happily on his crutches. His insurance company had offered him a like-for-like replacement car, but he had asked for an automatic version. He found that with the driver's seat pushed back and slightly reclined, he could rest his broken leg against the wheel arch and drive capably with just his left foot playing over the two pedals. It took a little while to get the braking pressure right, but he soon became adept at this race-and-rally driving left-foot technique. Freedom, at least, was his again, even though Amanda thoroughly disapproved and promised to 'nick him' if she saw him out on the road.

His return to the Onetelcall offices had caused much celebration and cheering. Max was deservedly popular and had become something of a talisman for the company. If Max was there to protect them, everyone would be safe, they believed. They all knew of the courage and ingenuity he and Duggie had shown in past showdowns against threats from cyber criminals made flesh, such as Moldovan drug runners, Triad crypto-frauds and even Hamas terrorists. They all knew that the Onetelcall buildings had been bombed twice but, with Max and Duggie on the ground, nobody feared an attack would be successful.

Max soon settled back in his office, his recovering leg resting on a footstool which was more theatrical than therapeutic. Duggie, pleased to have his friend back in the fold, tolerated Max's 'any chance of a coffee' pleas for an entire day until, seeing Max's crutch-supported agility, he told him exactly how to get his own coffee and where to pour it.

His first visitor was Dan, co-founder and now CEO of Onetelcall. Max and Dan had history, they had conspired to perpetrate a dire deepfake revenge on the Olderbury drug dealer who had attacked Jo, and that experience had created a lifelong bond between the two men.

"You don't have to be a bloody hero all the time," smiled Dan. "You can just as easily work from home until your leg is fully weight-bearing again. I know we'd be on shaky ground with our insurance company if you go arse over while you are on the premises."

"No, mate, I've had enough of remote working. I don't know how people do it. I can't stand the lack of involvement and, oh, I don't know, that sort of motivation you get from being in the thick of things."

"Ok, whatever, I know you are only here to soak up the adulation."

Duggie laughed, "He's getting precious little of that around here, I can tell you. I know him too well."

"Yeah, and me," nodded Dan. "So, chaps, what's the story, eh? I've had Jo bending my ear about attacks on the NHS - not one of our customers I hasten to point out - and that you and half the bloody company, to say nothing of the Olderbury police force, are tilting full speed into a major investigation. Is that a fair assessment?"

"Good question, boss. Duggie, would you care to answer our CEO?"

"Certainly Max, my pleasure. You see, Dan, Kathy has been vociferous about the vulnerability of the NHS, but, I tell her, the NHS isn't even a customer but still she says it should be investigated so, you see, Kathy tells me that she is working with Jo who says…"

"Yeah, yeah, yeah, very good Dug. I take the point. We are both mere playthings for our wives' greater purposes," laughed Dan.

"Ha, try being married to a police officer," said Max drily.

"Ok, so, Duggie, Max, is this a case Onetelcall should be getting on? I mean, I'm committed, as you know, to any fight against cybercrime and, candidly, whether the NHS is a customer or not, if we can track this hacking to its source and stop it, well, our stock hits the stratosphere. So, commercially, I suppose it is a supportable initiative."

"Well, boss, we know that this is coming from Russia, and we know that the chief hacker is busy blowing his trumpet all over the dark web and hacker chat rooms. Ok so far. We also know that there must be some inside assistance, or at least we think there must be, and we know we'll have the full backing of Olderbury Hospital for just about anything we ask of them. I've got loads of background, as has Jo, and I know Graham's goonhillies, the digital snooper girls and Kathy's lot are all keeping eyes on any suspicious traffic. So, let's have a planning roundtable and formulate our next plan of action, shall we?"

"In the national interest and, more importantly, for peace at home, I don't think we have a choice."

Dan was interrupted by the imperative shrill of Max's mobile. Over the speaker, they heard, "Max? It's Ben Barrington. Listen, you know we thought there would be more to this hacking? Well, there is and it's serious, really serious. Our internal drugs requisition system has just lost nearly a thousand packs! Our entire stock of opiates and opioids, all lost, gone and we don't know where or how. Man, this is a disaster!"

Max looked at his colleagues, "Well chaps, here we go again."

14

The results shocked Adam. His high-priced, beautifully packaged caviar, all varieties, contravened the CITES guidelines and contained only a trace amount of sturgeon roe. The rest was a blend of dried lumpfish and whitefish roe, all bulked up for added expensive weight with vegetable oil, tapioca pearls and other fish eggs. The County Scientific Services Laboratory was explicit. The products were illegal and shouldn't be used or resold, as both varieties also showed the presence of borax, a traditional caviar additive, now illegal.

It wasn't the wasted five thousand pounds that annoyed Adam, it was the realisation that despite his scrupulous checking, this supplier as recommended by his importer, was just a gang of rogues and thieves. He could already hear the voices of hindsight telling him he should have just gone to one of the major caviar houses. But Adam thought he had done that.

He called Pauline, "Remember our discussion about the pitfalls of trading in fish and caviar?"

Pauline could tell from his voice, "Oh no, Adam, oh no, not our lovely caviar? I so enjoyed that afternoon. Don't tell me it is duff. How bad is it? Can we still use it? Tell me, Adam."

"Our worst fears multiplied," said Adam miserably. "I sent some samples off for official testing. I thought I'd need a certificate for online selling, anyway. It came back with a bloody shopping list of our caviar's ingredients, all of which shouldn't be there, including borax which is a poisonous irritant to eat."

"Borax? Really, blimey, I thought borax was used in washing powders and the like, not as a recipe ingredient. How terrible. So, does this mean all that lovely- well what I thought was lovely, caviar has to be chucked?"

Adam's answer was distant and distracted, "Yeah, I suppose-no, a coincidence, well maybe…"

"Are you still talking to me?"

"Oh, sorry Pauline, my mind was just wandering for a moment. I was thinking about borax and detergents and what I was saying to your John about how cheap detergent powder is used to bulk up cocaine. It was a chat we had after I'd been to Rushian warehouse which, John said, was suspected of being a cocaine importer. See what I mean?"

"Not really Adam no, but that's not unusual."

In his Parkside office, Adam carefully wrapped up the remaining unopened tins of caviar, along with a letter demanding that his money be returned and exactly why. It was a vain hope, he knew, but he wanted to register his disgust. There was no return label, of course, but now Adam had two reasons to go back to Rushian importers and their suspicious roller-doored warehouse, with that extraordinarily safe safe. So safe that he needed to investigate.

"Hello Anna," he said, smiling his friendliest smile. "I came in a few days ago."

"Oh, 'hello luv, you're the caviar man. Yes, of course, I remember you. We don't get many polite and nice people in here, mainly just bad-tempered truck drivers and taxi drivers always in a rush. What can I do for you luv, more caviar? I don't think I've seen anything more come in for you."

"No Anna, it's quite the reverse. You see, the caviar that I collected from you, well frankly, it wasn't all it should be. So I want to return what's left after trying it, and I thought it would be best if I came to you and asked you to send it back to wherever it came from. Can you do that for me?"

"I'd be happy to do anything for you luv, just hang on will you?"

Anna tapped at her terminal and looked up, "There's nothing here about returns or anything, not prepaid or anything like that. So, you'd have to pay, luv, sorry, but that's all I can say."

"I see, but you do have a return address, don't you?"

"Yes, I've got an address, so I'm sure we can ship it back for you, but, as I said, it'll cost you. Oh, hang on again luv."

Anna's heels clickety-clacked as she went down the metal staircase and came swiftly back up again.

"Well, that's a thing luv, we've just got another consignment logged in to go to Moscow. So, what I can do is consolidate, you know put your box on the same load as the other lot and it will cost you loads less, ha!" Anna snickered at her little pun. "Mind you, it might take a day or two longer but, you know, cheaper and everything, that'd be good, wouldn't it?"

"You are wonderful Anna, thank you so much," Adam smiled again. "Can you fill out the paperwork and I'll pay you now by card if that's Ok. Oh, and could you give me the return address along with my receipt please?"

"Course I can luv, anything. If you want to wait a tick, I'll get it all done."

Adam duly waited as Anna tapped away again. Then, as he slotted his card into the reader, she said, "Your package then luv? I need your package now. Is it downstairs in your car?"

Anna followed him to the car park, past the open roller doors. "Busy then, are you?" he asked.

"Yeah, always busy. Shipments coming in and out from all over. It's a mare, luv, honestly, it is."

"And what do you keep in the safe? Do you import things of great value or is it just for, well, more delicate- what did you call it, yes, gear?" Adam had chosen his words specifically and noted Ann's slight flush in response.

"Oh, I couldn't really say, luv, not my place you see, and I'd get a strip torn off if I said more than I should."

"Well, we couldn't have that, thanks Anna for all you've done. I'm most grateful. Look, here is the box, it's all ready to ship, just needs the address and the right labels I suppose. Don't I have to fill out any declarations or anything?"

"Oh no luv, I always do all that, it's easier that way."

"I see, well that's great then," he said, staring directly into the warehouse. Right by the doors stood several boxes, all tightly taped up but, he noticed with surprise, that they appeared to be old NHS cartons. It didn't mean anything to him at the time, but it stuck in his mind.

He waved goodbye to Anna and drove off, his mind buzzing with possibilities which all sounded too movie-like to be real, but he couldn't ignore the facts, and he certainly couldn't dismiss Anna's unintended reactions.

He called John, "Look mate, sorry to bother you and I expect you'll laugh at me but, the thing is, I think the Rushian Import people are up to the top of their very tall, very secure 'fridge in something very illegal. I have every belief that it is importing and distributing drugs, possibly still coke."

"Probably, Adam, wouldn't surprise me at all, but what would I know? I'm out of that world now and me and my old girls don't have any need for drugs that don't come from the vet."

"I know, John, but I had to talk to someone. I still feel I have to talk to someone, and I thought you'd know who that someone should be. I mean, the police I suppose but I doubt they'd take me seriously. What do you think?"

"Honestly Adam, if you walked into Olderbury nick with that tale, they'd just ignore you. Every syllable you say would mean more effort and form-filling to the desk staff. So, they'd try to sound reassuring before saying goodbye. No mate, if I were you, I'd talk to someone who'd listen and the only cop I know who fits that bill is Amanda Golby. She's a detective and she's really good. Actually, she's married to that Max guy at Onetelcall. Anyway, I've still got her direct line and mobile. I'll text them over to you, yeah?"

Back in his unit, Adam chatted with the part-time staff he had employed to handle phone and online orders and dispatch them via their courier services. The administration department, next to his office, as always buzzed with the tapping of keyboards and people answering phones for enquiries and phone-in orders. The atmosphere of hectic activity and happy staff delighted him.

As he reached his office, he found himself rehearsing what he could say to the detective, a skilled and clever DCI, according to John. Adam was not used to feeling apprehensive. He had faced some intimidating and powerful people without flinching, but just the thought of reporting his suspicions of drug activity made him feel foolish.

The phone lines at Olderbury police station appeared exceptionally busy so Adam was put through without the standard cross-questioning. Screening was evidently arbitrary, he assumed.

"Golby."

Here goes, thought Adam. "Hello, my name is Huddard, Adam Huddard, I have a business called Adam Superfoods on the Parkside Industrial Estate. John Harrison, a former special PC holds you in very high regard; he gave me your name and I just hope what I have to say doesn't sound stupid. I really do believe I've stumbled across a drug import and distribution business, and I should tell somebody about it. John tells me that I should tell you," Adam shuddered to a stuttering halt.

"Thank you, Mr Huddard, would you like to breathe now?"

"Oh, yes," laughed Adam, "and it's Adam, please."

"Ok Adam, I'm Amanda. So, that's the formalities done with. You've found some evidence of drug activity, have you?"

"Yes, Amanda, I really believe I have, I'm not the sort…"

"No, Adam, I'm sure you're not. Do you want to give me a little more detail?"

"The short version, yeah. I imported some caviar, but, as it turned out, it was all dodgy. It came in via Rushian, an import and export warehouse, one of the older places with a big roller door, you know down on the light industrial area on the way to the river?"

"Yes, I am aware of Rushian," said Amanda, "and before you go any further, I must ask if you might have committed any infringement of our import regulations by bringing in some questionable caviar. I must ask as it may colour how I treat any evidence you give me; you understand?"

"Of course, I see exactly," replied Adam. "No, I haven't. I returned the goods after having them analysed so I'm very much on the right side of the law, but, you see, at Rushian, I saw…"

"Adam, sorry to interrupt again, but I feel we might have a more productive initial conversation if we met. Would that be possible?"

"Oh, really, well, yes, of course, yes, that is a good idea. Where do you meet usually for such conversations? I mean you are welcome to come to my unit, although it is quite busy and noisy, or I would be delighted to buy you a coffee or something somewhere more discreet. I know, how about the hotel in town, you know, The Royal George?"

"Yes Adam, perfect, they serve coffee in the reception lounge. It is open but there are areas which are quite private. If we need more privacy, then we can come to the nick. But, for now, the Royal will be ideal. When would you like to meet?"

"Amanda, you are undoubtedly busier than I am, and you are my priority now, so I'm free from the moment I put this phone down."

Considerate, thought Amanda appreciatively. "Well, Adam, it is late afternoon now, so how about this, I am about to leave work anyway so, half an hour from now? Would that work for you?"

As he walked into the hotel, Adam looked around the open seating area and appreciated its clever layout, designed to cater for any number from one to half a dozen, for formal or business meetings or just for a casual drink or coffee. He chose a secluded table and sat to wait for the DCI.

While Adam had been driving to the hotel, Amanda called Max, "Hello darling, you very busy?"

"Mand, you alright?" Max asked, surprised at the unexpected call.

"Yes, I'm fine. Look, could you fire up your high-speed crutches and hot foot it down to The Royal George, like about now?"

"Oh Mand, you've booked a room and you're planning on taking advantage of a poor defenceless one-legged man, right?"

"You wish, no Max, do you ever think of anything else? But no, not this time anyway, though, mmm, it's a nice idea, oh no, crikes, now you've got me at it, look, Max, I've just had a call from a guy who thinks he's spotted some funny goings on at Rushian."

"The importers? That wouldn't shock me much."

"No, I know, so I've invited him for a chat in the less formal atmosphere of the hotel's lounge and, well, he implied it could be a drugs distribution thing going on and I straight away thought of what Ben had said and wondered if there might be a link, which is why I think it would be useful to have you there too, to talk to this bloke, Ok?"

"I'm on my way."

Max was used to it by now. As Amanda strolled into the hotel's reception area, men who were busy talking stopped and gazed, following her into the room with their eyes. Adam too noticed her as soon as she appeared from the front doors.

Introductions soon dispensed with, she got down to business. "Adam, I've asked Max to join us because he is currently involved with a possible drugs theft. Not that this is the usual line of work for Onetelcall, there is usually a connection between drugs and IT tracking which can lead us to the culprits."

"Yes, of course, I understand that, but do you not have your own police cybercrime teams?"

"We do Adam, but in this case, there are more complex activities to consider, activities which Max and his colleagues are already pursuing. If, however, you'd rather…"

"Oh no, absolutely not, it's so good to see you again, Max. Not that you'll remember, we met briefly at one of the business meeting things, some time ago now but it's great, so good of both of you to meet me. I just hope I'm not wasting your time, my evidence, if I can call it that, is pretty thin."

"Tell us anyway, all you've got," said Amanda encouragingly.

Adam explained his sighting of the safe, the off-guard verbal slips made by Anna and the history of detergent presence with all the implications that might have.

Amanda listened without taking notes. "Thin would be a reasonable assessment of your case," she smiled. "I'm not sure there's enough for us to go on here; you've got a better case for food fraud than drug dealing."

"But Mand," interjected Max, "I've got a feeling about this. It might be slim as fact-filled indictments go but it does all make sense, doesn't it? And we know that drug dealing in Olderbury is back on the rise again, don't we? So, listen, if there isn't a good enough reason for you and your mates to go plodding in, how about I accompany Adam here for a repeat visit for some creatively imagined reason? I'm sure we can get Anna to open up a bit and I could have a sniff round too."

Max bought drinks and the three new collaborators enjoyed a general getting-to-know-you chat. As Adam was describing his annoyance at being sold duff goods, he remembered something that now seemed relevant.

"It's probably nothing, like most of my clues, but I saw something in the warehouse that stuck in my mind. As I said, probably nothing but why would an importer-exporter business like Rushian, be shipping boxes for the NHS?"

15

Adrian Simson was filled with awe at the skill, dexterity and learnedness of his mentor, Ben Barrington. Son of a primary school teacher mother, and a full-time union official father, Adrian had delighted his parents by being studious and clever, achieving top grades in maths, physics, chemistry and an A* in biology. An inclusive, diverse and sincere attitude helped him win through the admission tests and he studied for a Bachelor of Medicine and Bachelor of Surgery degree at the University of Bristol.

He met Ben during his first work experience session and spent the next two years studying general medical sciences followed by three years in clinical training. Now, as a junior doctor, he had been able to secure a position under Ben Barrington for the last of his six work placements in different environments. He loved his work and knew that in the fullness of time and once fully qualified as a consultant, he would earn significantly more than his current income, even when boosted by long stints of tiring but remunerative overtime.

And Adrian needed money. An exemplary young man in many ways, conscientious and kind, polite and empathetic, eloquent and resilient; he had all the prerequisites of a fine orthopaedic consultant, except for one flaw. He didn't drink, he didn't smoke, he didn't indulge in any luxuries, but he loved, just loved online roulette. He started gambling when he responded to a text on his mobile giving him twenty free roulette spins. To his delight, although in retrospect he recognised what a disaster it was, he won a very handy twenty pounds. His phone asked him for a credit card which he entered and enjoyed being able to have a flutter whenever the mood hit him. Online roulette, he found, was a welcome excitement, a relief from the stress of his work, the anxiety he suffered about his abilities and the grief he endured when a patient died.

The mathematician in Adrian believed he could be certain of winning and winning big over the longer term. Ignoring the possibility that such attitudes are common precursors of addiction, Adrian finely tuned a Fibonacci sequence, in which each number was the sum of the two preceding ones, to determine the size of bet he would make after each loss to create an overall running profit. Yes, of course, other punters had tried systems and lost to the inevitable house advantage, but they weren't Adrian Simson, grade-A maths star. Yes, others had lost because they lacked the self-discipline of a surgeon, the cold, calculating control required to resist a quick-buck win on outside higher-priced bets. Yes, some poor people became addicted, but they weren't him, the insuperable Adrian Simson.

Although shorter than they used to be, Adrian still worked long and arduous hours, often volunteering for additional shifts, his lifestyle left no time for any pastimes or hobbies. When he wasn't working, he was studying or sleeping. Online roulette fitted his schedule perfectly. He could play anywhere at any time. He didn't have to go to a casino, the wheel was in his pocket and always ready to spin. Ten minutes in the peace of a toilet cubicle, five minutes over a canteen coffee, a few spins before sleep, and a few more before leaving for work, Adrian could alleviate his anxiety and find comforting distraction whenever his mind needed relief. As time progressed, he found he was adjusting his daily routine to ensure he had sufficient time for his roulette session. He reduced his resting and sleeping time, cut back on time allowed for food and had no social life in or outside the hospital. His only extramural commitment was to the British Medical Association. He had been brought up to understand the power and importance of union representation and was pleased to work as a coordinator for the Association's Junior Doctors Committee.

Gary Pugh worked in BMA House as a senior organiser for the junior doctors' committee and any activities his committee might be in favour of arranging. He enjoyed his job, he enjoyed the power that he knew the BMA could wield and he found himself at home with those colleagues who shared his more radical values, standards and opinions. The BMA, a democratically structured union, relied on its active members, especially when local, regional or national negotiations for pay, conditions or NHS policies were being held. Gary could provide the ammunition, the view from BMA's standpoint, the arguments and the facts, but he needed his local coordinators to spread the word in each hospital or health service location.

Formerly a union activist at Manchester University's Students' Union, Gary had learned a lot about talent-spotting amongst union members. With over forty thousand members in Manchester, recognising who would be reliable and those who would be unmanageable agitators was a valuable skill. Agitators were splendid for whipping up outraged frenzy, but Gary looked for the calm and rational unionist to roll out his doctrine around the campuses and to organise effective flash mobs and parades of protest when needed. In Adrian, Gary knew he had a first-class local coordinator, but he had also noticed that in recent times, Adrian's response to requests for action, even minor events, had become lacklustre and unusually disinterested. Gary's instinct told him that Adrian had a problem and, sometimes, members with problems could be especially useful.

Adrian looked annoyed to see Gary sitting in his favoured hospital cafeteria. It was a public café, situated amongst the ground floor entrance shops that served the hospital's patients and visitors, as well as some passing local trade.

"Ah ha, I've been waiting for you Adrian. Good to see you, are you Ok?"

"Gary, hello, I wasn't expecting you. Look, I haven't got much time, is it important?"

Gary looked at Adrian. He was a different man from the bright-eyed dynamic young doctor he used to be, and Gary needed to know why.

"Look mate," Gary said soothingly, "the thing is, who looks after the people who look after us, eh? Not right, is it? I mean you work your arse off, you save lives, you take responsibility and make decisions that very few people would be prepared to make and for what, eh, for a fucking pittance. No thanks, no appreciation and a fucking insulting wage and that, mate, is what we are here for, your BMA, your family away from your family and you, especially you, a good union man and a valued friend and colleague, can depend on us if and when you need us, right mate? So, tell me, what's your prob eh?"

"What makes you think I've got any problems more than the usual ones we all suffer?" asked Adrian, stirring sugar into the hot Americano coffee just delivered to him.

"Aw c'mon mate, I know you, like, we've been buds for a while now, haven't we? I can tell something's up with you. I notice things, see, and I've noticed that your eagerness to be part of making a difference for all your colleagues is less, well, less, yeah, much less than it was a while ago. Now, I know, course I know, that you are knackered all the time, it's a grind what you do, a grind, but even so, you are not like the you I first knew."

"Is that so? Really? You know it's a grind and still wonder what's up with me. What do you think? I am, as you say, permanently, bloody knackered, I work all the hours and then a load more. What's worse is that I care, so I spend downtime worrying about patients on the edge of life; it gets to me, see? So sleep is a rare commodity, like money, you know that there's never enough sleep and there's never enough money is there?"

"I do understand Adrian, that's why I'm here, that's why the BMA is here, we try to make your life and the life of all your colleagues better by reducing your hours and increasing your pay, that's what we are all about."

"Bollocks Gary, I'm too tired to put up with your timeworn union-speak, your feeble justifications. The BMA is a political pressure group, you know it and I know it. You lot, you use junior doctors just like a mechanic uses a spanner, so don't come all holier-than-thou about trying to get a better deal for me, I know the truth, remember. And if you've come to talk about some more strike action, you can forget it. I'm up to my eyes in debt and strikes for more pay always end up costing more than I ever get back."

Gary knew that many junior doctors were given to self-medication. He understood why and didn't judge or criticise. He understood the demands of a junior doctor's working life and the need for some relief, some escapism. Many used alcohol, some found ways of acquiring quantities of painkillers and anaesthetic opiates, some developed a hunger for sex, some for food and some, he knew, found the same dopamine release and reward pathway stimulation from gambling. If he were a betting man, Gary would put Adrian down as a gambler, as none of the other likely respites from reality fitted his character or his demeanour.

"So, mate, is it money then? Is that the root of your evil, spending more than you earn or living the high life with fast cars and fancy parties?"

"Me, does that sound like me? I thought you said you knew me. So, look Gary, just bugger off now and leave me alone. I don't want to talk about any union activity, certainly not anything that means I get my pay docked. I mean you're bloody good at dragging us all out, but the union doesn't come up with any financial assistance, does it? Costs us poor mugs a fortune…"

"But you know it is all for the long-term good of your…"

"Yeah, yeah, when I'm dead and gone, junior doctors will all be paid what they deserve, but in my lifetime? Well, I've got debts to pay, see, so however much I support the union and its greater aims, I'm in no position to stand round a brazier, waving a placard and losing money, ok?"

"Ok, ok, I get you. Come on man, tell me, talk to me, how much do you owe and who do you owe it to?"

"None of your fucking business, Gary."

"But I can help. I might be able to help you and if I can, I will, but I can't do anything if you don't talk to me and tell me, honestly, what's going on. You are not the only one who cares for others, you know."

Adrian looked at the union man and wondered if talking to him might make his problems easier to address. "Gaz, you know that ads say 'gamble responsibly…'"

"Now there's an oxymoron if ever I heard one!"

"That's the truth, Gary, that's the real gospel. You see I enjoy the occasional flutter, online roulette mainly, it's a blast when I win but, well, at the mo, I'm not winning as often as I'm losing, see, that's the problem. It won't last of course, it's bound to change, my luck will come back, but to tide me over I've, well, you know, borrowed a few quid here and there and it is due for payback very soon, well, now actually."

"I see, Adrian, I see, and I do understand. Care to tell me how much you are in hock for?"

"Twenty-five grand and counting. Now you see why I'm a bit preoccupied and not so keen on any strike action."

"I do chum, I do indeed. That's a lot of wedge to come up with on the spot."

"Tell me about it."

"When's D-day, Ade? When do you have to pay these loans and what happens if you don't?"

"Yeah, loans is right, in the plural. I've got credit cards, bank loans, pay-day loans, you name it and just about all of them are due now, like today or very soon and you know what happens if I default, I'll be made insolvent and that'd screw my career well and truly."

"Yeah, there's always a lot more on the spin of a wheel than just a few quid," said Gary, immediately wishing he hadn't.

"Oh, how very fucking profound! How very full of wisdom. Just sling it Gary and come back when your beloved union has got twenty-five grand to give me for my services and loyalty, until then just fuck straight off will you."

"Sorry, Adrian. I'm sorry, I really didn't mean it like that, and I do realise that your job, presumably your home and life as you know it is pretty much at risk right now, isn't that right?"

"I'm not telling you again."

"So, I'll put twenty-five grand in your bank account today, no messing, the full amount straight away, no more questions, just your assurance that you'll pay off your debts and not use a penny of it for gambling again, ok?"

"You joking? That's not even remotely fucking funny, you complete tosser."

"No joke, Adrian. I'll need an assurance of being paid back over a reasonable period, of course. Although I might even be able to show you a way of keeping the loan and making a bit more on top of it; how would that sound?"

"Sounds bloody illegal to me. Is it Gaz? Is it illegal? What do I have to do, eh? What will you ask me to do in return for this dosh? It's not free, is it? You'll be expecting something, interest at a crazy rate, is that it, or something else?"

"Well, yes, Ade, but not what you think. No stupid high-interest rate, in fact, no interest at all, just a little help in fulfilling the aim of every union…"

"Which is?"

"Let's say the redistribution of wealth, except in this case, it is the redistribution of goods, a spot of rerouting of high-value goods to a place where they are more, you know, valued."

"Stealing? You want me to fucking steal for you?"

"No Adrian don't be a numpty, of course, not. All I'll want from you is a little information and the occasional helping hand with forms and the like, nothing dangerous, nothing like physically stealing, of course not, safe as houses and your saviour too."

16

Melor, unaware that he was making a powerful enemy in a distant country, continued to exploit techniques like those pioneered by Pal in his great Chatbot disruption. The AI facilities developed in conjunction with a major Chinese IT manufacturer, at the Moscow Institute of Physics and Technology, enabled Melor to insert his ever-more refined bugs over a larger number of devices in the UK's NHS services. The methodology Melor had designed looked for any open ports and auto-updates in networks known to serve hospital administration and functions processes and, to his delight, his constant cyber-searching in those networks had exposed many of the major suppliers to the NHS for hospitals and general practices across the UK. Now he could interrupt, on a random basis, many functions and could identify, create and redirect in-house requisitions for drugs and supplies on a massive scale throughout the entirety of the UK's health services.

Melor, like so many hackers, was addicted to creating chaos and, again echoing the brilliance of Agron and Pal's previous coups, planned to cause basic and practical disruptions at the same time as activating his primary hospital peripherals attacks. The General Practices made perfect targets. Permanently under pressure, constantly criticised and fighting to keep up with increasing demand, most General Practices had little resilience against cyber-attacks; *kak misheni*, thought Melor, easy target. The Major will be pleased.

As demanded, Luka collected Melor just one week after his last meeting and, as usual, Luka implied insider knowledge about Melor's fate.

"You hang by a thread, my friend. The Major gave you one week, and he is in no mood to be tolerant of any failure. I can tell you that for certain," the driver said as he slammed the liquorice-flavoured Moskvich's rear door on his passenger.

"You always fill me with such optimism, Luka," smiled Melor, feeling confident that his week's work would more than satisfy the Major's last ultimatum.

"I don't say these things lightly, young man," replied Luka with assumed authority. "Today the Major is feeling, how can I describe it, liverish, yes, he's feeling a little liverish, perhaps from last night's vodka. Anyway, his mood is not the best, his disposition not the most forgiving, if you know what I mean?"

Melor was not about to be knocked off balance by the driver's implications of a special, close understanding of the Major; it was all more aspirational imagination than reality.

"I'm not worried today, Luka, not at all. I have been more successful than the Major could have asked for and I am sure I will please him."

"Ok, young sir, ok, but then I ask you why today I am to deliver you to one of the secret rear entrances to Lubyanka and escort you personally to the Major's grand old KGB office, an office he reserves for the most serious of meetings?"

The Moskvich veered into Furkasovskiy Lane at the back of the large Lubyanka complex and then left, under the section on which the helipad sat, before drawing to a halt by a solid wooden door still adorned with the Soviet hammer and sickles. The splendour of the building's neo-Baroque exterior belied the austerity of much of its deeper interior. Melor, relishing his first visit to the famous building, had expected gold, crystal, old masters, tapestries and heavy antique furniture. Would he see some fabulous, looted treasures from the Tsar's palaces? Or would he be disappointed?

Luka marched Melor along a dark and dingy corridor, left and right, until they reached a more open space which Melor noted was rather grander. Through the large, secondary-glazed window he could see the column base which once supported a statue of Felix Dzerzhinsky, the fearsome Iron Felix, a leader of the Bolshevik Revolution and founder of Cheka, the first Soviet secret police organisation.

"Did I say to sit?"

"My apologies Major, I have been working very hard and am a little tired."

Melor rose from the guest's chair in Vasily Vassiliev's office and gazed around. If size was a measure of importance, then Major Vasily Vassiliev was not a man to be trifled with. If, however, quality was a more accurate yardstick, then the Major would be justified in harbouring some paranoia. The large room was workmanlike, threadbare and shabby. Where pictures of great figures from Russia's post-revolution history had once hung, stared images of Putin. Putin the KGB officer, Putin the huntsman, Putin the statesman, Putin the President and various other important, international groups starring the country's leader.

"You will sit when I say, you whelp. You will sit when you have convinced me that you have the viable proposition you promised me a week ago. If you don't have what you promised me, on pain of death you promised me, you will not sit, you will march from here to your doom. Do I make myself clear?"

"You do, Major Vassiliev, and as always you are succinct, and I hear both your words and your meanings. Happily, I come to you today to inform you that in the one week that you gave me, I have not only achieved but exceeded all of my promises to you. I think, no, I know, you will be pleased, perhaps even delighted and I hope I will bring a mood of happy optimism to you."

Major Vasily had been drinking Raf, a strong, sweet double-shot espresso coffee flavoured with citrus or lavender. Today it was astringent citrus, and it was particularly good, the Major found, for reducing the effects of last night's excesses. He felt less irritable and sluggish now than when he had scolded Luka for being five minutes late that morning.

"Then you have my attention, whelp, you have it for the next five minutes after which my tolerance of you will be fully expended."

Melor had mentally prepared for a colourful expose of his developments, a lengthy chronicle of his achievements, but his better sense told him that today was not a day for showboating.

"Then I too shall be succinct, Major. Promise Number One was to be ready to humble the already juddering mass of Britain's National Health Service. I am now ready to do exactly that throughout their hospitals and their local general practices - that is community doctors to us Major - and at your command, that process can begin immediately."

"You know I am having your work inspected, don't you? If you are overestimating your achievements, I shall discover very soon, and you are aware of what the penalty will be."

"I do know these things, Major. Your inspectors from the Institute and the University have been part of my work all week and I can assure you, Major, they are not only satisfied, they are also utterly amazed and in awe of what I can do."

Major Vasily was about to tear into Melor for being presumptuous and arrogant when it occurred to him that a man so knowingly close to prison, or worse, would not risk so much exaggeration about the estimation of his peers and Moscow's finest IT brains.

Noting the thoughtful pause, Melor jumped in again. "Promise Number Two, well more of an implication really, was that my attacks would be controllable, apparently random, untraceable and not risk lives unless such an added facility was to become desirable. I can, of course, confirm that this is the case."

"And what of the information I gathered for you from our friends in the UK?"

"Major, your help was invaluable, and I thank you profusely. When I promised to make you even more of a national hero than you already are, well, that is another promise I am keeping."

"Explain."

"Of course, Major, but please remember your promise to me, that if I do what I said I could do, you will pardon my previous, er, misdemeanour and allow me to continue to serve my country as a civilian and not a paroled convict."

"I am a man of my word, whelp. If you are to be of use to your country and our President, I shall ensure you can do so with as much freedom as any of us can claim."

It was Melor's turn for a pensive pause. Time to take a risk, he thought, a liverish major or not, it was time. "Major, we met, I admit, under less than favourable circumstances."

"For you."

"Yes, absolutely, less favourable for me but as you will see, extraordinarily favourable for you. Just how favourable is a matter for you to consider, whether what we can achieve together from now onwards should be exploited to favour your career, your promotion prospects and your public profile or, confidentially, whether it may, um, enhance your power base and, to a large extent, your, financial standing."

"What on earth are you wittering about, you whelp? Are you trying some half-brained bribery? Are you proposing to buy your release from my judgment?"

"Major, you castigated me for becoming Melor, the mythological genius, so well-spoken of on the dark web, in hacker chatrooms and the like. But think of this, you castigated me when I was still Bodgan, but now Bogdan is in the past and I truly am Melor, the hacker of great repute and I am not given such plaudits for no reason, certainly not for being half-brained. Even your own appointed experts acknowledge my gift, my expertise, my, yes, my genius."

"You are perilously close to the end of your days, you snail."

"Yes, Major, possibly, but listen, I am not bribing you, why would I? No, I am offering you some choices; I am saying that together we could accumulate power and wealth, very great wealth and very powerful influence. You will get to realise the greatness you know should be yours and I will become the most famous, most successful hacker in the world. That's what my half-brained proposal is all about."

"Words of fiction, at a time when your life is in great jeopardy, you choose to talk in words of some addled daydreamer. You had better explain yourself properly right now or this meeting and your life are both at an end."

"Then I shall, again, be succinct." Melor held out his hands and wiggled his fingers. "With just a few taps and clicks from these very fingers, I can provide you with limitless drugs to sell or to do with whatever you will. I can also provide you with data that is worth fortunes on the appropriate markets and, even better, I can provide you with data on some of the most important people in the UK, the wealthiest, the most famous, those who value their reputation and would be willing to pay to stop any unseemly medical information about them being leaked. How does that sound for starters?"

"For starters? If you have more to say, I suggest you say it now." Major Vasily was feeling a tremor of excitement. Could this worm be his passport to the world of his dreams?

"Of course, I have more. There will always be more but this time, I'll add just one more temptation for you. My system is a highly advanced, AI-driven version of the old ransomware that our hackers have been rolling out across the West for so long and with such success. Well, bluntly, my system can do all of that too. We can demand and receive bitcoin, or any currency, crypto or national, of your choice with every strike we make, millions for sure, possibly multi-millions over time. How does that sound for 'a one more thing'?"

"Is that it now? Have you said all you wish to say before I consider my position and your future?"

"No, Major, you accuse me of being presumptuous and now I shall prove you right. You see I am confident that you will come further on this journey with me and benefit, as you should, from its abundance. So, I will say that I ask for one more favour from you, a favour about information and it is this, how can I say it? To streamline my ability to redirect drugs, the right drugs, I need some further information, like all the in-house product codes and requisition forms and so on, so that I can reroute exactly what we want when we want it. Any junior doctor should be able to provide me with all that I need. I'll provide a specification for my needs of course."

Melor mentally smiled in triumph as he saw the look in the Major's eyes.

"Give me your wish list."

17

Adam couldn't let it go, "It's an itch that has to be scratched, a small voice asking questions that I have to answer," he explained to Amanda in a call to let her know he intended to go back to Rushian Import Export and see what information, if any, he could extract from the receptionist, Anna,

"I know we agreed that Max would come with me but, honestly, I feel I'll get further on my own if that's ok. We seemed to have a, well, rapport I suppose and I'm worried that being faced by two of us she'd turn all coy and secretive."

"I fully understand, Adam and I know Max will too. Good at being sniffy though he is, he is used to letting others do the digging when they have a better inroad than him. It works like that with him and Duggie all the time."

"Cool, that's that then, thanks. I will, of course, let you know what I find out, and, Amanda, is there anything you know of that I should be looking for? Do you or your colleagues have any particular suspicions which I might be able to follow up?"

"Oh, Adam, my answer to that would sound uncomfortably unprofessional. Since the raid your mate John told you about, we've all had suspicions about Rushian's range of imports and, truly, that's all we've got, suspicions. We've heard rumours about drugs coming in through Rushian, but no corroboration from any of the dealers, the very few dealers, we've nicked since the raid. We've heard about dodgy food, like your caviar but, so far, nothing concrete, not even a strong enough reason to justify a warrant. So, all I can say is, anything you find out will be more than we have at the moment, and it looks like food and drugs are the best bets for any import illegality."

"Well Amanda, the small voice in my head is asking about food so that's where I'll start."

Anna smiled happily when she saw Adam. "Hello luv, what brings you back here then, more caviar is it?"

"Hello Anna, look, I hope you don't mind but, well actually, I've come to ask if I might pick your brains."

Anna laughed, "Coo luv, that's what I call optimistic; most folk reckon I haven't got a brain to pick. But what on earth would you want to know from me? I mean you're a well-made-up sort of man, successful, clever and all that so what can my brain offer you, eh?"

"Anna, your modesty does you great credit, but I couldn't help noticing how at ease you are with all the paperwork and rigmarole that goes with importing and exporting and, no matter how much I read on the internet, it is all very foreign to me. I was hoping, if you don't mind, that I might buy you lunch or dinner in exchange for you explaining, as simply as possible, just what I should know and need to do to set up a regular import and export arrangement with Rushian. You know, an arrangement which includes all the usual legal declarations, valuations, insurances, carnets or whatever, all that sort of stuff. Well would you, please, very please? I really do need your help."

Anna laughed again, feeling an inner tingle of pleasure. "Well luv, there's a thing, me being able to help you, and, what's more, it's a pleasure to get nice people in here. So, yeah luv, if I can help you in any way, I'd love to. Yes, I would."

Anna had anticipated the next question and quickly planned her answer. She'd make the most of this unexpected opportunity.

"So, Anna, when would be best for you, lunch, or perhaps, dinner?"

"Thing is luv, I don't have a lunchtime as such, not really. It's always all go through the day here. Often, I don't have any lunch or just a coffee and biscuit or chocolate bar or something like that."

Adam returned to Rushian's yard as arranged at six-thirty and was surprised to see Anna looking very much the sophisticated dinner companion. She had changed from her office clothes into a chic dark green dress which complemented her long, wavy red hair, cascading down from her more usual simple topknot. Adam was impressed.

Hello, luv," she gushed. "Look, I have to say that just 'cos I couldn't do lunch, I don't expect a big dinner and all that. You know your caviar and whatever, a bar snack will be fine, honest."

Adam had booked a table at the recently remodelled Carpenters Arms. As a managed pubco establishment, it offered predictable food of a decent standard and a menu range which satisfied the needs of most midweek diners.

Anna expressed her delight, "Ooh, I love it here, how did you know? They do a seafood pasta which is delish, especially with a glass of white, I love it."

Adam obliged with a bottle of Pinot Grigio which Anna sipped appreciatively as they settled in, beginning with some introductory, exploratory small talk. They had more in common than he expected. Like Adam, Anna was single following a divorce some years earlier, but unlike Adam, her marriage was childless. At first sight, Adam had thought Anna was much younger but, she revealed self-consciously, that she was only eight years his junior, prompting Adam to offer a sincere, appreciative compliment.

She had trained as an accountant and acquired the foundations of a successful career until, at her husband's insistence, she started to work part-time and, when trying to start a family, she stopped working completely. Once single again and with what she believed to be only a miserly, mediocre settlement, she took a job with Rushian, a job for which she was over-qualified, but which paid better than any more professional vacancies at the time.

Adam also discovered that Anna, although attractive and amusing company, had a surprisingly limited social life. For her, supper at The Carpenters was something of an occasion. He also found out that she was an enthusiastic wine drinker. He poured and she talked.

"They'd be totally lost without me now, luv," she declared about her role at Rushian. "They were in a complete mess when I got there. The paper filing was all in overflowing boxes and their online organisation was all over the place too. Terrible really, considering how busy they are and how much stuff comes in and out, all around the world. Amazing they manage to get anything anywhere."

Adam sensed his opportunity. "It doesn't seem like a particularly large warehouse for so much shipping of goods. What sort of stuff do you mainly handle, or don't you get to know?"

"Oh, I get to know most things, luv, I have to you see, for all the paperwork and legal stuff. But I shouldn't really talk about it, I mean commercial secrets and all that. I know we have a company policy that nobody ever talks about what's in the boxes and crates that we handle; strict, they are about that, luv."

"Anna, so sorry, I didn't mean to pry. I'm just interested, that's all. Usually, you see, import and export shipping companies have huge great warehouses and lorry yards, and Rushian seems to be, you know, compact, limited for both storage and transport space but, of course, I couldn't ask you to break company policy on discretion, I wouldn't do that."

Anna's fingers played with the stem of her wine glass, twizzling it around as she looked across the table at her host. She had been off men since her divorce some three years ago, but this one was different. He was friendly, funny and courteous, he made her feel feminine again, a feeling she didn't get from any other colleagues or customers. She had to admit it, she was a little bit smitten.

"You can ask me whatever you like, luv. I can trust you, I know I can and it's good to be able to talk to someone, nobody else is interested in what I do."

"I know what you mean. When I tell people I sell food that is healthy and different from the supermarket run-of-the-mill bad-for-you products, I see their eyes glaze over and they suddenly need to talk to someone else."

"Oh, bless you luv," she smiled. "I think what we put in our bodies is vitally important..." For the second time in his company, Anna was caught off-guard by what she had said, and she flushed and giggled with a sudden embarrassment. He raised an enquiring eyebrow.

"Oh dear, luv, I didn't mean, you know anything rude, I meant what we eat, not any other sort of..."

"Anna, I know exactly what you meant, although I do have a weakness for the occasional double-entendre I must admit," he chuckled boyishly. "But you do give yourself away when realise you've said something risky. Remember the first time I met you? No, I don't suppose you do, but you did it when I said about 'shipping gear'. I think, you assumed I'd think you meant gear as in, well, gear of the dope variety, which I didn't at the time. Although I've since been told by a local chap that Rushian once had some sort of drug dealing accusations made against it, a long time ago I'm sure, but your sensitivity about the word 'gear' made me wonder, I have to say."

Suddenly, Anna's Pinot Grigio assisted easy happiness became sharp-eyed wariness, "Is that what this is about? Have you made a fuss about wanting me to help you understand import and export procedures, just so you can pump me for info about whether Rushian is some sort of player in bringing drugs into the country, is that it?"

"Gosh, no, that's not it, not it at all, I genuinely need to learn from you, you know that, and I must say I did have another reason but it isn't the one you suspect, it is... um, well, I very much liked the idea of, well, the thought of, you know, being with you for a while and seeing you away from work, like a date really but, to be honest, I'm so rusty about dating that I couldn't think of another way of tempting you to have dinner with me."

She flushed a little again, her eyes softened and her smile returned. "Oh, luv, I'm sorry, years of having to be suspicious of any man leaves a nasty stain on the brain. I'm sorry, I didn't mean anything, you know, just a bad reaction; it comes from being fooled and used so many times in the past, self-protection I suppose. I am sorry."

Adam felt guilty, given the true reason for the supper invitation but, to his astonishment, he found that he also meant what he said. He had looked forward to spending time with her for all the reasons he mentioned and, maybe, one or two still to be addressed. One more double-entendre from her might give him a jokingly masked opportunity, he thought, to move the relationship on a little. His guilt ruled. Adam's years had taught him that nothing worthwhile could be achieved from a false beginning.

"Anna, I have to be honest with you, everything I've just said is true and I think you know that. You know I wouldn't have approached you about this dinner if I hadn't wanted to be with you. You've guessed as much but my asking for your advice was a bit of a cover story. Just as I know you wouldn't have agreed if you thought spending an evening with me would be an unpleasant experience. I must confess there is something in your suspicions too. I am intrigued by Rushian, by my iffy caviar, the enormous fridge safe in the warehouse, questionable NHS cartons in the goods outwards area and, yes, it's true, by the fact that so many rumours still appear to be rife about Rushian's activities in general. That's it, the full and frank truth. You will always get that from me, the truth and nothing but."

She took a long sip of wine, her eyes not leaving his gaze. Eventually, she said, "You've no idea how much I'd like that to be true, but I've been dumped on by so many men, you'll understand why I am cautious, sceptical even. But I do thank you for being honest and for not treating me like some simple-minded office girl who can be duped with a bowl of pasta and a glass of wine."

"If we are to, perhaps, mean something to each other, we should start with complete openness and trust. It is important to me and everything I am building now is based on that principle. So, Anna, we could continue with what I think is a lovely evening together and not mention Rushian any more or we could put our heads together and see where we get, what do you say?"

"I'll say this luv, I'll say I'm all for openness and trust, though it takes time for trust to build, doesn't it?"

He nodded.

"Ok luv, I still think you have something on your mind you haven't told me. I think you've got more on the business than your inquisitive nature and some knock-off caviar. Why don't you tell me and then I'll decide how much I trust you and how much I don't trust the company I work for."

Adam leaned forward conspiratorially and described his conversations with Amanda and Max. He admitted that he would share whatever information she supplied with the police officer and her cyber-scam specialist husband, so that, together, they could decide what to do next.

"Adam," she said earnestly, "you are on to something but it's not what you think. I can't be sure because although I process all the paperwork and electronic transfer stuff in Rushian, I believe some of it is doctored before I ever get it. So, I might think I'm transhipping a consignment of, what, cleaning chemicals for example, but in actual fact, the package contains something different altogether. And I suspect, almost know but not quite provable, that the something else coming in from, say, Russia or India or Pakistan might be fake drugs, not the gear that you think it is like heroin or whatever, but fake medical drugs which get fed into the health service distribution network or sold on the street if they have value. I also believe that the process operates in reverse, that good, real medical drugs straight from our chemists are being shipped out again mainly to Russia, but also with false paperwork and fake contents descriptions. Anyway, in a nutshell, that's what I suspect. Does that answer any of your private-eye questions?"

"Not nearly as many as it raises. I've got questions tumbling over themselves in my mind, but I don't want to ruin the evening by cross-questioning you all the time. I'll just ask one more thing, do you think that fake pharmaceuticals are the only illicit products that Rushian handles? I ask because I've been reading about food fraud and just how big a problem it is around the world, and it seems to me, after my caviar experience, that it might be a scam an importer-exporter might easily exploit."

"You know, for a clever chap, you haven't rumbled the obvious, have you?"

"Clearly not as clever as I'd like to think. What haven't I rumbled?"

"You think that the Rushian's warehouse, limited in size as you've already said, is their only facility, that all their business comes in and goes out through just one place."

"Oh, I say, I see. You're right, I'm not that bright, am I? I don't suppose you know where else Rushian operates from?"

"Who do you think does all the admin, Adam? Looks like you scored more than you planned for when you asked me out to pick my brains eh?"

"Oh, Anna, I didn't even know I'd scored!"

For a third time in Adam's presence, Anna blushed and giggled, much to his delight.

18

Adrian confounded Gary's clouded expectation by using twenty of the twenty-five thousand pounds to repay his most demanding debts. Gary had expected him to gamble all of it but Adrian, with all the willpower he could muster, gave himself just five grand to play with. Back on the online spinning wheels, his short-term well-being was much enhanced; he felt more peaceful and relaxed, he'd even managed to sleep and eat and his concentration at work had returned to its full capacity. He put to the back of his mind any worries about what Gary would demand from him in return for all that cash. He worried even less after a winning streak saw his funds increase by nearly half of what Gary had supplied. His common sense said, 'Bank it' but the addict in him said 'Let's win even bigger' and so Adrian decided to increase his standing bets.

Again, he won and was on a powerful mental high when Gary appeared in the hospital café.

"You look like a new man, Ade. Life improved has it, since our last meeting? I hope my financial assistance has made a difference; it certainly looks that way."

"Hi, Gazza, yes, I'm loads better than I was, thanks. What brings you here? As if I couldn't guess, come to give me some of the labours of Hercules in recompense, have you?"

"Nothing quite so strenuous, Ade. Don't worry, the Nemean lion can live another day, but yes, I have a small request, an instalment if you like. In return for the favour we have done for you, you can now do one for your union."

"Well, it had to come I suppose," said Adrian with a breezy lightness which rapidly faded, as he saw the union officer's serious expression.

"Yes, Ade, it had to come, everything comes with a price, that's life don't you find?"

"Yeah, I suppose it does. Anyway, I'm on a bit of a roll at the moment, what about I pay you back, you know, in real money rather than lots of favours as you call them?"

"You could, Ade, you could give me some money but, let's be honest, it isn't a likely occurrence. And anyway, it won't be long before you're back in the shit again and I'd just have to give it back to you. Besides, it won't make any difference now, you know, to the favours. You see you owe me, us, and whether you pay back or not you still have to help us when we ask; better than getting the sack for being an irresponsible gambler, what do you reckon?"

"Lovely, the British Blackmailers Association, eh? The Union of Extortion, yeah? You make the old-style debt collectors look compassionate."

"Aw, not really, I mean we don't break legs or anything like that, we just ask you to help from time to time, as any good union member might be more than willing to do, see. It's just a small ask in comparison with the enormous amount of money you've had from us."

"So, no escape then, I see. I should have guessed, money has no morality in union eyes, just another tool of disruption."

"That horse you're riding is way too high for a man in your position, a gambler, an addict, a danger to life even. You know Ade, a word of friendly advice, for as long as you gamble, you'll lose and for as long as you lose, you'll be in hock to people who lend you more money to lose until there is no more, nothing other than a dark, ignominious end."

"Thank you, vicar, when I want advice, I'll ask for it ok? So cut the matey shit and just tell me what you want me to do."

"Your call, Ade. Here," Gary handed him a sheaf of papers.

"What's this then? It's just forms and stuff, internal hospital stuff, what's this crap got to do with anything?"

"So, you are familiar with these forms and the terms they list, the codes, the requisition numbers and so on, yeah?"

"Course I am, I use them every day. I fill in the reqs for each patient's medication regimes and sign them off to go to the pharmacy for action."

"And that's all I'm asking you to do. Fill 'em in, sign 'em off and give a direction for the delivery points, wards or whatever, where the drugs will be sent, or do they get collected?"

"Varies, sometimes they come to the wards in a regular delivery run and sometimes, if the drugs are highly controlled, we send a ward nurse to pick them up, a proper handover for safety, see?"

"Do you ever collect them, Ade?"

"Occasionally, depends on what's going on. So, what's the deal Gaz, what's going on here?"

"I need you to make all these requisitions, properly and using all the right codes and whatever. I want you to order the popular stuff, you know Diazepam, Librium and any other benzos, painkiller opioids and opiates too, tramadol, fentanyl and the like, oh yeah, and the usual anti-depressants, sleeping pills and weight loss pills, you know semaglutides and the like, yeah, get the idea? Simply, you pick drugs being used already so it doesn't ring any bells, and you'll see you have targets for each class of drug in that list, make sure you hit 'em, ok?"

"Then what? No, let me guess, I order the drugs, then I collect them or get them delivered to a ward where I'm working and then I sneak 'em out and deliver them to you or some other lowlife peddler, right?"

"That horse is getting too high again. Remember who's the addict around here, gambling, booze, drugs, whatever, it's addiction so look at it this way, you are just helping fellow addicts, right? So, sometimes I'll pick up the packages from you and sometimes you'll do us one more favour and cabby the whole lot to an address I'll give you. It's a warehouse here in Olderbury, so no great effort needed from you."

"Then what? What happens to all this dangerous drug when I pass it over?"

"What's it to you? The less you know, the better, just be careful and don't do anything which might get you caught. Remember, the longer you keep doing this for us, the longer you can keep on spinning those beautiful roulette wheels; think smart and hit your targets and we'll all be just fine and dandy."

"And you think you'll get away with all this, do you? You think that nobody will notice a sudden increase in drug requisitions, you think no one will notice me suddenly making an increased and regular number of drug collections, you think that the hospital's infallible drug movement reconciliation systems won't spot such a change in usage patterns? If you think you can do all that and not be noticed in a jiffy, or me being noticed in no time, you're bloody barking Gary, bloody insane."

"Oh, doubting Adrian. First off, you will only do a few runs for us, the rest of the time you will simply feed me with sequential and random requisition numbers and so on by text, on-demand and I'll do the rest. Secondly, you just leave your infallible systems to me. I can assure you, they aren't infallible at all; the people I know have ways of dealing with such systems so that this activity will go untraced, untraceable and you'll stay as innocent as a newborn lamb."

"As in 'to the slaughter'," he replied, bitterly.

Adrian studied the lists and the targets he'd been set. Every atom of his being objected to what he was being coerced into doing, but he knew he had no options and would do exactly as he was told. The targets for his personal actions were not too huge and were spread sensibly over a rolling schedule. He could see that this wasn't a quick-hit crime, this was a carefully considered long-term plan, not too greedy, not too noticeable, just a reasonable increase across the range of medication that he wrote up every day.

He had no idea what else would be happening when he wasn't collecting drugs in person or what would be done with the requisition orders and numbers he would supply to Gary. As there was nothing he could do about any other drug orders, he would simply have to ensure he did what he had to do without getting caught. How could he know that a hacker in Moscow was orchestrating his life and creating a decoy, a just-in-case patsy to blame if something went wrong when the massive drug heist hit full speed and drove Olderbury hospital, amongst so many others, into a blind, helpless panic? All he knew was that for as long as he was careful with the cross-check paper, and digital tracking and recording copies he might, just might, no, certainly would get away with it.

The day after Gary's visit, Adrian tested his plans and, without notice or question, easily collected his order from the hospital's always hectic pharmacy. His requisition dockets, paper and electronic, were all in order; the dispensing chemist had no way of knowing that the top copy form had no other copies for tracking or drug audit taking. Adrian didn't know that an external interrupter would adjust the ward patient drug regime records to conceal the inevitable difference in drugs issued and drugs consumed.

He had, in all, a dozen large cartons of blister-packed valuable, powerful pills all of which fitted, just, into his backpack. Of course, nobody noticed him leaving the hospital with his bounty and, with a sigh of relief, Adrian drove slowly and legally to the light industrial unit by the river.

"Hello, luv," said the welcoming receptionist at Rushian Import-Export.

"Hello," said Adrian. "I have a small consignment for you, it should be expected under the name of Gary Pugh at a London address."

"Oh, alright luv, just pop your boxes into the cross-hatched area by our roller doors downstairs and I'll do the rest. Do you have a delivery note for me to sign?"

Adrian's instructions had been explicit up to that point but didn't supply him with any paperwork.

"Er, no sorry, do you need one?"

"Me luv? Need one? Oh no, I don't but I thought your people would. Never mind, don't worry, I'll meet you downstairs so you can be sure your packages will be ok with me when you leave them."

Adrian began to understand the scale of Gary's redistribution of drugs when he placed his boxes in Rushian's goods inwards section and saw four more boxes, all with NHS identities like his, ready for forward shipping.

"Do you know where these came from?" he asked as innocently as possible.

"Not really luv, they came by courier about two hours ago. They are a lot like yours, aren't they?"

"Yes, mine are for emergency relief aid, I believe. My boxes, I understand, go to London for consolidation with other donations to be forwarded."

"Yes, of course, I see. I thought it would be something like that. We've been asked to expect a regular delivery for onward shipping so I thought it must be for some disaster aid or something like that. We usually do all the forward shipping ourselves, but I suppose your London colleagues have their own arrangements. You might be better off just using one of the local courier services, luv."

"Thanks for the advice but I've been told to come to you."

Something was going on that Adrian didn't understand and the presence of more NHS boxes had startled him. He sent a text to Gary, "WTF? I C + NHS box at Rush. Mad"

The reply was quick, "10 reqs now 10 tomoz."

Adrian's imagination began to flow, but he had no idea of the enormity of the operation in which he was an unwilling, expendable component and how much more his unknown Russian puppet master had in store for him, and others like him across the UK.

19

"Max? Ben. Oh, fuck Max, I need to talk to you now, right now, can I come over?"

"Of course, Ben, has something else happened? I mean the last time we spoke you told me about the stolen drugs, but I can tell from your voice that the matter has escalated even further, yeah?"

"Yeah, and then some."

Ben was shown into Onetelcall's meeting room. He looked every bit the worried man. No smile, no jocularity, he glowered at members of the meeting Max had hurriedly assembled. Jo, Duggie and Indira, taking their lead from Max, remained solemn too as Ben began to pour out his woes.

"It's serious, it's fucking serious, and I don't know who else to talk to. I was hoping Amanda might be here too."

"She's on her way right now, Ben, five minutes away tops," Max confirmed.

"Ok, I'll start anyway, shall I? We can always catch up if she has any questions."

"Yep, of course," said Jo, "and I'll keep a record of this meeting anyway. But, before you start, Ben, can we use these moments for me to explain what we've been up to since your last call to Max about your internal requisition system being compromised?"

"Looks like it's more than that, compromised sounds too gentle," blustered Ben, red-faced with anxiety.

"Oh, right. Well, we'll come to that in a minute, but first, you should know we have been running some surveillance and remote monitoring on the network and mobile traffic in and out of your locations, as much as we can access at short notice anyway. So, we have made a start on figuring out who is attacking you."

"Attacking, that's the truth Jo, we are under attack and it's getting worse!"

"Sorry, people, couldn't get here any faster with lights and sirens," announced Amanda as she burst past the receptionist into the meeting room. "Hope I haven't delayed your meeting too much. What have I missed, anything important?"

"Amanda, so good of you to come. You haven't missed anything except my being far too rude. Sorry, everyone, it's just that I'm in a panic and I know I'm way out of my depth," said Ben, trying hard to regain his composure.

"Now that Amanda's here, why don't you just spill all the beans right now, Ben? Talking it out might help," smiled Jo.

"Yes, well, I told you, didn't I, about the apparent theft of drugs and how it seems like someone, God knows who, can take over the functions of our internal ward drugs ordering system? I don't know how the drugs that are falsely ordered get from our pharmacy to wherever they have been taken, but gone they have, and we have no idea how to prevent the same from happening again."

"Ok," said Jo, "so let's look…"

"Hang on, sorry Jo, but that's not all. You see one of our systems, it's a patient record function, not life-threatening but important, has also been got at by an outsider. And, well, in a way it's even more serious because, I should explain that the system in question is an external system run by a specialist outfit, appointed and paid for by the NHS nationally. They say that they have been blocked from sectors of the patient records and have to pay a huge amount of money to be able to use their own systems again. See what I'm saying, does it make any sense to you?"

"Ben, may I call you Ben? I am Indira and I work for part of the intelligence group in Onetelcall, specifically in mobile networks but, I stray into other areas too."

"Of course, Indira, call me whatever you want," smiled Ben for the first time. "But I have a feeling that I'm not going to understand most of what you are about to tell me."

Indira smiled back at him, her sympathy and understanding clear in her expression. "I fear I may disappoint you, Ben, because, at this early stage, I haven't got a great deal to report. What would make a big difference is if you could give me a few details?"

"Anything, anything at all."

"Amazing, thanks. Well first, could you give me a list of everyone in the ward where the drugs were stolen? Names and, if you can, their mobile phone numbers too, that alone will save hours of investigation."

"Indira is our ace digital snooper," smiled Max, lightening the mood as usual. "And the closer she can get to the inside information, the more she will be able to reveal. Quite how she and her fellow spy, Sue, do it, I just don't know."

Ben, visibly more relaxed replied, "All of this is so very far beyond anything I know but I will do all I can to give you anything you need."

"Awesome, thanks. Can you, then, also give me details of the drugs that were requisitioned illegally and when? Like what day and time, if possible, the pharmacist who released them. Then, Ben, can you give me any login details you have for the patient record system that has been hacked with ransomware, and, if it's not too technical, the type of records the system keeps? Like are they a spreadsheet, a formatted form, or free-access notes? That type of thing. I'd like to know a bit more about the network too but, if I may say, I expect that will be too technical for you to find out."

"Hang on chaps," said Max with an edge of excitement, "we can give Ben a breather on the network info 'cos we know a man who knows it all, don't we Duggie?"

"We do indeed. My mate Perry. The chap who fixed you up with network access while you were laid up. Yeah, I'll call him as soon as we are through here."

"Excellent," said Max. "Now, Ben, you've given us the gen on the thefts and the new ransom development, is there anything else we should know?"

"Not yet, Max, no but I shall go back and call around my colleagues to see if I can find out if we are alone in being attacked in this way or whether there are other departments like mine suffering the same problems."

"Great," said Jo, "one more thing, Ben, can you call the company that runs your ransomed patient service and tell them that we will be in touch with them? A word from you will guarantee their full cooperation."

"Jo, I think you overestimate my influence, but I'll certainly call. It is OceanwaveData by the way, the company is called OD, OceanwaveData, based in Birmingham. I know the medical director, slightly."

"That's just the job, Ben, thanks," said Max. "Just to be clear, because we have to sign off on all this, let me confirm that you are asking us to investigate on your behalf, and on behalf of the hospital, and you will allow us to investigate your colleagues, departments, processes and IT infrastructure to trace the hackers, the thieves and the ransom perpetrators, is that right?"

"Yes please," replied Ben. "I have come to you for help because I know you and what your brilliant company does, but I don't have any official mandate from the hospital or NHS to do this and I'd rather keep this on the low-down, involving as few people as possible."

"Quite right," confirmed Jo.

"Oh, and before the subject comes up, you must know I don't have any budget for this. If you need paying, well, I don't know, well I simply have no idea, how we could manage that."

"I know, Ben, I know," said Max. "We've discussed it before and I stand by what I said, we'll do all we can for you. If we succeed, I'll put my lucky salesman trousers on and hit the NHS Trusts for some contracts. If we don't, then something so dreadful will have happened that I'll quit this business for good. In the meantime, the full force of Onetelcall is behind you and will stay that way unless someone very powerful tells us to stop and even then, we probably won't."

"Max, thank you. I don't know what else to say, but all of you, thank you."

20

"Adam?"

"Anna, how lovely to hear your voice."

"Adam, look, I think I've got something odd to tell you about."

"You've found out who's selling sham caviar, don't tell me!"

"I won't tell you that 'cos I haven't. But I have spotted something too strange not to tell you about."

"How about the Carpenters again? Shall I pick you up from work?"

Back at 'their' table, Adam poured a generous amount of her preferred Pinot Grigio, and a zero Leffe for himself, as he was driving.

"I'm just dying to know what this is all about," he said. "Not that I'm not very happy to see you again. I am, truly, but you have piqued my interest. I can't resist a mystery."

"It was you who made me suspicious in the first place. Remember, you asked me about some boxes filled with cartons all with NHS identity on them? Yeah, you remember?"

"I do. I saw the boxes in your goods inwards area by the doors, and it crossed my mind that NHS goods had no good reason to be in an export bay for shipment by a, you know, independent, small shipper, even if you do have other warehouses. I didn't think Rushian might be the sort of company the NHS would use, even if it was intended for emergency care or aid or whatever."

"Well, you started me thinking luv, that's for sure and the more I thought about it, the more it seemed, well, suspicious and altogether not the right way of doing things for a massive outfit like the NHS."

"We agree on that. So, what else have you spotted?"

Anna looked into Adam's honest, appreciative eyes and knew she was confiding in the right person.

"It's more of a who than a what, although there is some 'what' too luv, if you see what I mean. I hadn't paid any notice until you said about the boxes and then there's this chap; he started coming in a little while ago, about the same time as you saw the NHS boxes. He's been in again a couple of times and the thing is he brings in boxes, well, packs more like, just like the ones you saw, and he always seems to be, I don't know, nervy, shifty. He says his stuff is for foreign aid, but if that's right why doesn't it come in by courier like all the other boxes? I mean, it's fishy, isn't it?"

"It certainly is Anna, it certainly is. There's something fishy about the whole thing. Do you have a name for him or an idea of where he comes from, where he works perhaps?"

He poured her another glass of wine, and she wrinkled her nose by way of thanks as she thought about her answer.

"I honestly don't know, that's the problem. I mean he's a young man, clearly educated and, honest luv, I'd bet he's a medical man. He just has that air about him or maybe it's because he brings in medicine or whatever. But now you've asked, I will have a name for him on a form. Of course, he might be using a false one, but we could at least have a look, couldn't we?"

"Can you get in at this time; is the warehouse still open?"

"Doesn't matter luv, I can get into the offices even if the warehouse is closed. I've got a key for the admin bit you see; the warehouse is on a separate security set-up, alarms and all that. I'm sorry, I should have thought…"

"Don't worry, it was brave of you to talk to me about it. You had no reason to think you'd need to bring evidence with you, but it does occur to me that you might well remember another key fact, like where the boxes are going. They must have a destination location; did you see where that might be?"

"Oh crikey, yes, of course! I filled the forms in, didn't I? They were for an address in London. Funny that 'cos most of our shipping is overseas, but he said he'd been told, yes, told to get us to courier it to a place in London."

She smiled and took a big slurp of wine.

"Brilliant, that is interesting. Why not use a usual courier or a contracted NHS delivery service?"

"He said it would go to this place in London to be sent on with other donations, to some medical charity somewhere." She paused, screwed up her eyes then opened them wide, "Devon Square! That was it. I can't remember the name of the company or organisation or whatever, but I'm pretty sure the addressee was a Gary, Gary Pugh, that's it, stuck in my mind, don't know why, yes, I do, you know, Pugh, Pugh Barney McGrew… the song?"

Adam looked blank but grinned appreciatively.

They decided against returning to Rushian as Anna could easily text the name of her mystery man to Adam in the morning. He drove her home to her stylish flat in one of the converted mills in Olderbury's former wharf.

"You look surprised, luv," she laughed. "Divorce isn't all bad. I didn't get what I should have but it was alright. Mind you, if you measured it as a salary for hard labour my settlement wasn't great."

"It's a lovely spot, very stylish and elegant, it suits you perfectly."

"Don't please," she said, "don't be even nicer. I don't know how to handle 'nice' but thank you anyway. It's been a long time since anyone said anything nice to me."

"I understand, really I do. I felt estranged from the world of compliments, however well-meant, when I got divorced. I'm sorry; no more mister nice guy, ok?"

She chuckled, leaned across and kissed him on the cheek. She wanted to invite him in but didn't, afraid he'd say no and even more afraid he'd say yes. She thought about him most of the night and went to work early so she could call him and talk to him again.

"Morning," she chirped, "not too early in the day for you is it, luv?"

"Hello Anna, not at all. I couldn't sleep so I was up and about early anyway."

She wondered if his sleeplessness was for the same reason. "I know, I didn't sleep much either, you know, my mind was in a bit of a whirl…"

"Thinking about matey and the NHS boxes?"

"Yes, luv, that's it, yeah thinking about all sorts of things really, not just that, but all of last night."

Adam felt an almost forgotten frisson, a tensing of his senses and a rush of desire. "Me too, Anna, me too."

He could hear the tightening in her voice as she said, "Yes, well enough of that. Listen luv, I've got more of a scribble than a name, that's why I couldn't remember it, see?"

"Enough of what?"

"Don't Adam, please, teasing goes along with being nice, you know that."

"I do, sorry, so what does the scribble say? Can you read it?"

"Only just. I asked him to sign and print. It was for authority for me to complete all the forms for him. That was early on when I thought he was asking us to export his boxes, see, and anyway, he signed alright but didn't print, so all I've got is a wiggle which does, I'm sure it does, begins with Dr. It's unusual to have any title, you know, nobody signs like Mister John Smith, I mean, do they, so his squiggle almost certainly begins with Dr and the rest well, I think it starts with an A, like Adam, yeah, and it looks like Ad but it could be Al or At, not sure but it is a longer squiggle that, say, Alan, maybe as long as something like Alastair, not sure. The surname looks like it starts with an 'S' but then it's just a wavy line with a dot at the end."

"Thanks, Anna. I think it's time I reported all of this to Amanda at Olderbury Police and Max at Onetelcall. They are on the same trail at Rushian as you forced me to admit..."

"Ha, forced you indeed, as if; but, yes, it makes sense to keep everyone informed, especially the police, 'cos if our suspicions are right, we could be looking at some theft or drug dealing and, I suppose, I could be implicated as I sign so many forms for so many people. I'd feel safer if the law knew I was on the side of the goodies."

"It would help if I could have a copy of the signature, would that be ok, could you photocopy it?"

"Of course, luv, I could hand it over to you tonight."

"Just what I was thinking."

Anna laughed again, "Now we've got the excuse to see each other again out of the way, I'll scan the signature and email it to you within half an hour."

"Now who's teasing!"

21

Luka was noticeably more deferential, thought Melor. Perhaps the Major is being less disparaging about me now, he mused, knowing Luka to be an inadvertent barometer of the Major's thoughts and moods.

"You have done good, I think," said Luka giving some confirmation to Melor's thoughts. "He is, I think, going to buy you a very fine lunch at the Grand Café."

"Is he? Is he? The Grand Café, eh? He doesn't stray far from the Kremlin does he, our Major Vassiliev?"

"No young sir, the National Hotel is an easy walk for him, although sometimes I must drive him after lunch. He enjoys vodka at lunchtime and sometimes the walk back is a lot longer than the walk there, if you understand me."

Melor saw the Major, already seated and, this time, he sat opposite him without being invited.

"I shall now call you by the name you give yourself, you have earned it. So, I say, welcome Melor and for this lunch, you will address me as Vasily. It is a lunch to say, thank… no, to celebrate, that you have absolved yourself of any previous misdemeanours and indeed, fulfilled your initial promises to me. It is, of course, to be hoped that your endeavours continue with a growing level of success and efficiency. I am sure you understand me."

"I do, Maj- er, Vasily. I am grateful for all this and grateful to you for allowing me the freedom and the reprieve to be able to do the work I wish to do for my country."

"There is no need to creep any further, Melor. You no longer have to crawl to gain my favour, you should only continue your work and extend its scope, which, I assume, is what you wish to do anyway."

"Yes, Vasily, that is my intention. I shall make you a powerful man, indeed, I shall make my country even more revered and feared and I shall, if I may say so, make the name Melor a byword in cyber genius."

From a distance, the two men could have been friends enjoying a sociable lunch. They both drank several vodkas and tucked into Pozharsky cutlets, a buttery, creamy ground chicken classic and a speciality of the restaurant.

"Our plan is working well, I have to admit," said Vasily grudgingly. "It has been noticed with approval by many of the president's closer advisers. He is, I believe, pleased that we are delivering such costly disruption and audacious manipulation of the vile West's weak infrastructure. We know that the president believes that such activity as ours is as much of a weapon as a gun. It costs the targets a great deal in money and time, both commodities which have to be diverted from efforts which may be made in support of our enemies or rightful land reclamation."

Melor smiled to himself at the Major's new use of 'our' and 'we' but he didn't comment. Despite his improved relationship, he would still take no risks with the Major's capricious temper.

"I am pleased that your name is spoken of in the high offices of our president, Vasily. It was my promise to you, and you will now know that I have kept my word."

"Others too now see that our initiative carries an opportunity for self-promotion, and, in some cases, I have to say for self-aggrandisement. By this, I refer to General Savva Komarov. You will have heard of him I think, he is excellent at making his name known to everyone. He achieves this by assuming intellectual ownership of others' clever ideas and being a loud post-event detractor of enterprises which fail."

"I have heard of him, yes, but I suggest those who understand these matters are not all impressed by the General's evident conceit and bombast."

"Really, is that the case, Melor? You must be careful about sharing such a view because the General has plans, I believe, to come for a free ride in our playground and I must tell you that I am not an enthusiast or supporter of this manoeuvre."

"How does he propose to insinuate himself into my- that is, our activities? It is not easy to jump on and provide a new perspective on such a complex, sophisticated and technically advanced campaign as this."

"You underestimate the General's guile. He has proposed an amendment to our process, one which, as I've said, I do not approve of, but which has met with some support from others in his coterie."

"Am I to be told what this amendment might be?"

"I will tell you now, the General has made the point that we are removing stocks of drugs, and this in itself will become a self-fulfilling disaster because they are quickly missed and it is therefore logical that the supply of those whose drugs we steal will stop very quickly, limiting the longevity of the programme."

"So, he obviously doesn't understand the architecture of our strategy," said Melor with disdain.

"Maybe not but he has suggested something which I must put to you. As you will know, here in Russia, along with friends we have in India and Pakistan, we have a flourishing industry in manufacturing fake drugs and whilst the contents don't emulate the original drug, the packaging is cleverly and convincingly imitated."

"So," Melor said, anticipating the inevitable, "he thinks we should replace the real drugs with the fake products when we arrange to have them, er, redistributed as we are now. That's it isn't it?"

"That is indeed it, in a short form anyway."

"The General is aware of course that this will lead to certain deaths, multiple deaths of innocent people. Our activities at the moment disrupt a country's infrastructure, they inflict cost and disruption as intended, but they do not, nor should they, simply kill people needlessly, gratuitously and wantonly."

"That, I'm afraid Melor, is exactly the General's ambition. He is, as many cowards are, vicious and without any conscience. He is, as you might know, not alone and his views about inflicting widespread lethal terror in the UK have gathered some significant support."

Melor sipped more vodka. "I am in the same position all over again, am I not? If I demur, I will, I suppose, be locked up as a dissenter?"

"Your grasp of the situation is, as always, accurate."

"And you will support the General's murderous intervention because your survival in the higher ranks of government, and the plush life that comes with it, would be at risk if you don't."

"Excellent, Melor, excellent insight and appreciation of the matter."

"Then Major, we must work out how best we can deliver what the General and his barbarian cohort demand, and refrain from pointing out that just as our removal of drugs will be noticed, so will deaths caused by his fake drugs."

"Exactly so. Your antipathy is noted as is your return to addressing me as Major. Melor, you may show your displeasure to me, as I may to you, but both of us, that is you and me together, are caught in this dangerous, political connivance and we must jointly tread carefully if we are to survive."

"Well, the thing is, Vasily, it is easily done technically but to succeed we need two factors to work efficiently. The first is easier, I need to emulate more accurately all of the real products, paper and digital information associated with each drug that we steal and replace. Secondly, and you know this already, your friends on the ground will have to be physically involved in the logistics of removing and replacing the products at each pharmacy and that, may I say, is a major undertaking, Major."

"It is Melor, it is indeed but I am more than equal to the task. I have people who have access to every location we target, although I should add that you will have to delete any of the current locations where I don't have such access ability."

Melor's initial reaction softened as he understood his lunch companion's perilous position. "Then Vasily, I suggest we do the intelligent thing right now."

"Which is?"

"Vodka, Vasily, we drink vodka until the world hurts a little less."

22

"Gary? Adrian."

"Alright mate?" answered Pugh on his private mobile.

"No, I'm not fucking alright. I want to know what's going on. I did my bit for you, I've scammed your drugs, I've carried them to your shippers, and I've done everything you asked but the hospital is still being attacked. We've got random outages all over the place and we are losing way more drugs than I've handled for you; I want to know what's going on."

"What's going on is that you've done a few little jobs as part of a very modest repayment schedule, for the large amount of money you accepted from me to keep the money-lending hounds off your backside. How's it going, by the way? Still losing I suppose?"

"Ok, ok, but even so, I want to know what the story is, why Olderbury Hospital is being targeted for cyber-attacks, drug theft and God knows what else?"

"Oh, there's nothing special about your place mate; there is a wave of hacking attacks and drug redistribution, as it's called, happening in hospitals, clinics, care centres and any NHS facility you can name all across the country. Haven't you read any news recently?"

"But blocking our systems and demanding huge amounts of money to unblock them, is that part of the same action by whoever is pulling your strings, who gave you the money to buy me?"

"Whatever it's worth to you, but yeah, it is a coordinated effort, and it is working brilliantly. You've done your bit, and you will keep on doing it because you don't have any options. I've been easy on you, Adrian 'cos I like you. I see you as a mate and like mates do, we are both doing what we have to do for whatever reasons, gambling in your case and my reasons are my own and nothing to do with anyone else."

"So, what's next then, eh? I assume you are going to carry on in the same way. Drugs I can understand and what you all call ransoming, I can understand, but the shutting down of crappy processes like patients' records for no apparent reason seems crazy and pointless to me."

"For a clever man, you are a simple soul, Adrian, so you'll not understand why I need you to continue to requisition drugs as I request and keep quiet about what you know and do. You are up to your bollocks in it now, so being discreet is the only option you've got. You will have worked out already that we have ways of getting into most of the hospital systems electronically, like how we change all your drug records, but it will soon be the case that we change how we work, and I'll need a bit more help from you. Who do you know in your pharmacy? Got any mates or a girl you meet for a drink or coffee occasionally, anything like that?"

"No Gaz, not really, I hardly know them at all, and since you've put me under the cosh I'm trying to keep a very low profile in the pharmacy in case they start to take notice and ask questions. I don't want to get caught you know."

"Oh well, worth a shot. So, look, Adrian, I'm coming to Olderbury very soon to do a spot more recruiting, I need someone in the pharmacy to put back what we take out, like-for-like sort of thing, but not quite."

"Do I understand you? Have I got it right, you intend to replace the drugs you steal with some counterfeit crap, is that right?"

"It's part of a possible plan, yeah."

"But, Christ Gazza, that's bloody criminal. I mean criminal like bad; nicking a few pills is one thing but knowingly killing people is quite another."

"Is it, Adrian, is it really? Are you trying to tell me that stealing heavyweight opiates which you know will be sold on to addicts is any different? Addicts die from their addiction, you know that, so there is no difference between feeding poison to a defenceless addict or feeding sugar pills or whatever to someone who is probably dying anyway."

"I don't like it all, Gary. You may think you've got a clever point, but you know as well as I do that fake medication is a whole different matter from the pusher and user world of mind-altering drugs. I'll have nothing to do with it, understand me, I'll do what you ask along the lines we've been working so far but I won't help you put fake drugs in our pharmacy, I just won't and remember if you take me down, I'll take you with me, sounds trite when I say it but boy, Gary do I mean it."

"So, how much in debt are you now Ade? I don't need to take you down, you are doing it to yourself, like any addict, your demise becomes a self-fulfilling prophecy, death by your own hand, damn nearly suicide. You are an addict and you simply feed your addiction in the same as what you steal for me feeds other addicts. So, don't come it with me, mate, you are as tainted as any pusher whether the drugs are real or fake."

"Probably so but supplying drugs to addicts is a very different thing from making people who have sworn to save lives administer, unwittingly, fake, useless medication to people, patients, who desperately need the real thing, whose lives depend on what we give them. I won't do it Gary; I will not be part of any scheme which randomly kills innocent people, and which turns dedicated clinicians into involuntary murderers."

"Pretty words Adrian, but you are still trying to apply morals despite your immorality, and it is getting you nowhere. Look man, I hate to be the heavy here but well, you've got no choice. I'm not asking you to dose anyone with phoney meds, just to figure out a route for one lot of cartons to replace another lot of cartons…"

"Yeah, I see that, but the effect is just the same, it is still the foundation of what could be a massacre. I'll have no part of it, I won't, I won't," Adrian paused, his previous high spirits shrivelled into a ball of bitterness. He cursed his gambling as his mind raced to work out how to extract himself from this desperate predicament.

His subconscious told him that he was falling into the basement beneath his rock bottom. His addiction had driven him to a place where he was considering, knowingly, to enable manslaughter. How could this be possible? A life dedicated to saving life was being debased to actions which would endanger life instead. But he had no options, did he? No, he thought no options at all. Ignoring the stark choice of rejecting Gary's exhortations would mean telling the authorities about his misdemeanours to date and then having to face, even beat, his gambling demons. In its desperation, Adrian's mind flooded with cortisol and serotonin, fuelling his search for a solution which would appease Gary and offer a stay of the inevitable for him, that day of reckoning which must eventually face all addicts.

"Adrian, you still with me?"

"Just thinking, Gary, just thinking how amateur and ill-conceived your plot is. I mean, do you seriously expect to recruit pharmacy personnel in hospitals and dispensaries to switch stocks of dangerous drugs for you? Even if you throw lots of money at them, it's just a stupid plan numerically and for secure longevity, stupid."

"Oh, really mastermind, that's your view, is it? And I suppose you've got a better idea, have you?"

"Actually yes, I have a much better plan which is achievable and workable over time and places, but to make it work you'll need to convince the power behind you. I mean, the people who supply the money, the technology and who have the motivation to execute such an outrageous, immoral, evil act."

"For fuck's sake, Adrian, stop with the moralising, will you. Your sudden holier-than-thou attitude is enough to make me throw up. I won't be judged by an out-of-control gambler who would sell his own mother for one more spin of the wheel, so if you've got a suggestion, you'd better lay it on me now and it had better be amazing."

"Oh, it is Gary, it is."

23

The Adam Superfoods meeting room looked pleasingly professional, with a blend of competence and hospitality.

"Brilliant, thanks," said Adam as Pauline showed him what she and Estelle had done.

"I've put name cards out, don't know if that's what you high-powered people usually do for meetings, but it's what I do," said Pauline slightly defensively.

"Amanda, Max, Duggie there and Anna, me, you here. What about Estelle?"

"She's not keen on, I don't know, just sitting and not knowing when to speak or what to say, so she's decided she'd rather be a kind of waitress and join in if she feels she has anything useful to say."

"Works for me," smiled Adam, "as long as she's here and happy then that's great. Having someone hovering with drinks or samples or whatever is a lovely touch."

Adam had called a meeting to explain what he and Anna had discovered and to share their suspicions.

"This is lovely, thank you, Pauline, Estelle, Adam. It's a great spread and I'm looking forward to tasting some of your products," said Amanda, as she arranged herself on her chair at the laden table.

"Me too," chuckled Max, "I don't get fed at home you know."

As Amanda threw a rude look at her husband, Adam saw Anna visibly relax at Max's joke and he moved quickly to strengthen her confidence for a meeting that, he knew, had made her feel nervous.

"Thank you all for coming here. I hope we will achieve more in these less formal surroundings than we would at the Olderbury police station, if I may say, Amanda."

"Oh, too true Adam. No, this is great and as we don't have an active, official police investigation running right now, this under-the-radar approach is spot on."

"Good, so let's crack on. Anna and I will report what we have found out and what we suspect. I must add that all of this has been made possible by Anna; without her help and insight a lot of what we are about to tell you would have gone unnoticed. We owe her a lot."

Anna blushed as mutterings of appreciation echoed around the table.

"Please, no, don't, I mean, I've done nothing apart from talk to Adam and he's bought me some super meals for my efforts. I suppose you could say I sang for my supper…"

Amanda kicked Max under the table before he could comment.

"Anna is being too modest. Our first contact was when I picked up and then returned that adulterated caviar. I was slightly suspicious after what John said, that he thought the shipping agents, Rushian, were as bent as a violinist's elbow. He's Pauline's husband for those of you who don't know him. He spent a while as a 'special'."

"Well, he's quite right of course," confirmed Amanda. "We have deep suspicions about Rushian. We believe they have more premises than we know about, but we haven't got anything solid on them, certainly not enough to act on, or even investigate more thoroughly."

"You're right about the number of warehouses," said Anna. "Although they keep very quiet about them, they move around empty warehouses and factory units quite often."

"Do you have any addresses?"

"Yes, Amanda. I mean not on me right now but I'm sure I could get a list of our current locations for you. Shall I email it?"

"Thanks, that'd be good."

"Anyway," continued Adam, "since I was at Rushian and noticed that safe-cum-freezer unit and the NHS boxes, Anna has been keeping her eyes open. It all amounts to what could be a major NHS scam. We are not sure what, why, or how, but we are certain something is very, very wrong and Anna has spotted at least one man who could be involved. We don't know his full name, but we have these clues," he showed them a note of his hangman-style letters and dashes from the signature sample, "and we think- it's just hunch really, that this man must work at Olderbury hospital."

"Hey Max, this signature, it sort of fits, it could be Adrian, the nice doctor who works with Ben, couldn't it?" said Amanda.

"Anna, is your hangman in his early to mid-thirties, same height as me, thin, gaunt even, with dark, almost black hair and tired looking, slightly hooded blue eyes with eyebrows that look like he plucks at the centre?"

Anna giggled, "Well, I don't know about his plucking habits but as descriptions go, I'd say that's the man. My man is a bit too thin, you know, skin and bone rather than healthy-slim."

"Let's say it is him; what is he up to Anna, what have you got on him?"

"I like sounding like a detective," said Anna, warming to her subject. "So far, I've not got a lot to be honest. He turns up with boxes of cartons all wrapped carefully and discreetly and they are always to be sent to an address in London for a recipient called Pugh. The boxes, says our man, are to be added to a bulk delivery of charitable medical aid bound for somewhere else, quite where or for whom he never says but that's the story."

"It gets better though, doesn't it Anna," said Adam, "because other consignments of similar boxes come into you by cab or courier, all to be sent on to the same London address. I looked it up and guess what, the address is a holding address for the British Medical Association. I phoned them and asked for Gary Pugh who was out of his office that day."

"Good stuff…" responded Max.

"But that's not all," interrupted Anna, then looked embarrassed for jumping in. "Sorry, Max, but there is more. We are now shipping in boxes, almost identical boxes, I'm not sure where they originate but they are to be forwarded to the hospital and a variety of health centres, clinics and other medical facilities in the area, like about a twenty- or thirty-mile radius from our warehouse and that's a lot of locations, maybe over a dozen."

"Oh really?" Amanda sounded surprised. "We suspected some satellite units, but we hadn't reckoned on so many."

"Seems so," said Adam. "We are still working on what goes in and out of them, but we don't think all of the digital records are kept centrally and Anna doesn't get to see all the documentation. We can only surmise that fake goods are coming in and pukka, nicked stuff is going out. That's the pattern as it seems to us right now."

"Um," Anna hesitated, "I don't know if this helps much, I don't even know if I'm right. All the boxes and cartons coming into my depot are so realistic, they even have all the computer codes- constantly changing computer codes at that, not the sort of static, printed look-alikes, but what easily pass for the real thing. They identify the product and all the details as well as place or origin and place of destination, stock numbers and all that. So, you see, if this inbound traffic is fake, it seems to me that the essential codes are the real thing and that surely suggests a great deal of inside cooperation, doesn't it?"

As usual, Duggie had been sitting quietly, absorbing all the information before launching, "Ok, here's the deal as I see it. Number one, we've got a bloke, a doctor known to Max and Amanda, who's part of a conspiracy to steal pharmaceuticals from the NHS, presumably for further forwarding. Number two, we have a freight forwarder and import-export company which is evidently complicit in this conspiracy. Number three, we have the name and address of a London-based link in the chain and, Number four, we have circumstantial evidence that fake drugs, albeit well-dressed and documented fakes, are coming back into the same import-export company for onward delivery to local NHS facilities. Does that about sum it up, folks?"

"Succinct as always me old mate," said Max to general approval.

"Ok," continued Duggie, "well, I might be able to add a morsel of meat to these bones, courtesy of Kathy. She and her team have been keeping an eye on digital and mobile communication in and out of Rushian and, with a lot of help from Perry, in and out of the hospital too. Anyone want to make any guesses?"

"From Russia with malice?" ventured Adam.

"Great film," grinned Duggie. "Spot on, yes, of course, it's Russia. We've known for some time that Russia has been hacking some of the NHS legacy systems, but it looks very much like they are stepping up their offensive against our health systems. Kathy says to tell you, and I paraphrase here, that Onetelcall now has quite definitive proof of a high-level plan, a strategy to do just as has been suggested here, steal street value drugs and replace them with phoney pharmaceuticals. Although this is a new tactic, she says."

"Interesting to have some proof of this," said Adam, "but I think we have enough to go on already. Does Onetelcall have any other intelligence for us? Names, locations, quantities, targeted drugs, you know, that sort of thing?"

"Can I just say something?" Pauline looked around the guests with an expression of anxiety. "I can see why Adam Superfoods might help the authorities about fraudulent caviar imports, we'd all like to help stamp out that trade, but what has a Russian campaign to hack into NHS computers and steal medicines got to do with a small superfoods business? I mean, it's nothing to do with us and, well I don't know about you Estelle, but I'm not keen on swapping my kitchen for something like 'the Berlin desk' or a secret squirrel spy ring, I'm just a farmer's wife and a mum. See what I'm saying, Estelle and I, we aren't cut out to be like Atomic Blond are we?"

"Oh, I don't know Pauli," said Estelle, looking slightly flushed, "I rather fancy a bit of adventure. How about a Venus spy trap or a bit of honey-trapping, I'd like a bit of that, not sure that Tim would approve though."

After a general round of laughter, Amanda piped up,

"Pauline, Estelle and you too, Adam, funny though that is, there is a serious point here. I don't sell superfoods and none of you, including Anna, are law enforcers, so I suggest we stick to what we do best. I can't allow any of you to start any investigation which would lead you into danger or muddy the waters for professional detectives and policemen. I am hugely impressed by what Adam and Anna have found out and I'm grateful for your suppositions too. With what you have told me, I can now mount an authorised, official investigation."

"Understood Ma'am," grinned Adam, "but you must know that we shall keep on looking and telling you what we either think or know is going on. We can't stop now, can we Anna, we just can't; it's not human nature to stop now."

"And, Amanda," added Anna, "you need us, and you know you need us, don't you? You need someone on the inside and you need a legitimate Rushian customer to find out things you couldn't possibly get to know without some heavy-handed police operation. If you charge in waving your warrants or whatever you do, you'll lose all the major players and end up with a few minor crimes against the import laws or whatever, but you won't get anywhere close to the big players, the English end of this Russian attack, will you Amanda? I mean, honestly, will you?"

"Oh, for God's sake, I have enough trouble keeping my husband alive without you queuing up to be bloody heroes. I give up, I do, but listen to me very carefully, if I catch any of you wandering over the line of the law or interfering with a police investigation, I'll nick you, ok? I'll bloody well bang you up."

Max interrupted, "I say Mand, steady on, Anna's got a damn good point, and you know, of course you know, that you need all the help you can get. You won't get much in the way of extra resources from your…"

"Max, let me finish will you. I have one more thing to say, she paused and looked carefully at Anna and Adam. "I am so grateful to you. It is people like you who make policing possible these days. I might not be able to condone what you are suggesting but I sure as hell appreciate it, thank you, thank you very much."

Max smiled proudly, "She's awfully good, isn't she."

24

"This arsehole Melor is some basic wanker, can't you do something to smash him? What's the use of being a great words man, Agron, if you can't rip him to shreds wherever he posts, eh?"

"I know Pal, he is pushing his luck. All this bragging is going to end badly for him, I just know it is. I think it is better to remain aloof for a while rather than weigh in with verbal fists flying, frustrating though that is for you I know but we live to fight another day in another way. You don't get a champion boxer scrapping with some cheap street fighters, do you? No, you don't and that's the view we should take."

"Alright, alright, I hear you but I'm not happy, I tell you, I'm not, I just want to drill a whole new asshole into this fucker. I mean, what's all this Melor's Gambit like he's some fucking chess champion? He's a wanker, that's what he is and the more he posts about his brilliance, the more of a wanker he sounds."

"That's exactly my point and like everyone who blows up a big balloon, it will explode in his face. I've been thinking, Max and Duggie must be on his case too, but I've only had a brief text back from Max saying he'll be in touch. Not a squeak since. I'll give him a nudge I think."

"Hello Max, it's Agron."

"Agron, good to hear from you. Sorry I haven't come back to you about this NHS action, but we are making progress, and I can easily see a joint operation with you could be a good plan very soon, Anyway, how are you both?"

"Pissed off, Max. Pal is doing his pieces and wants to get at this Russian hacker."

"Yeah?"

"Oh yeah, he's massively pissed. I don't suppose you see it but this Melor is the hacker who's doing it to you. He's all over the hacker sites and dark web forums, bragging how much of a fucking genius he is. You can imagine, Pal is feeling well dissed, to say the least. A pissed off Pal is not a pretty thing, that's for sure."

"We should talk, swap notes and all that. I don't suppose you ever come to England, do you?"

"Max, you know better than that, we are nice and safe here in the hills over Mattinata and that's where we intend to stay. But look, you and Duggie are always very welcome to come here, why don't you pop over?"

"Be with you in a couple of days then and we'll work out a plan, I just need to talk to some people first."

Max called Duggie, "Pack your shades and straw-hat chap, we're off to Mattinata again."

Then he called Ben and explained that as he had a big meeting coming up in a day or two, he needed the latest update on the current level of known theft and was shocked at the answer.

"Am I glad to hear from you, Max, it's going from bad to bloody terrible here. None of us knows what to do about it, not even Perry. He admits we're being infiltrated but doesn't know how to stop it. It seems not only are drugs going out from here, but we've traced fake drugs which have somehow got into the system. So far, we've caught it all in time, but someone is going to die soon because of this counterfeiting."

"It's escalated pretty quickly then?"

"Yes, from when we last spoke, what three days ago, it's got so bad we are considering emergency measures to safeguard lives. That's a bad place to be, Max. You and your team must do something soon, we are floundering, and we are not alone, what's happening to us is happening all over the country, it's like an epidemic."

"What do you know about your junior, Adrian, isn't it?"

"Yes, Adrian, why do you ask?"

"Just answer me, please Ben. Have you noticed anything about him recently that strikes you are being, oh I don't know, different?"

"Well, now you ask, yes. He has been distracted and depressed one moment and on cloud nine the next. I can tell you in confidence that I wonder if he is overdoing the little narco helper pills. A lot of junior doctors do, you know, they are under huge pressures."

"Ok, keep an eye on him, yeah? We have no proof, just suspicions. He may be involved, I hope not, he's such a nice fellow, but there is a chance…"

"I see, tell you what, how about I give Adrian some time off? Heaven knows he could do with it and it would keep him away from whatever you suspect him of doing until you've had whatever meeting it is that you are having."

"Good plan, thanks. I'll let Amanda and our digital snoopers know. It will be interesting to eavesdrop on his activities while he's off duty."

"Good lord, Max, are you watching him, listening in to his calls and all that? I mean, is that legal? More importantly, what have you overheard so far?"

"Legal? Ben, I ask you, what's legal when you are fighting a battle like this? So, yes, we are keeping an ear on him but, sorry, I can't tell you more than that, not yet anyway, soon but not now."

Max and Amanda had a dinnertime debriefing.

"Well, Mand, we need a plan. There are too many plates spinning, and I feel like we are losing control. Neither of us has complete authority to act, to intervene, to fight back, and yet that is what we know we must do. If we put Rushian, Adam and all that to one side, we could concentrate on what I see as the biggest threat, drugs, real and fake, sloshing around all over the place and that is where I think we should put our effort right now."

"I agree," she nodded, "no matter what else is going on, a potential threat to life is where we should be. What have you got in mind?"

"It's not much of a plan at all but is a starting point if you agree."

"Ok."

"I'm flying off to Mattinata tomorrow, taking Dug with me of course, for what you might call a recruitment drive. I'm going to set Agron and Pal up to go into battle against this Russian hacker; those two are so angry they'll leap at a chance to make a counterattack, I know it."

"That's a start but a slow one. I'm sure you're right, some counter-hacking will work but it's no super-fast fix, is it? While you're scoffing spaghetti, our hospitals are being flooded with counterfeit drugs and deaths will, for sure, follow. So how many might die in the meantime, eh? Oh, Max, it makes me feel so helpless and I'm damned if I'll just sit by and do nothing, authority or not, approval or not."

"Well, here's a ruse for you, an idea which doesn't need any top cop sanction."

"What can I do without approval? I'm a police officer, not a freelance equaliser!"

"Ah, but you are a woman, well-practised, if I may say, in the art of seduction. I'm living proof of that, aren't I? Why don't you see if you can get closer to our Adrian, find out a bit more about him at um, a personal level, eh, good idea?"

"Fuckin' hell, Max, I don't know whether to be complimented or affronted, pimping me out again like some old slapper."

"Aw, c'mon, you know it gives you a thrill, that power over men, that ability to wrap us all around your little finger."

"Well, now you mention it, I do quite enjoy leading men by their wil…"

"Mand… oh, cold hands!"

25

Roof down, sun shining, engine singing, Max and Duggie revelled in their hour-long journey from Foggia airport as their hired Alfa Spyder sped through the beautiful Gargano scenery. During their flight from Gatwick, they had discussed tactics for the upcoming meeting with the two friendly, but often testy Albanian renegades.

"It's another tap dance," declared Max, "we'll just have to make it up as we go along."

"That's what I call preplanning and being prepared," chuckled Duggie, knowing that whatever plans they made would change the moment his intuitive friend started talking.

"Something else too," said Duggie, "you can still only just bend your knee properly, and we've got a manual sports car?"

"Yes, to both me old chum."

"I'm driving."

Their welcome was like a family reunion. "You stay, we drink," announced Agron, clutching a bottle of gin.

The Starlink satellite dish gave a clue to the technology that lurked behind the hillside cottage's front door.

"Even better now," announced Pal in the proud tone of a new father. "We have power, all the power I need to make my entrance to any network in the world, to harness all the quantum AI anyone could need, this, my friends, is the supreme of all supreme hacker's workplaces."

"And yes," smiled Agron knowingly, "before you ask the questions, it does work both ways. We can track and trace any hack from anywhere to anywhere if we have just a scrap of information to start with. So, yes, my friends, we know all about your health service hack, but especially who is behind it all."

"Yes," growled Pal, his voice laced with frothing, fermenting poison, "we know the bastard Melor. His name is Melor, not his original name of course, some fancy stage name from a self-promoting actor who believes he has a talent, who believes he can compete with me, Pal, the greatest hacker who ever lived, and he thinks he can live my life, breathe my air…" He fell back into his chair, his face suffused, his breathing deep and erratic, such was his anger.

"Now fellas," said Duggie soothingly, "you'll be aware that Max here has a bit of a reputation for wreaking revenge on cyber-criminals who deserve a hefty dose of comeuppance. The reason we are here now is to offer you a way of delivering your wrath against this Melor character with the full support and approval of Max, me, Onetelcall and, most probably, the entire combined European police forces and health services around the world."

"Duggie, as always, is right," said Max, "and if my guesses are correct, we can not only finish off your Melor for good, but we can also take down everyone who is working with him in Russia and the UK. Now that would make you feel a bit better wouldn't it, Pal?"

"Catch, Mr Max, where is catch?" demanded Pal, fixing his guests with a suspicious glare.

"His English always slips when he's agitated," smiled Agron, "and we know you two well enough now, you are men of your words, like us. You may bend rules and sometimes break laws which need to be broken, but between us, we are all men of our words to each other."

Pal stood and very solemnly held out his hand, "Ok, we shake, then I know."

They shook hands several times as well as swearing oaths of lifelong allegiances. By the time they hit the second bottle of gin, they felt confident of all-round mutual goodwill.

Clinging on to his last vestiges of sobriety, Max explained that before launching any reprisal strikes, they should combine their listening and tracking resources to widen the net over everyone and anyone who was implicated with Melor.

"We know some names," chirped Pal, cheered immensely by the excitement of impending action and the numerous large gins. "We have traced much of the scum in Melor's electronic messaging and although we know we aren't as good as your girls, Indira and Sue, we have captured quite a lot. I have it all locally, so you can see for yourself. Some names mean nothing to us, but you and your contacts may be able to identify them and their jobs, their roles in this pathetic attempt to copy my genius."

"Brilliant," observed Duggie, only marginally avoiding slurring, "shall we inspect your intel in the morning?"

With several cups of strong early-morning coffee, some cornetti and pastries, the four men studied all the eavesdropped transcripts. After a very short while, they established that Major Vasily Vassiliev and General Savva Komarov were key players along with Melor, also referred to in some notes made by the Major, as Bogdan Belov. Satisfied that no more names could be gleaned, Max sent them, with a little context and background from Pal and Agron, to Jo knowing that the moment she received them, the full team would start examining every digital uttering in forensic detail.

It seemed obvious from Pal and Agron's intelligence capture that 'Melor' was the 'Nomme de keyboard' of the hacker-in-chief and he took orders from the Major. Max and Duggie couldn't see where and how the Komarov character fitted in, but they knew the full story would soon emerge.

26

Doctor Nathanial Hetherton, nearing retirement, was the lead GP in a practice that cared for patients in the small market town of Broderton. And he hated it. In fact, he had come to hate most things in life. Long gone were those idyllic days of adventure, ambition and excitement. He had been a student doctor when they enjoyed a reputation as fun-fuelled hellraisers and put much effort into maintaining the reputation. He studied almost as hard as he played and chased his career as fervently as he pursued fun at the university and various medical locations he attended in his quest for full qualification.

Nat had a calling, perhaps from watching television medical shows as a boy when the doctors were all debonair and heroic, surrounded by adoring nurses, or perhaps because he believed that he should dedicate his life to being of use and making life better for other people. Whatever the original motivation, he longed to be a doctor and although less glamorous than some disciplines, the role of GP appealed to him the most.

Three wives and thirty years in a job which offered surprisingly little variety, gradually eroded his idealism, replacing it with cynicism and resentment. Doctor Hetherton was known and generally liked in Broderton where he had a lengthy list of patients, the majority of whom were better than averagely fit and suffered only from ailments and debilitations created by their age and over-indulgences. His once effusive sympathy had been ground down to blunt insensitivity.

"Eat less," was his advice to the overweight. "Drink less," his standard recommendation for those who sought help for alcohol dependency. "Get a job or a hobby," became his common prescription for anyone suffering from depression. He declared to all that he would no longer accept any patient who smoked and would not offer any support for those who were seeking to quit, telling them, "Just don't set fire to the damn thing." The curmudgeonly doctor had compassion for only one addiction, gambling. His favourite father-in-law had been captivated, totally consumed by all forms of gambling. He had adored the thrill of on-course betting at any track, the live racing, the badinage and the excitement and in the process, gambled away everything he had and more.

At first, Nathanial told his second wife's father not to be such an asshole, to stop throwing his wealth away. He spent hours proving beyond any doubt that he could never win, that only the bookies and the bankers made any money from gambling and was aghast to see that even faced with incontrovertible proof, the man just kept on gambling, ignoring the facts, confident that one day he would win, as he put it, 'Charlie big time'.

Nat's overwhelming need to mend people took charge and he produced a plan which he believed would save his wife's amiable and genial father from a terrible end. He based it on the Minnesota Method and Alcoholics Anonymous's Twelve Steps programme. In the fight against most addictions, complete abstinence is essential but in the doctor's version, he replaced the bookie with his own created hypothetical wager-and-reward system based on praise and self-improvement points. He talked to his subject until there was an established, total acceptance of the problem and until he got him to admit openly that he was powerless over his gambling addiction. Then he was able to gain a full commitment to an extended programme of recovery.

To Nathaniel's amazement, the programme began to work. It took an unreal amount of his time that, as a working GP, he could ill afford but the results made it compellingly fulfilling and exciting. For a while, Nathanial considered starting a private practice for gambling addicts and even posted some professional papers about his methods and his findings. His next step was to advertise on selected social media and could soon tell by the sheer number of desperate responders that he was on to a winner. But misanthropy vanquished ambition and avarice He just couldn't stand the whining, pleading neediness of the many gamblers who approached him for help. He did overcome his distaste to help a small number whose requests for help were more positive than pitiful, especially one new applicant, a fellow medical man.

Uncharacteristically and despite his gruff intolerance, Dr Hetherton also had an alter ego as Doc Nat, the after-dinner speaker. "Hello Mrs Jones, I haven't seen you for some time… No, sorry Doctor, I've been ill," was his standard opening joke, enough to elicit a polite titter from his usually merry, wined and dined audiences. His blend of real-life horror stories, startling facts, debunked myths and searing descriptions of some of his more idiosyncratic patients and their unspeakable ailments was a successful formula. He valued the additional public speaking income. Three divorce settlements had denuded his wealth dramatically but the increasingly healthy speaker fees he could command meant that retirement would soon be viable.

Doc Nat enjoyed the irony that one of his jokes about the triteness of doctor-receptionist love affairs was exactly the relationship he had with Jane Coles, the patient services manager at the Broderton GP Centre. Both he and she wore a protective emotional carapace, a hard shell moulded by the pain of multiple relationship failures. Each found condescension and aloof superiority to be the crutches they needed to shore up their flagging self-esteem and each needed the other if anything worthwhile was to be rescued from their ever-shortening futures.

Jane, usually poised and controlled, had lost her composure and looked alarmed. She almost fell into his consulting room, one hand holding back some fly-away hair, the other clutching a printout.

"Nat, oh, Nat, it's a disaster, what shall we do? Oh, Nat, we are in big, big trouble."

Nathanial was shocked to see his unflappable assistant and lover so distraught. He leapt up, took her by the elbow and steered her towards his patient's chair.

"Hold on, Jane, it can't be that bad, here, come and sit down; breathe, that's it, breathe slowly and tell me what's so terrible?"

"Look, Nat, it's from Travers, that techie from our IT management company. Just look, it's a list of all our patients who have email accounts with us, and Nat, we, they, all of us, we've all been hacked. Some bastards have hacked our server or whatever it is and stolen all the details of patients whose email addresses are held by us, every damn one of them, stolen, hacked and, and, oh, it's a disaster Nat."

She sobbed and Nathanial's mind raced as he tried to assess the possible fallout from such an intrusion. "Did Travers say anything about how the hackers got into our server and, more importantly, what else have they stolen? I mean what about practice records, patient records, prescriptions and all that admin sort of stuff we've got?"

"I'm sorry, you'll have to call him. I just lost it when he phoned to say he'd sent me this," she waved the printout dramatically above her head. "He was talking but I stopped listening, I just panicked, sorry. Can you speak to him?"

"Hey Geepee, bunch of canine poo innit?" said the irrepressible Travers. "Up to your kneecaps in it, I'd say. Still, Geep, you're not alone, if that's any comfort."

"What's the damage, Travers? Tell me in simple terms what has happened."

"Well, like I said to your lady Jane, like wow lady Jane…"

"Travers, you're bloody certifiable!"

"Yeah, anyways Geep, you've been royally rogered, your IT system that is, hacked to high heaven. Amazing, so clever, sent in a bug via an auto-update from your appointment and diary application and vacuumed out all the data it could find, like all of it, that is, the lot, all she wrote."

"Are you not paid the equivalent of a bank theft by me every month to ensure that this sort of thing never happens? How did it happen Travers, why were we not protected like I seem to remember you promised?"

"Listen Geep, we're good here, ever so, but we can't protect against the unknown and we have never seen anything like this before. It isn't just us caught with our danglers in the air, from what's buzzin' it seems that hundreds of practices have been rinsed like you in the last day or so. But I can tell you that all those who've been hit shared the same front desk app that you use and all of them have open comms channels with Olderbury Hospital, which, I happen to know, is being hacked so much it might as well keep its secret data on fuckin social media."

"I didn't know that…"

"Sure Geep, I don't know how to cure STIs, that's why I do what I do, and you do what you do. So, I know that Olderbury hospital and it's not limited to just them, is in a crisis of ransom and theft, so much so they've mugged Onetelcall for some heavyweight assistance."

"I see, so what should we little practices do now? I mean what can we do to put right what's been damaged and how can we protect ourselves from it all happening again?"

"Ok, here's the word, you pay me for my super-tech services, and I do everything I can for you now, right? I've blocked all traffic in and out of the practice's systems, the items that are sensitive, like prescription orders, patient records and stuff like that. I've got a small team on it, and we'll monitor you in microscopic detail for at least a few days. You should be safe now but, if I'm to be honest, I'm still at a loss to know how deep we are infected and what worms, bots, spiders and other crap might still be active but I'll sure as hell keep a constant lookout for you."

"Can't say I'm much mollified," said Nat crossly, "but I suppose I can't ask for more. What about the patients, are they in any danger?"

"Nah Nat, almost none. Most of them have details of their gory bits listed with you but nobody who hacks at this level is interested in Mr Bilbow's bunions, I mean, really. It's true too that almost none of them have any financial details stored with you, so they can't be turned over via their banks. So, Geep, if it was up to me, I'd keep shtum about all this and not panic the horses. See what I mean, keep the faith man, let them keep the faith."

"Travers, you aren't as good as you think you are. So, tell me now what you're not telling me. You are hiding something that I know I won't like."

"Yeah, well, there is one small thing I should tell you."

"Come on."

"It looks like you signed something like five thousand prescriptions, mostly for packs of one hundred tabs of pregabalin, like half a million pills Geep, spread across pharmacies in the county and all for distribution delivery points which, by the looks of it, the chemists are fulfilling without question. Why wouldn't they, they don't see the big picture, just a spike in orders which ain't all that unusual to them, I guess."

"And you left that news until last, did you? Can't you see what this means? You're an imbecile, Travers, you know that?"

"Whatever Geep, I got your back now and I'm not in the business of fighting big-scale drug theft. Nobody I know can fight this, not even those hotshots at Onetelcall 'cos I can tell you for sure that this comes from Russia, and the hit on you and the other practices is an infinitesimal occurrence in a big, big, big attack on the UK's healthcare services, and probably one of the biggest prescription drug heists the world has seen."

27

"It's terrifying, talk about walking a tightrope, bloody terrifying, we might be killing people as we dole out drugs without knowing for sure if they are the real thing or some fake shit."

Ben was hunched over a large glass of wine in The Royal George's hunt bar. He looked at Max and Amanda and it was clear that he was a man close to breakdown.

"I mean, we're chronically under-staffed as it is and now, we have to divert analysts to test every batch of suspect drugs before we can prescribe them. At least we know what is being stolen and replaced, so it could be worse but, honestly you two, we are close to imploding or making a lethal mistake. It's bound to happen eventually, small fingers, big dyke, know what I mean?"

"I don't know what to say, Ben, it's awful but at least whoever is doing this hasn't claimed any lives yet, so that's something I suppose," said Amanda, knowing how thin her words of consolation sounded.

"Do we, do we really? I don't know," responded the gloomy surgeon. "My guess is that any deaths from counterfeit drugs will have been hushed up, you know, put down to heart attack or whatever, probably bloody Covid. I don't know but it is the NHS's way when its back is against the wall."

"What? To lie?" she asked.

"Well, I wouldn't go that far, perhaps the word 'complications' sounds better than hospital-acquired toxicity, wouldn't you say? We don't want mass panic, that's the very last thing we want and anything like that would be an even bigger win for whoever is doing this to us."

"It's a bigger win than you know," commented Max seriously. "Even we don't know the full extent of the damage. But we do know the whole of the UK's NHS is under a concerted cyberattack from Russia. It's the cleverest we've come across at Onetelcall. It differs from the usual array of state-sponsored digital warfare and criminal hacking opportunism, this time we are finding overwhelming evidence that some egomaniac whom we believe to be tagged 'Melor' is masterminding a multi-faceted, strategic cyber offensive. What makes this so different is the sheer scale of the operation. It's not a bit of delinquent bug-planting, this Melor character seems to have a complex network of support in the NHS, in goods shipment, in distribution, in product intelligence and, well, I hardly know how many more 'ands' there are. We've got a fight here that is much bigger than any of us ever thought. And it's growing exponentially."

"Our IT teams have been working with Max's specialists," said Amanda. "They all agree that this nationwide crisis started here in Olderbury, and we have now confirmed that one of the original inside moles, if that's the right description, I can think of others, is, sadly your own very pleasant and likeable Adrian Simson."

"Are you now completely sure?" asked Ben, miserably.

"Sure, we are sure," she replied. "We have a witness description, a signature, we have phone records and, it's a slam dunker, Adrian Simson has been complicit at some significant level."

"Are you going to arrest him?"

"No, not yet at any rate. We are getting some useful information by tracking him, but it is only a matter of time. We want to have a solid case against him, of course, but we also want enough to effect a meaningful arrest of his contact, a man called Gary Pugh, a BMA staff member who doubles as an activist for whoever in Russia has recruited him. If that's what's happened, we need to know a bit more before we jump."

"I've met Pugh with Adrian," said Ben. "They appear to be mates, though I wouldn't trust him as far as I can spit. I did suspect something was going on between them not so long ago when Adrian was a bit depressed and, lo, after a meeting with Pugh, he was flying high again. Odd, I thought, very odd."

"Max, can you explain?" asked Amanda. "I really shouldn't."

"Certainly, Mandy. You see, Ben, what has also been discovered is that your clever, ambitious and caring young doctor is also a gambler, a serious gambler, an addicted gambler who, like all gamblers, ended up owing a lot of money to a lot of people. We believe Pugh gave him a bung big enough to get out of the clag. It doesn't take a genius to figure that Pugh would have demanded something significant in return, and it is highly possible that Pugh forced Simson into being his insider agent."

"Well, it's pretty bloody self-evident, isn't it?" blurted Ben. "I mean as far as I'm concerned it seems clear that this Pugh, this fucking terrorist in our midst, has forced our boy to falsify prescriptions, to divert drugs, reduced him to being some sort of local mule. I mean, God, Pugh has bullied, blackmailed, coerced and intimidated an essentially good man into betraying all that he believes in."

"You are such a good man, Ben but I have to say the jury is still out on how voluntarily culpable our Mr Simson is," replied Amanda, "and we must look at the facts. First, he's a gambler who sold out to save his neck and get creditors off his back, yeah? Second, he took money knowing there would have to be a price to be paid and then, without scruple as far as we know, played a significant part in one of the most severe drug and digital crimes this country has seen. He's not attempted to warn any authority of the carnage about to hit us. So sorry, Ben, no matter how great the pressure on him, Adrian will struggle to get any sympathy from me. I reckon what he's done through weakness and greed deserves the harshest of judgement and I shall do all I can to ensure that's exactly what he gets. Until that time, we have the small problem of how to put a stop to this escalating emergency across the entire, goddam country and that's not going to happen simply by nicking a couple of small cogs. We need a bigger plan. I already have some of the weapons in place to beat these bastards and put in an effective revenge strategy too."

"Revenge?" asked Ben.

"Yeah, smart, merciless, unexpected revenge against the major players, this Melor and the evil shits he is working with in his fucking gulag. I say revenge because I want payback. I want them to suffer for their sins, but I also know we'll never physically catch, arrest and bring them to justice, so justice has to find another route and believe me, Ben, what I have in mind will destroy this inhuman offensive and feed the perpetrators to the pitiless judgement of Mother Russia's cruellest eminence-rouge."

"I'm at a total loss now guys," Ben admitted. "I will bow out of this conversation and leave it to you and your various teams. But I'll do anything I can to help, you know that."

"Yes, Ben, we know," replied Max gently, "and we appreciate all you've done so far. The information you and Perry gave us was crucial in creating our ability to monitor so many communication conduits and we are grateful for all you've done so far. It isn't easy for you I know. But I think we would both stress right now how important it is that Adrian Simson isn't tipped off, that he doesn't get even an inkling that we are closing in on him, right? So, while he's there, treat him, if you can, as you normally do, absolutely business as usual. No hint of what you know leaking to him by word, comment, expression or mood. It's a big and difficult ask but it is completely vital."

"It's Ok, he's taking some downtime like I said. You'll keep me fully informed of your progress, will you?" asked Ben, expecting a yes.

"No, Ben, from now on you concentrate on doing what you do so brilliantly and leave us to do what we can, ok?"

28

"Lap of the gods old son, lap of the gods," said Gary. "I've passed on your idea through my, er, handler, I suppose, and it's out of my hands now. If it's a goer, we'll be heroes, if it isn't, well, never say I didn't try, old mate."

Gary and Adrian were sipping flat whites in the hospital's street-access public coffee shop. It had been a week since Adrian offered Gary an alternative to the wanton killing of patients by replacing the high-quality drugs they were stealing with useless, dangerous counterfeits. His suggestion had been born of desperation. His conscience and his belief in the oath he had taken as a doctor forced him to try, at least, to divert the influx of dangerous, useless faux medication from the intended destination of hospital pharmacies to the open market where gangs would buy almost any pills and powders to sell on to their user and addict customers.

Although Gary knew better than Adrian that the planting of fake drugs in the NHS was part of a greater plan, he could see the appeal of disrupting the street market and gang power in a way which might favour his Russian paymasters even more. To offer them a method of creating gang warfare with only the Russian-backed narcotic distribution organisations having a chance of winning was not without merit. Within a day of Adrian's desperate spur-of-a-moment inspiration, the idea was put to Major Vasily Vassiliev by his SVR coordinator for the UK. In less than fifteen minutes after that, his driver, Luka, delivered Melor to his Lubyanka office.

"Melor," said Major Vasily, only just getting used to treating his tame hacker without contempt, "it seems that someone in the ranks of our UK supporters shares your view about us feeding counterfeit medicines into hospital pharmacies."

"I'm not surprised, Major," replied Melor, remembering that the Major's first name could be used only by invitation. "Random murder, which is what it amounts to, does not appeal to many people, I find."

"Is that what you find? Perhaps you could explain your view to General Komarov who is a zealous promoter of such wilful slaughter, especially when it is connected with us and our notable successes in the UK, so far."

"Major, I'm sure you are not wasting your time with me unless you feel there is a discussion to be had in which I may be of some small value."

"We have been offered an alternative strategy by some NHS insider our supporters have recruited."

"Major, strategies in my programme are determined by me, with your valuable advice and authority, of course, but we need no further contributions, not from opportunist egocentric generals or weak, traitorous English NHS workers," Melor was irritated and it showed.

"Do not let your remission lead you to indulge in unwise boldness, Melor, and do not deceive yourself into thinking that you have the power of independent policy making. Nor, if I were you, would I be unguarded about my opinions of senior political figures; open windows and tall buildings will soon cease to be safe for you if you are overheard."

"I know, Major, I know. Thank you for your sagacity. Let me ask again, is there more to this meeting than you have told me so far?"

"Some of our less principled countrymen have found great success with partners from perhaps, Eastern Europe, Pakistan and areas of Africa, in providing UK citizens with the various drugs they seem so enthusiastic about consuming."

"This is not big news, Major."

"Patience, let me elucidate. The desperate NHS operative has, out of panic I suspect, come up with an interesting idea. Instead of the pharmacies, he suggests we flood the competitors of our drug distribution compatriots in Britain so that their customers react by using our people rather than the scum who would vie with us for this, ah, lucrative market. It is an idea which I can see finding favour in some quarters of our hierarchy, those closer to the more criminal factions of the regime."

"I see, a bloody turf war in which addicts die and gang members stab and shoot one another is a civilised alternative to killing ill people, is that right?"

"Most of the people who choose to describe themselves as my superiors would say yes. They would say that any dissolute Western life is worth taking and it is them to whom we must listen, not our personal views, beliefs or consciences."

Briefly, Melor thought about the hidden costs of becoming the world's greatest hacker. Was becoming a killer by proxy part of his youthful dream? If he had known, would he have changed course?

"Well, Major, I suppose every aggressive offensive, military or cyber, will have casualties. It is a fact and I must suspend my distaste for indiscriminate murder. You will accuse me of hypocrisy anyway so I shall, instead, concentrate on delivering what I am commanded to deliver, whether it is as planned, against the UK's drug gangs or both, I shall, as always, prove my genius and enhance your reputation, Major, even further."

"Your ability to overcome your principles for the sake of personal advancement is impressive, even by the standards of the duplicitous, devious and deceitful hierarchy we serve. Melor, you may indeed live longer than currently expected," the Major snickered ironically.

"If I may say, Major, the way I see it is this; for as long as I succeed in pleasing you and elevating your profile amongst that hierarchy, I shall survive, because you will survive and for as long as you enable me to do what I do next, I shall remain at the pinnacle of the world's greatest hackers and that, I believe, affords me a charmed physical existence and an immortal virtual life."

"Good, shall we drop all this existential bullshit now and talk about the issue at hand?"

"As you say," grinned Melor, "but if you are to ask me if I can think of ways of enabling this gangland disruption, then my answer is of course I can. I believe I know exactly how to achieve what is required and, if you were about to ask if I can still deliver my magic on both fronts simultaneously, again my answer is of course I can. Although I may need to involve some additional social media people if that is allowed."

"Social media?"

"Yes, Major, social media. Trust me."

29

Pal was the first to spot the new initiative, even before the might of Onetelcall's snoopers and way ahead of the police IT surveillance teams.

"Hey, Agron, "we are being plagiarised again."

"Must be bad for you to use a big word."

"Fuck off, this is serious, that fuckin' half-arsed hack in Moscow is stealing our social media techniques for some sort of assault on the big drug gangs everywhere in the UK. You know, like the message-in-message, hidden in most of the message boards stoking the rise in racial violence, the cryptic code, the dark web links, the camouflage chatter, encrypted Telegram groups, all of it, Agron, fuckin' all of it."

"For why, I mean to what purpose?"

"Far as I can see, they are changing tack. They moved focus from the NHS attack to some sort of troublemaking amongst drug runner outfits. I can't make it all out yet, but my guess is they are trying to get gangs to buy their fake drugs, you know, a new source, super-cheap, massive profits, safe and all that shit."

"Gimme a sec, I'll look over all the recent traffic and see if I can get any more info, right?"

"Right. Call Max too, give him a heads-up, yeah?"

"Yes, sure, Pal."

Agron scoured the monitors and believed he could make some sense of the new development. He had a newsman's second sight in dot-joining and adding accurate hypotheses. When he called Max, he had a strong feel for what was happening.

"Max, Agron, hi."

Max was always surprisingly pleased to hear from this foe-turned-friend; his visits to Mattinata had become highlights of escapist fun in his busy schedule.

"What's the word?"

"Not words, headlines, big, blazing headline news straight from our intel sweeps and it is this, are you ready?"

"Poised and coiled for action chum."

"They've changed direction, and it looks like they are manipulating some sort of gangland war by pushing fake pharmaceuticals into distribution networks, ones not controlled by the Russians or their allies, and that, let me tell you, can only have one conclusion."

"Fuck," exclaimed Max, "I haven't had an inkling about this yet. I know I don't have to ask, but are you sure, like certain?"

"Yeah, we are sure. It's like from the horse's mouth 'cos that's where we got it, direct comms intercepted by Pal, so it's the real deal for sure."

"Ok, can you give me a little time, an hour or so to do some checking around and a bit of thinking? This isn't an anticipated development, and we might need to re-arrange some of our plans."

"Sure, Max."

Max let his mind freewheel. This could be a pivotal moment in whatever war was being fought, a game changer, a changed game, or fake news, a dummy manoeuvre. He tried to assimilate dependable facts. Attacks on NHS equipment, yep, that was a fact; stealing drugs from the NHS also indisputable; an insider in Olderbury, yes, Adrian Simson is involved but only a bit player being pushed about by the guy Gary. Rushian? A conduit, culpable in many ways but not important in the greater scheme of things… probably.

Max had originally believed it was about money. Most crimes like this orchestrated attack look sophisticated but eventually, it is always only about money. That could still be true but there must be a more valuable goal, a bigger prize to justify all the effort and organisation of the whole operation. Did the answer lie in Moscow? Yes, surely. But why? What was the end game? Destroy the NHS, undermine the UK economy, tie up time and resources? Probably all of those but, to Max's mind something was missing. It didn't feel right, it didn't have the hallmarks of a state-sponsored incursion. And who were the real players? Melor, the technical whizzkid, Vassiliev, the Major with the power, or Komorov, a latecomer with his own agenda, from what Max could infer from the eavesdropped evidence. And now drug gangs were set against each other. Part of a strategy or a change in ambition? So why? Flood the NHS with damaged addicts? Force increased police activity? Why use fake drugs when the perpetrators have already stolen the good stuff?

Max needed to focus. He got into his car and drove to the exact point of impact of his car crash. Eyes closed, he relived those terrible moments, and his mind wheeled in a mental reset. Shaking and slightly sweaty, he drove onwards from the crash site and stopped in a gateway a few hundred yards away. Relishing every breath, he gave silent thanks for his life. As he did so, he felt calm and vital. He was in control again; he had been given the rest of his life and it was his to use to his best ability. In that gateway, in his introspection, the clues in his conundrum began to take shape, not yet fully formed but definitely in a discernible pattern.

He sat in deep deliberation until the daylight started to fade and then he called Agron.

"Sorry to have been so long, I had a lot of thinking to do."

"Ok, we've been doing the same. Tell me where you've got to."

"Not sure that I know to be honest, but I'll have a stab. Let me start with what we know."

Max took less than ten minutes to share his knowledge of the circumstances.

"Yeah," said Agron, "as a skim across the surface that seems about it. You have rowed your ducks well. Now I think we must dig deeper into the comrades' chit-chat, not that there is much chatting, everything we intercept is all very short, sharp and business-like."

"Hmm, yes, that's what we see, although our abilities to listen in on mobile conversations in Russia is, well, limited and strictly speaking I shouldn't share any of our techniques with you, trust you though I do… now…" Max heard Agron chuckle, "…but as part of a covert alliance with Five Eyes, we have been able to seriously upgrade an existing technology, the old Pegasus spyware if you know it?"

"Pal will."

"Yeah, anyway, we are now getting some better-quality conversations. Indira is transcribing some of them for you, and they all confirm what we all suspect."

"Which is what?"

"Aw, c'mon, you know. This isn't a Russian government initiative, this is a personal power grab in the Kremlin hierarchy and your bogeyman Melor is a tool being used in a battle of, what, egos, power and wealth or simply survival, we can't quite tell."

"Are you saying that this Melor clown is no longer our prime target? Cos if you are, we will have to think again about our joint action with you. I'll never be able to sell anything to Pal that doesn't include the annihilation or total humiliation of Melor."

"Actually, I am and I'm not, and I think I might have an idea. My head has been in the clouds today and that is exactly where our solution lies."

30

For a bleak moment, Adrian considered ending it all. It was just after five in the morning, the sky was beginning to lighten, it was always his worst time. He awoke from the happy release of sleep to face the reality of his predicaments and, as so often happened, a consuming depression overwhelmed his thoughts. He didn't fear death, it was living and ageing that he dreaded. He could, of course, prescribe himself any one of hundreds of drugs to release him from his misery, but even in his despair, he knew the only solution would come from within, not by pill or injection and certainly not from the momentary rush of gambling. Without consciously knowing why, he picked up his phone and rang a number he hadn't called for a long time.

"This had better be an emergency."

"It is doc, believe me, it is."

Adrian jumped in his car and by nine o'clock was sitting in Nathanial Hetherington's kitchen, clutching a medically prescribed large brandy.

When Nathanial first got Adrian's call, he his normal reaction of curt dismissal was quelled by the sheer desperation in the young doctor's voice.

"You need to come here right now my boy," he said, wondering where this sudden spurt of altruism had come from.

As Adrian sat in front of him, pale, shaking and suffering a self-imposed deep mental trauma, Nathanial knew that he still had his calling's instinct to help a fellow in need, to tend to the sick, especially to a young man who reminded him so much of his more youthful self. He knew he had to drain Adrian's mind of the poison which threatened his very sanity. Jane came up with the solution.

"Nat, darling, he needs to talk, he needs to get whatever it is off his chest and he needs to do it now, while it is all so real and I don't think there is a better way of getting him to relax and start talking than a generous dose of Napoleon's favourite."

Adrian gulped the first drink and sat silently staring into the middle distance, while Jane sat beside him, a comforting arm around him. Nathanial sat opposite, bottle at the ready, observing and waiting until the time was right to get the troubled young man to talk freely. Finally, Adrian slumped forward, his silence giving way to a soul-wrenching sobbing, as Jane gently rocked him to and fro, humming quietly to console and reassure him.

By ten o'clock, Adrian had regained some of his self-control and seeing the improvement, Jane set about making toast and coffee.

"Well, my boy," said Nathaniel, "now we are all safe and relaxed why not tell us your story? Start at the very beginning, leave nothing out and remember that nobody here will judge or comment, the important thing is that you talk it all out."

Adrian drained the remnants of his third large brandy. The alcohol had done its work. More relaxed and certainly more garrulous, he spoke non-stop, pausing only for more toast and coffee, until way past midday. He omitted nothing, hid nothing, apologised for nothing and justified nothing, it was the whole, unabridged story. When he stopped speaking, he felt a sense of freedom. Nathanial could see the look of relief in his eyes, but he knew better than to offer false optimism. He stood up and moved behind Adrian, placing his hands on the hunched shoulders.

"When you first came to me about your love of the spinning wheel, I had hoped you'd overcome it, but I was wrong. I should have kept track of you, but I consider grown people capable of leading their own lives. Of course, that is seldom true for any of us and now, my boy, I owe you an apology. I feel I have let you down in the past but now I'm about to tell you what you certainly won't want to hear…"

Jane failed to exercise similar constraint, "You fucking little shit, do you have any understanding of the havoc you and, oh, you and your putrid mates of Satan have caused us? Let alone all those vulnerable people in hospital. And you come here, spilling your guts about how terrible your life is. It isn't nearly terrible enough!" she raged. "You should be fucking horsewhipped and then horsewhipped again and again until the fucking devil himself takes you."

Nathanial placed a conciliatory hand on Jane's tense, shaking shoulder and looked fixedly at Adrian. "You see, m'boy, we have been victims of the shenanigans you have got yourself involved with and the fallout from what might be a jolly jape to your Russian paymasters is a matter of great importance to us, mere plebs that we are, your collateral damage."

Adrian looked away, not able to meet Nathanial's eye.

"However, that damage is now done, and we must look ahead, we must decide what is best for everyone involved in the story you have just told us."

"I had no idea it had gone so far," pleaded Adrian, "that so much harm has been done to so many people. I really didn't know, I was just caught in a trap and, I know, it was a trap of my own making and you've no idea how much I regret it all now, how much remorse I feel, how much guilt and, Nathanial, Jane, I think I know what you will both say and I know it is the only course of action open to me, I shall hand myself in to the police."

"No need old boy, I've already called them."

It took an unnecessary three hours for the police internal communication network to pass the crucial news of Adrian's capture through to the Olderbury task force and then considerably more time for the unmarked police car to get him from the doctor's Broderton kitchen to Olderbury police's new secure interview quarters.

Amanda called Max to tell him about this unexpected breakthrough. Duggie, during a quick update meeting at

Onetelcall's boardroom, suggested they should sweep up all the known Olderbury participants in what they now called, a little disparagingly, the Hospital Basket Case.

Amanda was unimpressed by this suggestion and its implication that she should be doing more. "Do thank Duggie for his inspired insight into policing in such matters," she told Max. "But we have neither the right nor the reason to barge around like the Sweeney nicking anyone we fancy fitting up, understood? When we can move, we will, until then you do the techno snooping and I'll do the professional policing, ok?"

"No need to get shirty, Mand. We know the constraints you have to work with, and Duggie wasn't even implying that he knows better or that you are deficient in your duties. He was suggesting that we can do what you can't, see? We can, you know, apprehend some faces and keep them nice and safe until you cut your way through all those red tapes."

"Working with you lot is like managing a bunch of delinquents," she moaned with an audible grin in her voice. "You know I can't sanction private action against any suspects and if you tell me what I think you are about to tell me, I should probably arrest you and your playmates instead."

"Ha, you know you need us, and what's more, I know you wouldn't arrest Angel and Jesus, now, would you?"

"Dear God, those two? Really? Oh Max, take care, give 'em my love and ask them to keep the body and bullet counts to a minimum, will you?"

31

Mary and Nigel Binns, accompanied as always by Harry Stotle, commonly called Haza, their exuberant cockerpoo, shook their heads in disapproval as the sound of a Mariachi band played full volume across the serene route of their wildlife ramble.

"I mean, really," moaned Mary. "What sort of people inflict such noise pollution on decent countryside lovers like us? Inconsiderate doesn't cover it, downright disgusting and someone ought to do something about it. It's just so un-English."

"You're right my flower, as always, you are so right. Let me tell you, if I could get my hands on them, they'd be sorry."

"Are you looking for me, signor?"

Nigel half-turned to see who had spoken and found himself confronted by an intimidating hulk, a sliver under 1.8m and a muscular 100 kg dressed in a typical country squire's tweed suit. With his eyes hidden behind his mirrored sunglasses, Angel, looked positively threatening.

"My apologies, signor, I thought I heard you say you wished to lay your hands on me. Well, here I am, please, be my guest."

"Are you responsible for this appalling din?" demanded Mary who found nothing intimidating.

"I must confess that I am. It is the sound of my homeland and sometimes, even in all this beauty, I miss my home."

"Well bloody well go back there and leave our countryside to those of us who love it."

"But I own this land madam, with my brother, we are the custodians of this beauty and spend much time and money keeping it as you see it today. We close gates, we collect litter, we clear up dogs' mess, we return it to its natural state after it has been badly treated by careless walkers and inconsiderate picnickers. So, you see, it is my land, it is land I love as much as I love my homeland and I don't feel I should be told to leave it, do you?"

"Are you going to let him talk to me like that Nigel? Say something!"

Angel squared his shoulders and advanced menacingly on Nigel. "Yes, Nigel, say something, put me in my place, oh dear, I am in my place, so what else do you have to say, Nigel?"

"Well, I mean," Nigel took a step back and looked as though he might be sick.

"I am the naughty teenager with the loud music, I am to be told off and sent to my room, is that it? Are you going to send me to my room Nigel? It might be difficult if I don't want to go, you know."

Angel held out his arms in a beckoning manner, baiting the hapless Nigel into a confrontation. With some distaste for her husband's weakness, Mary decided to intervene.

"Very well Mr Country-Landowner, I concede that you are exactly where you should be, on your land, bullying anyone you can and throwing your weight around just because you can. Come on Nigel, I don't want to spend any more time with this self-entitled thug."

They turned and marched off like petulant children, looking back to call Haza who was busy peeing on Angel's shoe. Mary burst into a shrieking laugh as Nigel scurried onwards, not wanting to be responsible for his dog's indiscretion. Angel looked down, tickled Haza behind his ears and looked at Nigel. Then his gaze lingered on Mary, and with a laugh in his voice he said, "I see you have had your dog's balls chopped off as well as…" He looked back at Nigel and shook his head sadly.

Angel and Jesus, brothers born in poverty in Mexico and former hitmen for a drugs cartel, had made a fabulous fortune from their very special abilities. They settled in England following many visits to the country to act as bodyguards and action heroes for Max and Duggie, in previous battles against digital criminals. They were rarely impressed by anyone but had great regard for Max and especially Duggie, the quiet man who had shown impressive resolve and 'big cajónes', courage in tight, potentially lethal trouble.

When Max called again, both brothers were delighted to hear from him, knowing that some interesting action would be sure to follow.

"Hey, you two, what's happening?"

"Max, our friend, how good it is to hear you. It has been some time since we showed that private army a thing or two about warfare in the Iranian cyber revenge shoot-out. Oh, how my brother and I loved that, real good fun man, you always give us real good fun."

"Happy to be of service, my friend. Duggie says hi too, by the way, and so does Amanda who told me to tell you not to overdo the body count or the bullets."

"Sounds good so far compadre. What is that we can do for you this time?"

"You're going to love this, we are going to do the work that our wonderful police force can't do, we are going to gather up some bad guys and keep them safe until the forces of law and order are ready to receive them more formally."

"Why can't you speak in fuckin' Spanish you goddam gringo? I only got a bit of what you said!"

"We are hitting some baddies and locking them up, right?"

"Oh yeah, for sure, right? You comin' over to fill us in?"

It was a family reunion, Mexican style. Laughter, hugs, beer, food, music and reminiscences. Angel, Jesus, Max and Duggie recalled so many memories from the days of Spray Wilson. He was the founder of Onetelcall and a powerful drug supplier until the cartels forced him into exile. Then there came the appalling

Sniff Taylor who had tried to attack Jo. Not to mention the bomb-crazed femme fatale from Chisinau who nearly ensnared Max, and the Triads crypto frauds. So many adventures and they all agreed it was no wonder that Max was so well remembered in Olderbury Hospital.

"Ok boys, here is our shopping list. We lift 'em and keep 'em safe and secure."

"Hey man, that's no probs for us English aristos," grinned Jesus. "We got fuckin' outbuildings built to keep mad bulls, horny stallions and local thieves safe and secure. A few scrawny limeys will be no problem, that's for sure."

"This is Number One on our most wanted list. Gary Pugh, he works in London, and this is the best, well only, photo we have of him."

"Doozey."

"This, we believe, is a guy called Paul Preston, one of Pugh's known contacts, and this is Neil Handly who we think is a go-between for Pugh and whoever gives the orders. We got them off his phone records and traced their pictures through social media. We think they're part of the network between the Russian guys and the distribution people here in the UK."

"Fuckwits."

"Ok, these people are closer to home here in Olderbury. These three, according to quality inside information, are the top guys in a firm called Rushian, a well bent import and export shipper we know to be one of the main routes for getting stolen drugs out and fake drugs into the country."

"Assholes."

Jesus looked disappointed, "Y'know man, I can see that you'd need us to help you snatch these assholes but, well, it ain't exactly thrilling, is it? Where's the action?"

"Not much," agreed Max. "But these people are at the front end of an organisation we don't know much about. We know it is clever and we know from experience that wherever drug movement happens, violence is never far behind. We can guess that the Gary character will be a pushover but after that, we have no way of knowing what resistance we might face. I'm just taking the finest precautions any man could ask for and that's you two."

"Yeah man, we hope for the best and tool up for the worst, is that it? We can be ready real quick. When do you want to roll?"

"Soon, Jesus, very soon. I'll be in touch tomorrow with, I hope, the final details."

"Cool man, let's have more beer."

32

It had become a tradition. Every time Onetelcall was involved in a fight against cyber criminality, their councils of war were held around the garden table in Jo and Dan's very English cottage garden.

Dan was the founder of an international and high-level anonymous alliance which investigated and shared intelligence on all matters to do with digital and cyber security. He also oversaw the increasingly successful business he and the original founder, Spray Wilson had imagined when they started Onetelcall. Frequently too busy to be involved on a daily basis with his most trusted colleagues' activities, he insisted on attending meetings which he knew might involve risk and danger.

Ever since he and Max had collaborated on a most ingenious deepfake sting against the man who had attacked Jo and the drugs empire behind him, resulting in Spray's downfall, Dan had understood the vital importance of occasional risky, courageous, direct-action initiatives to defeat darker forces. He knew that in his team, courage was never in short supply, and he loved the buccaneering feeling that such fights gave him.

He looked round at his guests. His trusted friend Max, Max's best buddy, Dug, who would lay down his life for any of them. Sue and Indira, two extraordinarily skilled and intuitive backroom digital analysts who had proved their commitment under extreme circumstances in the past. Kathy, Duggie's wife and an emerging technologies genius with a massive brain and an even bigger love for her man and her beliefs in right and wrong. Jo, of course, scurrying around as usual, getting food and drinks, laughing and leg-pulling. She had once been his special events organiser, arranging VIP meetings for high-level Onetelcall customers and some of the most senior cyber intelligence leaders in the world. Now his wife, she and Dan had become the industry's power couple, devoted to each other and devastatingly effective in both business and covert, often perilous confrontations.

Dan opened the meeting, "I can see from the popular choice of zero-alcohol beers just how seriously we are all taking this outrage against our NHS and our society. Tonight, we are about to begin the fight back and to exact some revenge on those bastards who attack us."

"Not 'arf boss," grinned Max, "and may I add that Phase One is already in place and just awaits your approval, gang. I have a sort of go-ahead from Amanda, so effectively we have informal police support for my plan, with some reservations of course as part of my plot involves two guys from Mexico."

"I feel safer already," smiled Jo.

"What was Amanda's reservation?" asked Dan.

"Oh, only that they should be frugal with their bullets, and she'd rather interview our targets than bury them."

As if on cue, his phone rang. "Excuse me, I'll take this, it's Mand… Hi Mand, what's up?"

Everyone sitting around Dan's garden table saw the usually unperturbable Max look panic-stricken.

"Oh fuck," he said several times as Amanda broke her news.

And shocking news it was, as Max relayed to the others.

"This thing just got a whole lot bigger and a whole lot more threatening," he said with obvious emotion. "We knew there was odd social media activity between drug suppliers and their networks. The chaps in Mattinata have been all over it and shared their intel with us, but, well, to be honest, I think we've all been so focused on the clear and present threat that we didn't give this development the attention we should have. According to Amanda and her police intel, there have been stabbings and shootings all over the country as county-line bosses turn against each other. There's been a spate of drive-by shootings in

Birmingham and London and stabbings, apparently in multiple locations."

"It's been calculatingly brilliant really," said Jo. "I've been in close contact with Agron, sweet boy- sorry, this is not time for levity, and I've seen the strategy unfold. The Russian operation, whoever or whatever it really is, changed course and instead of placing fake drugs in the NHS system, it started flooding the drug supply chain with its hooky dope. Now, all the distributors are suspecting that their competitors are behind the supply of useless gear and started fighting each other in blind reprisal."

Max's phone sounded again, "Yes Mand… oh no, oh Christ, anyone… fuck…"

"You'll not believe this, the Rushian warehouse has just been firebombed. It's totally ablaze and the fire services don't think much will be left when they eventually get the fire out. What is more important is that the building was empty and so no one, especially Anna, has been hurt which is some blessing I suppose."

"So, Max," said Duggie, "how do you see this affecting the grand plan? I mean are we still going to, er, apprehend the three targets we've identified who are behind the Rushian operation?"

"Off the top of my head Dug, I think it is even more vital that we do just that. This whole war is escalating and if we can remove some key players from the arena, well, it can only be for the good."

"Am I right in thinking that you plan to illegally imprison anyone you fancy who might or might not be involved in this whole mess?" asked Dan. "Am I right? Because if I am, I must ask whether acting outside the law, even if Amanda and her colleagues are aware of your action, is a wise strategy. Might it be that when the day comes it will be us who get banged up whilst the bad guys scuttle off unscathed by our laws?"

"Yeah, I know what you are saying boss and it's all a bit Mission Impossible, like the police know what we intend to do.

They know why and how important it is but, if the fan gets hit, they will disavow any knowledge and even Mand can't save us from that. It is a calculated risk because if we don't mop up as many players here as we can, we can't go ahead with phase two, which I won't tell you about in detail now, but it will be the best revenge sting ever, honest. We will let Pal off his leash - God, he's cross - and he will create a kind of metaverse Armageddon which will not only defeat the bastards behind this but will also have them bloody crucified in their own country."

Dan looked at Max, the man he trusted and who he knew to be smart and audacious. "Max, I don't think I want to know any more, just don't get yourself or any of us killed, ok?"

"Ok, boss."

33

Communication between Onetelcall and Mattinata had become intense. Graham Carter, head of Onetelcall's Deepmatters AI cyber intelligence function had not originally approved of consorting with known psychopathic criminal hackers. However, as time progressed, his liaison with Pal, the self-proclaimed best hacker of all time, had moderated his view and he had come to appreciate the impressive skills the exiled Albanian displayed. He was also staggered by the depths of Pal's fury at being plagiarised and amazed at the technical genius and complexity of his retribution.

Although Pal needed no help in his work, he, too, found his new alliance with Graham and the rest of the Onetelcall team rewarding, motivating and, he had to admit, sometimes enlightening. On the second flank, Agron, reprising his role as social media manipulator and wordsmith stayed deeply in cahoots with Jo and, when needed, Sue, Indira and Kathy, as the eavesdropped intelligence dossiers grew and the depth of information about the Russian offensive developed. Max, for his part, adopted a position on his Mount Olympus, determined to orchestrate everything he surveyed with his ungodly baton of revenge.

The overall strategy had been dynamic and changed as circumstances and threats developed. Originally, the idea was to immobilise Rushian by having Adam report them to the authorities for importing illegal produce, stopping them or at least impeding their trading. The firebomb had made that ploy unnecessary, and, reactively, the idea of arranging the short-term disappearance of key players until the police could handle them had become more crucial; anything to stop them from fleeing before the authorities could arrest them.

Max knew, as Amanda had confirmed, that there was insufficient evidence to precipitate a wave of arrests, especially potentially politically sensitive arrests, but there was full agreement that action had to be taken while the police compiled their cases. With as many UK suspects as possible removed from daily activity, the Russian programme would necessarily falter and that would necessitate unusual activity over all the intercepted digital communication conduits that, between them, Mattinata and Olderbury monitored and analysed constantly.

The strategy had come from a simple passing comment when Max and Duggie had been indulging in a long supper on Pal and Agron's mountainside terrace. Pal was moaning, again, about his work being emulated and Duggie said,

"You know the old saying about imitation being the sincerest form of flattery…"

"You have it, my little English friend, you have it! Of course, that's the way," exclaimed an excited Pal. "This shit Melor wants to be me, does he? Well, see how he likes it when I am him!"

Now, from his imaginary seat on his notional Mount Olympus, Max could see that phase one, Pal's turn-the-tables attack was ready to go. All he needed was a catalyst, the silver bullet which would precipitate an irreversible course of action, an unstoppable programme which would exact the greatest revenge of all. And he knew what that spur would be.

When the time was right, General Savva Komorov would be made aware of evidence that Major Vasily Vassiliev and his functionary were not playing by the rules and that they were acting against the best interest of Russia and its president. The final killer tactic would emerge when, if the plan worked, Komarov would send in the goons to inspect every nook and cranny of Melor's work. Then Pal, supported by Kathy and her newly acquired knowledge of the looks and technologies of Melor's systems, would show those state spooks a dramatically different version of Melor's creation. Their exact and cunningly modified replica of the audit trail of drugs and money would be revealed, and, for extra pain and retaliation, it would ensure that Major Vasily was totally enmeshed too.

Being Zeus was too lonely for Max as he went through time and time again each and every detail of the multi-pronged plan. At home that night, he held Amanda's hand and said, "You know, this is far too complex, there are far too many people involved, far too many things to go wrong, to backfire, to make matters worse, to fail dismally. Mand, for once in my life, I am beginning to have doubts."

"Oh, my darling man, what can I tell you? If it fails, if it all goes wrong, you will have falsely imprisoned several people and, don't worry, I will nick you for it."

"You're such a comfort," laughed Max, "but I can't do or think any more. I'm just going to have to roll the dice and hope I'm cleverer than I think I am." And with that, Max sent the first text of 'Operation Russian Revenge'.

Only five miles away and within distant sight of the flames as they danced in the night sky above Rushian's burning warehouse, Jesus and Angel readied themselves. With the sort of second-sight anticipation which had saved their lives more than once, the two brothers guessed that Max's 'Go' message would be on its way any time now. Professional as always, the brothers had modified a seven-seater Land Rover Discovery to ensure that any occupants of the rear seats would be restrained and secure. The darkened windows and interior blinds would keep them invisible from prying eyes, as well as keeping the route and destination secret.

The visible external panels of the Discovery had been wrapped with an experimental polychromatic adhesive material which could change colour, depending on the voltage being fed through it. In daylight, it wasn't perfect yet but at nighttime and on CCTV lenses it was completely convincing. They could drive a red Land Rover into a multi-storey car park and drive out again in a blue vehicle. For added sneakiness, they'd carry a range of different number plates.

Of course, eventually, someone would figure out the ruse by watching cars in and out and spotting the difference of entry and exit Land Rovers' colours and numbers but, by then, the brothers would be long gone and so would their people carrier. Always armed with small pistols, they saw no need for any additional artillery, this was just a simple collection job. They had their GPS set, the tank filled, photos of their quarry in hand and embedded in their minds; they were ready to go hunting in London.

As anticipated, Max's 'Go' text pinged at about eleven o'clock. Jesus and Angel were pleased, they would work through the night and be back home with their three guests before breakfast.

34

Despite his increasing wealth, power and acknowledged success, Melor was content to remain in the student flat Vassiliev had provided. The fact that he was wealthier than most Russians outside oligarchy or government pleased him at an abstract level; that he was now becoming influential and talked about in high places also made him happy but was not important to him. His self-esteem and self-importance, however, knew no limits as he was, without any doubt, a great hacker who had achieved a truly seismic coup in the competitive field of digital disruption and institutional interference.

As his systems and processes advanced and developed he, like most players in his maliciously esoteric endeavours, had moved all his operations to the cloud where he had space and scope to achieve even more impossible feats of technological chicanery. He wasn't to know that this transition meant the beginning of his downfall or that cloud security was a speciality for Pal and even more so for Kathy's emerging technologies team at the very edge of innovation.

It was ego, however, that led him to underestimate the threat of external interest in his creation, a threat that had shown on his monitors very quickly after his final phase of transition to cloud-based operations.

"Ah, you see, that is other hackers just trying to share in my glory," he told a junior software engineer co-opted to his project.

"But Melor, it is more than that. I think it is people actually breaking in and copying segments of your master codes and designs," replied the young intern.

"You are ridiculous! Nobody would dare, nobody can crack my security. Who could even get close to understanding my base code or techniques to copy them? Never mind use them! Too many built-in ratholes. I will hear no more of it! You will see, Melor is invincible."

As Kathy had guessed when the evidence of cloud transition was first spotted, Melor had selected a giant Asian cloud service for his platform. He avoided Western companies like Amazon or Google, choosing instead a supplier which knew a thing or two about using collected data for cyber-attacks. As Kathy and Pal both knew, this supplier was not impenetrable either via hacking or by engaging with disillusioned or greedy employees. Such people were readily accessible to Pal over his dark web contacts network, people who were honoured to work with Pal and knew his gratitude would be generous.

The cloud service welcomed Melor with enthusiasm. They would offer all the support they could, believing over the long term, he was bound to fail, and they would easily pick up value from his legacy techniques and his precious data.

The idea had emerged when Max and Pal had been talking about films. Max explained a plot in which the crooks created an exact replica of a casino's safe vault where they staged an imitation robbery whilst performing an ingenious robbery in the real strongroom.

"It amazes me that this sort of thing doesn't happen more often, especially now we have such opportunities in a metaverse-type environment," said Max, not sure whether he was being far-sighted or simply stupid.

Pal's eyes closed and his head rocked slowly from side to side. Then he laughed, "Oh Max, my newest oldest friend, sometimes you are an inspiration even to me."

It took a team effort to predict or even guess what a search might look like when the authorities descended on Melor and Vassiliev to determine the scope of their activities. Had they been doing what they proclaimed or taken their country for millions? At the end of it, Pal was satisfied that he had created as exact a copy of the significant functions of Melor's critical infrastructure as possible. He had also developed a brilliant switching capability which would display his metaverse style version on any screen, at any time, where the real version was being accessed and it would transfer seamlessly and, to an untrained eye, identically.

The trick would be to identify when inspectors were delving into the systems, and not Melor and his team working away quite normally. The question bounced to and forth as Pal became ever more delighted, collaborating with a company once his enemy.

Sue, an experienced digital interceptor and expert in key-logging analysis suggested a solution. "Patterns," she said, "users always work in similar patterns. We feed user key-log data into old Deepmatters here, or your AI facility, if you prefer Pal, and we will instantly have a way of knowing which user is online, and who is a newcomer."

Pal knew this was a good idea. He had already installed a key-log analyser in his solution, but Sue didn't know this, and good ideas should be appreciated and rewarded in Pal's view. Knowing he was in severe danger of becoming affable, he sent her a ticket for two to the Florida Keys. Agran suggested this was a bit too flash, but Pal said,

"When you have the amount of money we have, does it matter? And she deserves a special treat. I can't spend it, I don't want for anything, let me, for once, be a nice guy. I quite like the feeling."

At the same time, Agron and Jo had enjoyed an indulgent time preparing social media content for a variety of platforms and purposes. Agron had achieved remarkable success with social media cluster-bombing at the time of Pal's chatbot campaign. They decided to use the same technique to attack the UK drug gangs, the NHS insider moles and the drug distributors. Using WhatsApp, Telegram, Vkontakte, Moi Mir and the rest, they would post an avalanche of disinformation about Melor and Vassiliev. One of Graham's team found a Russian TV interview with Major Vasily Vassiliev and used it to create a damning deepfake video of Vassiliev rerouting drug consignments to his own warehouse.

Max surveyed his empire appreciatively. "It's all in place Dug, it's all ready to go. We just need the word from Angel and Jesus, and, oh Christ, we'll hit the go button and pray, my old chum, pray."

35

"I fucking hate this place," said Angel as he steered his chameleon car through the London suburb, firing ULEZ cameras as he went. "Who could live in this shitfight? It reminds me of downtown Mexico City."

"We are spoiled bro, living where we do."

"I guess, and I'm sure many people just love it here, just as I now love our countryside house and surroundings."

"I'm sure."

At the first address, a bright streetlight through the curtains identified the sleeping man within as Gary Pugh. He didn't hear the click of the skeleton key, the snipping of his security chain or the silencing of the house alarm. He heard nothing as the two brothers approached his slumbering form. The pressure of a chloroform mouth patch disturbed him, but it happened so fast, that he didn't wake up fully before the chemical knocked him out again. He wouldn't feel the pinprick of the hypodermic needle or the delivery of a carefully measured dose of Valium, enough to keep him asleep for the required length of time, but not so much as to interfere with his breathing. They carried his limp body silently through the house, out onto the deserted residential street and into the Land Rover where he sat securely restrained, in guest seat number one.

They drove swiftly to the next address. Using Pugh's phone, Jesus found Preston's number. He rang it and then hung up.

"Now that's a wake-up call," he sniggered as he sent a text: 'Emergency I am outside NOW come quick.'

He rang and hung up again. An upstairs light came on and Angel, concealed under a plane tree, waved frantically. Preston assuming it was Pugh, ran straight out into a wodge of chloroform.

The last address belonged to the suspect, Neil Handly. Another house turned into flats and the brothers simply repeated the proven process, using Preston's phone, with the same satisfying result.

Their 20-plate red Discovery became a 21-plate green Discovery in a deserted factory yard only half a mile from the last collection point, and off they all set; next stop, Olderbury.

"Do you think picking up these Rushian hombres will be as simple, bro? You know, like just as boring, man?" yawned Angel.

"How should I know?" replied Jesus. "Shall we hit them tonight or take these dudes back and go straight out again for the next consignment in daylight?"

"Well man, I say we go back. After we've locked these dudes up, I could eat and freshen up and after that I'm easy, you know, don't mind either way. What do you choose?"

"I'm guessing Max would like this over and done ASAP. He's strung out like I've not seen him before. I'd go for speed here, let's do it fast."

"Cool, bro. Tell you what though, these next assholes ain't going to be beddy-byes are they? They'll likely be at the ruins of their place looking at the damage and wondering what the fuck to do next."

"Good thinking man, we'll recce first yeah? Tell you what, Angel, you take the Healey and have a good sniff around and I'll hang back in the wagon ready for your word and some action, yeah, that a plan?"

36

A tearful Anna looked at the imposing man in his elegant country tweed suit and unnecessary sunglasses.

"Can I help you, luv?" she asked.

"I guess my parcel ain't ready for collection then," said Angel wryly, "it was being shipped in from the States, machine parts you see, but I guess they are just lumps of metal in a burned-out box by now. Christ… er, beg pardon ma'am, what goddam mess."

"I think you are right on all fronts, sir. I'm so sorry, it seems someone, an arsonist obviously, set fire to the building last night and I'm afraid just about everything has perished. We aren't allowed in to inspect yet, fire inspectors, police and forensics all have their jobs to do first."

"I see, what a bummer, beg pardon ma'am, you must be the boss lady round here, right?"

"Oh no, I'm only a minion, that's the boss, over there, Mick Turvey if you want to talk to him but, really sir, I can answer as many questions as he can."

"I don't doubt it ma'am and I'd much rather talk to you, but I guess there's not much to say is there. It'll be an insurance job now and not my bag anymore. So, the two guys with your boss, fire department, are they?"

"No, they work here too, well here and at our other warehouses. That's Terry and the big bloke is called Bear- it's Brian really but somehow Bear suits him."

"I can see that ma'am; I think I'd agree with anything he says."

"Oh no, he's a pussy cat, a big softie really, never seen him lose his temper or throw his weight about at all."

"You're a lovely, kind lady ma'am, it's a pleasure just talking with you. Seems kinda deserted round here now. I mean apart from you, me and those three guys, it seems like the place is empty."

"Yes, it is, everyone else has gone now, the forensic people are coming back when everything is properly cold, or so I'm told."

"Are you on your way too now, ma'am?"

"Well, I'm…"

"I'd recommend you be on your way now, ma'am, if I may." Angel allowed his jacket to fall open and reveal his shoulder-holstered pistol.

Anna's face drained of all colour and she started to shake.

"No ma'am, no, I'd never hurt you. You are safer now than you'll ever be, you have my word as a Mexican and a CIA drugs enforcer, get the idea?"

Anna nodded. She felt oddly confident in this charismatic if a little strange, stranger.

"You're going to arrest them, aren't you?"

"Something like that, ma'am."

"You know they are already being investigated here by the UK authorities, don't you?"

"Yes ma'am, we are here in their full knowledge and with their approval, don't worry about that. Have you been involved with the investigation then, ma'am?"

"I have a little, I must confess. It's all quite exciting in a frightening way."

"Stay a little frightened and stay alive, that's my motto, ma'am. Now, I must do my job, and I do recommend you take yourself away to somewhere nice and safe. Will you do that for me now, ma'am?"

Anna scurried off but not too far. She squatted behind a parked car on the factory road and watched Angel tap his phone. In seconds, a blue Discovery sped into Rushian's yard and an almost identical man, right down to the sunglasses, leapt out. She watched as the two men sauntered up to Mick, Terry and Bear. Just out of arm's reach, they stopped and started talking. Crikey, she thought, they look menacing. She could see Mick reacting badly. Then the man she had been talking to put his hand in his jacket and Mick buckled at the sight of his gun. The three men, looking like naughty schoolboys, trudged unwillingly towards the Land Rover. Neatly done, though Anna as the men were loaded into the back of the vehicle.

Angel and Jesus also believed they'd done a good job. They only had to secure the rear seat restraints and they'd be home in no time.

The first shot flew past Angel's ear and into Bear's shoulder. As he screamed in pain, the second shot caught Jesus's thigh and ended up in Mick's knee. Jesus fell and spun around, gun in hand. No matter how much his thigh howled at him, he wasn't about to be plugged by some dumbass sniper. He spotted the shooter who was already running. Jesus fired but, unusually, missed. Angel was sighting up as the man ran lickety-split away from the scene.

He'll be out of range of my little Glock in a second, he thought, torn between giving chase or staying with his brother and his guests. Never indecisive for long, Angel sprang up, nobody gets away from the Soto brothers. At that moment Anna jumped out from behind the car and screamed at the running man. Shocked, he stopped and strained to see where the screaming was coming from. He stopped just long enough to feel the bullet enter his lower back.

Anna ran to tend to Jesus, who was suffering only from a surface wound. The bullet had scored his leg as it went on its way. She stemmed the bleeding with her hanky which she then fixed to his wound with the ribbon holding her small cameo pendant. Throughout everything, Angel had his gun on the three men, but they weren't going anywhere. Both Bear and Mick were in acute pain and Terry did all he could to care for them, which amounted to, "Bloody hell, don't fucking die you bastards."

Jesus looked at Anna. "That was brave, lady; stupid but brave. I don't think I'd have popped him if you hadn't acted when you did. Me and my bro, well, we owe you some."

"May I suggest something, sir?"

"Yeah lady, anything."

"You and your, er yeah, brother? Well, you both take that gorgeous sports car and bugger off somewhere else pdq and take that Terry bloke with you. I'll drive the Land Rover to hospital and get these chaps tended to."

"What about bro's wound?"

"Take him home, clean it, disinfect it and bandage it. It's not deep enough to need stitches and I'm sure you've both had worse, in what I imagine has been colourful lives."

As Jesus was able to stand and walk, the brothers bundled Terry into the small rear space of the Healy sports car, roof down to accommodate his bulk and sped off just as the sirens and blue lights were approaching.

Amanda in the second patrol car saw the Healy but said nothing. So much for bullets and body counts, she thought with a smile. Anna greeted her warmly and with a sense of relief. She was worried that her two former colleagues would see this greeting and suspect her of being a traitor, but the two men were so involved with their own self-pity that she needn't have worried.

"I didn't see much really, Amanda. I was just passing, and I screamed when I saw a man with a gun. Then three other men roared off in some sports car I think and left these two fellas here."

"We are on the same side, Anna. You needn't protect Jesus and Angel from me, though I do admire your diplomacy," grinned Amanda.

"Are those their names? You know them? What now, do you want a statement or something?"

"No, not now, the ambulance will see to these men here and I'll follow them just to see if I can get any sense from the man shot in the back. He's a sniper I guess and probably a gang specialist looking at his weapon. He'll go in a separate ambulance."

"Yes, makes sense," said Anna hoping that Amanda didn't think she was taking the mickey.

"Is this your Land Rover, Anna?"

"Er no, not strictly speaking. I was- that is, I'm just using it before I give it back to a friend."

"You are a terrible liar, Anna, but it doesn't matter to me now. I suggest you go home in it and let the boys have it back later."

"I'm not playing cards with you, Amanda," she said. "You've got a third eye."

"I'll see you soon. Take care, I suspect you've done something gutsy here, but I don't quite know what. Anyway, bye for now."

Anna phoned Adam from the Land Rover and Amanda phoned Max from the ambulance. Neither conversation lasted long. Adam said he would be at Anna's place at warp speed.

Max said, "It's not ideal but it's better than nothing. I'll go to Angel and Jesus's place now. Sorry about the bullets and bodies, but you know how it is..."

"Oh yeah, Max, I know. Give the boys my love. Tell them I'll try to work out a way not to arrest them."

Terry was almost gibbering when Angel and Jesus got him back to their repurposed remand cell. "We were shot at for Christ's sake! We could have been killed; I mean I might have been dead now."

"Shut it asshole, what do you expect when you play in the big boys' drugs game eh? Candy fucking floss and birthday cards. Dumbfuck."

"Tell you something though bro," said Angel, "I mean, asswipe here has a point. Like why ain't he dead? Why aren't they all dead, why aren't we? I ask you, two shots, just two shots and bad shots at that."

"You know why, bro; it was intended to be a warning, a painful warning, but you know, the torching, the shooting, someone wants them out of business, not dead, not yet anyway, just off the streets for good."

"It's all this fake dope flying about," growled Angel. "It's making bad blood everywhere, gang against gang. I tell you, we ain't seen the worst of it yet. It'll get more and more fucking deadly as these fake pharms keep coming in. I just hope Max knows what he's doing."

"Max always knows what he's doing," said Max, strolling into the old stable block.

"Hey dude, didn't hear you. Really am losing my grip," said Jesus.

"Yeah," chuckled Max, "going deaf, are you? And I heard someone shot you. You look ok now though."

"For sure man, some broad called Anna fixed me up on the ground and bro here has done the rest. Just a flesh wound, nothing to get excited about."

"Anna is on our team," said Max. "A brave girl. We all owe her a big thanks."

"Ain't that right. So, what's the deal with these fuckwit hostages, eh? You want us to do some persuading, or what? Me and Jesus have a neat line in, you know encouraging folk to give us answers."

Terry groaned in fright.

"See, it's working already."

"The way I see it, you hoodlums, is that Amanda has enough people to interrogate right now. She has the hospital junior doctor who was the gofer guy for that Pugh character, the sniper who winged your mate; and Terry's two mates in hospital also waiting to be questioned. She's got her hands full, and I reckon we just keep this lot on ice for a day or so, until Mand or the task force are ready to arrest them, like officially."

"Ok, Max, whatever you say. We are well-trained hoodlums, ain't we? You sure you don't want us to soften 'em up just a bit? Jesus could do with some light entertainment."

Terry almost yelped, while the other three, still spaced out on Valium, looked vacant and confused.

"No, we have to be very careful here, let's just keep them locked up nice and tight. We don't hurt them, we feed them give them a drink and let them sleep, no waterboarding, electric shock to the bollocks or any other games, you understand?"

"You just ain't no fun anymore."

"As long as we've got this lot and Mand has got her arrests and the guys in hospital, the UK, well Olderbury anyway, arm of this Russian bullshit is shut down. There are others involved across the country, but from Gary Pugh downwards, and Mick from Rushian, we've got the key players, enough to screw this part of the UK operation."

"And then what man?"

"And then, Jesus, we go for the kill and take the whole fucking lot of them down right where they stand in their festering den of evil."

"You sure you know what you're doin' man? I've said it before, I reckon you're either a genius or totally deranged."

"Or both, bro, or both," laughed Angel.

37

General Savva Komorov, fifty-six years old and looking ten years older, was a functioning alcoholic of some years. His daily diet included at least two bottles of vodka, premium grade now he could afford it, not the evil one hundred per cent plus, homebrewed Samogon of his formative years on the Plains and in the army. Decades of dependency had dictated his character. Reality and Savva remained distant strangers, any empathy and compassion he might have shown had been drowned out and his ability to maintain normal human relationships was just an old memory, lost but not missed. As his ego inflated, his ability diminished. His judgement appeared erratic and frequently driven by the callousness of a moral and mental coward. His climb through the ranks had been achieved by treading on others more capable than himself and his duplicity and paranoia had worked in his favour, keeping him safe from various coups against him.

The General did not stand out amongst his peers. Dependency on alcohol and drugs in the senior army ranks of the Russian army was as common as in the regiments of unwilling conscripts. On the day the message popped into his inbox, General Savva was treating himself to generous pourings of a fine old cognac, it made a luxurious change from his habitual daily vodka. The brandy made him volatile and unpredictable, he always resented any interruption to his daily routine, especially now, in his state of unstable excitability.

He read the message several times, his fury rising:

Komarov, you are being fooled. Vassiliev and his lackey are laughing at you. They make millions while you get nothing. They steal your idea and make a fortune while you get nothing. Now they are plotting against you. Be warned. <!>

He had no idea these were some of Agron's finest words of agitation, guaranteed to force him to react in his well-publicised mercurial way. Agron had hit Savva Komarov's hot buttons. He slammed his big hand down over all the keys on his 1980s-style office intercom key and lamp unit. He scowled with anger as his staff, alarmed and fearful ran into his office. From a junior administrator to his senior military aide-de-camp, a captain, they all stood in front of their red-faced, incandescent boss.

He shouted and screamed at them all for over ten minutes. He had been betrayed and undermined, threatened and ridiculed and it was all their faults. They would pay with their jobs, their ranks, and their lives. If they were to save themselves, they must join him in routing his enemies. He demanded absolute allegiance and mortal commitment to exacting revenge on his enemies.

The Captain spoke up, "I am loyal to you, General, and always will be, but you cannot order us to attack another senior officer and his department. It is against the rules of the Russian army. Internecine battles are banned. A statute exists that internal differences must be satisfied using the appropriate mediation channels or by the judgement of a board of appointed independent generals."

"You argue with me? I am one of those generals, you fool! You refuse to follow my orders? Think before you choose such a path, know that to dissent now is to be a traitor, a deserter and inevitably shot, by me if necessary." Komarov waved a copy of the printed-out email in their faces. "See, see for yourselves! If I am being ridiculed, then all of you are. Your careers, your political standing, all destroyed by one plundering, devious Major and his lackey scum. We must act, we must act to save our reputations and to use our enemies to add to the power I have, and you share."

"But General," ventured the Captain, "Do you trust this email? You could be being duped, double-bluffed, manoeuvred, manipulated…" he paused, hoping he hadn't gone too far.

The General glowered, his hand shaking visibly as he reached for his tumbler of brandy. "The difference between a great man like me and an overpromoted minnow like you, Captain, is guts, the courage to know what is right and what is bullshit, what is to be ignored and what is to be acted on with an iron fist, a good, old, traditional Soviet Russia *serp I molot,* sickle and hammer fist."

Despite being half the General's age, the young Captain had learned which battles to fight and when to acquiesce. It was this diplomatic sense and a highly developed dose of self-preservation which had powered his rapid rise up the ranks.

"General, I assume you recognise the symbol used to sign this note? You will know, of course, it is a symbol used by the Horned Horse hacking group and that makes a degree of sense, doesn't it, Sir? Because if this note refers to Vassiliev's initiative, they will be furious because he and this shadowy Melor creature have trampled all over the Horned Horse's hunting ground, threatening their patch, invading their space."

"At last, you say something of use, and yes, of course, I knew the moment I saw the symbol who sent this email. I have known this organisation since they first successfully ransomed a series of banks in the USA. I have been aware of their authenticating symbol, originally known by only a few of us. That is why I shall act on it mercilessly with all the power of my rank and my fury."

"What are your orders, General?"

Years of alcohol consumption had depleted Komarov's logic process making him anxious, delusional, obsessive and egocentric. Dominant in his mind was a persecution complex which drove him to punish anyone he thought to be an enemy, and that involved most of the people he knew. He had no tones of grey, no facility for strategic planning, no room left for guile, just the animal survival instinct of attack and destroy. Now, feeling threatened and victimised, Komorov's mind could offer nothing more than a violent, emphatic offensive.

"So, your sycophancy has overcome your regimented principles has it, Captain," he sneered, "and you want my orders? I shall give you my orders now, no need for discussion, no need for opinion from anyone, just be sure you do as I say and remember the price of failure."

38

Everyone heard Pal's whoop of delight. The connection between Mattinata's nerve centre and Onetelcall's operations room via an encrypted constant coms link meant that as soon as any action started, nothing would delay team information.

"Am I right," asked Pal in an atypical burst of collaborative teamwork, "does this look like a new user, a change of keystroke usage?"

A unanimous chorus of agreement erupted, confirmed instantly by Deepmatters. Immediately Pal, with an equally atypical tremor of nerves, hit his pet 'metaverse switch' and bet his entire reputation that within five-hundredths of a second whoever was accessing Melor's cloud estate, was now unknowingly, exploring a replica parallel virtual world. Within seconds they knew Pal had been correct on both counts. Firstly, that Melor's cyberworld was being traipsed over with the heavy fingerprint of investigation and, secondly, that the investigator had no suspicion that what he saw onscreen was anything but the real thing.

Max felt taut with apprehension. The success of his plan depended on total belief in the mimic system's authenticity, ensuring that the perpetrators of the egregious campaigns and attacks on the UK health systems would be destroyed by their own compatriots. It was a long shot, his only shot and now he would have to watch as the screens displaying masterpieces of fakery unveiled the process of revenge.

After half an hour, it was obvious that the unseen scrutineer was executing a forensic analysis of every available shred of communication, transaction, instruction, tracking and administration, from pharmacy identities to product codes and NHS inventory details. After an hour, the search had moved to the system's financial records which showed payments in and out by region, by operative and by purpose. Funds for Gary Pugh created some lingering interest, noted the Onetelcall onlookers, especially Max who was recording all relevant intelligence for Amanda.

It had been Agron's puckish idea to design 'Melorworld' as an accurate replica for superficial appraisal and to conceal condemning evidence in files behind layers of additional security. Pal and Agron watched eagerly as the cursor moved to hover over an icon identifying a video directory. The icon was clicked, immediately displaying a pop-up, inviting the user to access 'MelorLock', an invitation which was not refused.

Relaxing slightly, Max and the team looked on as revelation after revelation popped up on increasingly rapidly moving screens. Accounts, videos, money transfers, false reports, records of funds and drugs being diverted, evidence of multiple private Swiss and Caymen Island accounts and vast cryptocurrency holdings in the names of 'Bogdan' and 'Vassil', all graphically revealed. Next, the inspectors found evidence of millions of pounds, dollars and roubles diverted to Cyprus and onwards into the laundering chain.

Just as the screens had been reviewed at speed, so were they then lingered over on second and third inspections. Pal had tiered his revelations, to be discovered gem by gem by any ordered and logical analyst. To his added delight he could see that whoever was searching the cyber estate knew a thing or two about it. Finding the concealed directories spurred the visitor on to further digging and exploration.

Like a tourist following a brolly-waving guide, the inquisitive user dutifully navigated to some fake audio files of phone conversations, suggesting that Komorov would be groomed as a scapegoat, blamed for the collapse of Melor's organisation because of his insistence on replacing real drugs with fake drugs. It would be easy to do, agreed the two voices, one of which was easily recognisable as Vassilev. The voices went on to plan how, by showing a false large-scale clamp down by the British authorities caused by the fake drug placements, they could reasonably and legitimately shut down the operation. Then, they agreed, they could transfer to a remote new centre of operations run by and for the benefit of Melor and Vassiliev, whilst Komarov would face the consequences of what would be perceived as his failure.

A series of messages, seemingly between Melor and Vassiliev on Telegram and VK, proved damning indeed. They made outrageous allegations of misbehaviour, financial and sexual, by some of the senior members of the cabinet. They also made vicious personal attacks on Komarov and intimated their plans to flee from Russia as soon as any cracks began to show and to start up again from a safer location, like the scenic coast of Türkiye.

Max assessed the amount of damaging information the Russian inspectors had discovered. It was obvious that the key players, Melor and Vassiliev, had intended to steal the entire operation for themselves, that Komarov was being set up, and framed, and that very little of the massive profits from the stolen drugs and added ransom income went to any government or authority, as had been expected and agreed by the State Duma officers who had sanctioned it. With the added spice of offending many high-ranking ministers, the evidence displayed on the replica infrastructure was enough to have Vassiliev tried for multiple offences, including life-imprisonable treason. Everyone knew, of course, that mysterious sudden death was a more likely outcome.

After two hours, with the replica Melorland still being scoured, one of the phones Max had confiscated from Gary Pugh and his two fellow conspirators, announced an incoming call. Max looked at the illuminated screen and saw a +79 number waiting, a Russian cell phone, he knew.

"Yes?"

"Pugh?

"Yes."

"I call for Melor, he tells you to close down and run. No questions, That's all. Understand?"

"Yes."

"We've done it!" shouted Max in high excitement, "we've only fucking done it. They are closing it all down. It's over, for us, for them, for the NHS, for all the subsidiary companies that have been hacked and ransomed, for the drug gangs, for the pharmacies, for the GPs, for every bloody one of us, it is over!"

He called Amanda to give her the good news, knowing that the police could now act, taking the three men held by Angel and Jesus straight into custody, to commence their full, detailed questioning.

Agron announced that Pal had left his desk for a while, last seen heading to his favourite spot in their extensive mountainside grounds clutching a bottle of his favourite Raki and, said Agron conspiratorially, possibly a tear in his eye.

"He will want to know what is happening in Moscow, you know. He will want to know what happens to the shit who had the temerity to attempt to emulate him. He will want more than justice; it is the Albanian way."

Max laughed, "Oh yes, I understand revenge. I understand that punishment should fit the crime, that's the job of punishment, our job, our revenge goes much further. It goes for atonement, for retribution, for reparation."

Kathy looked up and smiled, "You know, with all the listening, hacking, tapping and eavesdropping we've got in place, we will likely know exactly what is going on."

39

As Luka drove, far too fast, towards Lubyanka, Melor felt struck again by the sheer scale, the massiveness of the neo-baroque building. He looked up to its roofline and reflected on how the floor below, the top floor with no windows, was a prison area.

Luka followed Melor's gaze. "You know, young sir, that prisoners of Lubyanka thought they were being held in the basement because there are no windows. They used to say that Lubyanka must be the tallest building in the world because you can see Siberia from its cellar."

Melor smiled at the grim humour, "Poor bastards, Siberia or death, not much of a choice, eh?"

"Be glad, young sir, that you are as free a man as any of us," said Luka guardedly, "to be detained even today is a prospect so awful it cannot be imagined."

Melor felt smug. The man who would once have imprisoned him had become his greatest ally. Between them, they held fortunes, and the money kept rolling in. He knew too that they were pushing their luck, the time had come to close the operation and get out, to go somewhere, anywhere safe and live in luxury.

In his impressive office, Vasily Vassiliev paced and plotted. Independently, he too had decided to shut up shop, close operations and disappear. He had heard mutterings of discontent from General Komorov's department and knew that the bellicose General would soon become a real danger. Komarov was not a man easily dissuaded from putting the boot into others, any others. Throughout their association, Vassiliev had come to like Melor. He admired his ability to create such a complex and clever cyber-structure, producing so much money, quite unreal amounts of money. More than that, he admired the young man's gall. It had taken some sizeable balls to fight his corner as Melor had done when he was still Bogdan and facing possible, probable, death or imprisonment.

Vassilev's door resounded with the weight of heavy knocking.

"Melor, don't bang so hard, just come in, will you?"

Sensing something unusual, Vassiliev turned from refilling his glass to see, not Melor as expected, but four, armed FSB security forces officers.

"What is this? I am your superior officer and a senior official of the FSB, I demand to know on who's authority, you come to my office like this."

Another figure entered behind the four guards. "Sir, I am Captain Arkadi Kozlov, senior officer in charge for General Savva Komorov and I have permission and authority from the highest level, from the Minister for Internal Affairs himself, to enter your offices and seize or inspect anything that we feel may be suspicious. Do you understand, Sir?"

"No, I damn well don't understand, Sir."

Vassiliev picked up the phone and called his colleague, the Internal Affairs minister. Pale and subdued, he replaced the receiver and nodded to the Captain. "It seems your authority is correct. You have my permission and cooperation."

Suddenly, the door burst open again, and an indignant Melor entered, forcibly escorted by two more FSB guards.

"What the fuck is all this?" demanded the outraged self-proclaimed genius. "I am Melor, I am above such treatment, your petty laws do not apply to me, know your place you nonentities, release me now."

"Bogdan," said Vassiliev, quite deliberately, "we appear to be under investigation by order of General Komarov with the authority of the Minister to whom I have just spoken. I fear we have no choice but to submit to the Captain's instructions."

Melor sat and accepted the large measure of vodka that Vassiliev offered.

"What do you want to do? What is that you need to see Captain?" asked Vassiliev.

"I need access to your computers; to that array of machines and screens you have so professionally installed over there." The Captain waved his hand towards the access and monitoring stations that Melor had fitted in the office, at Vassiliev's request as soon as the NHS mission started to bear fruit.

The Captain turned to Melor, "Belov Bogdan, you are I believe the architect and creator of the assault mounted on behalf of your country against the National Health Service in Great Britain?"

Melor nodded glumly.

"Can you assure me that everything, and I mean everything that is involved or associated with this NHS attack is available to view on these machines?"

"Of course, it is called the internet, it is the cloud, if you have the right digital credentials, you can go anywhere and see anything. On the other hand, if you are computer illiterate then, Captain, you are fucked."

"I see that in the shining light of your brilliance, you are blinded to the abilities of other people," said the Captain with a hint of disgust.

Vassiliev looked at Melor with concern and desperation in his eyes. Melor remained calm and sanguine. Vassiliev didn't know why.

"The master password, now."

"Take a guess," muttered Melor, still defiant.

The pistol whip drew blood from above his right eye and Melor shouted out in pain and anger.

"Now, Melor, now."

Melor complied and wrote down the chain of numbers, letters in leet and symbols for the administrator's access. He knew that to equivocate further would only cause him more pain. He didn't doubt the purpose and intent of this young, resolute Captain. His face showed, he hoped, his capitulation.

The Captain, accompanied by two young specialists from the FSB technical team, whom both Melor and Vassiliev recognised, started their work.

Melor stood and walked to Vassiliev, holding out his glass for a refill. "Now they will see what we want them to see," he whispered. Vassiliev looked questioningly and Melor smiled.

"Is this installation safe and secure?" asked the Captain.

"Captain, I am unquestionably the best hacker in the world, do you really think I would allow some inferior keyboard soldier easy access to my creation? I can assure you that nobody is looking over your shoulder at my genius."

The Captain threw Melor another disparaging look. "How impressed should I be? But then if there is a hacker in the space, he or she will only confirm that your genius comes a poor second to your criminality."

Melor smiled, it was a cocky smile and far too confident for the Captain's liking. It was a mistake.

Slowly, the Captain and his team inspected every file, every directory and where necessary, every page and spreadsheet. Much against his wishes, the Captain felt impressed by the audacity and digital skills Melor had exercised in cracking every NHS target, identified to cause disruption and allow all manner of Melor-designed bugs, trojan horses, malware and ransomware to be fed into the entire NHS network of networks.

The overview accounts seemed, at first glance, to reflect the rapid movement of large quantities of money, cryptocurrencies and various other currencies from non-UK buyers of initially real, stolen drugs, and subsequently the fake offerings. The Captain had not been given access to any of the government accounts into which the illegal funds should have been deposited, but it was clear the proceeds had gone in and out again, out to the correct accounts in the Kremlin's multi-layered coffers.

Beginning to doubt that he would ever find a smoking gun, the Captain wondered if Vassiliev and Belov were really the outrageous villains his General had labelled them. Could he be chasing a figment of Komarov's alcohol-fuelled imagination? But that smile. He couldn't overcome that smile. Melor was too clever to create such a complex structure without building in traps, nooks, crannies and big black holes in which he could hide the truth. The Captain's cursor hovered over a video file icon and saw the pop-up that Pal and the Onetelcall team were so pleased with, Melorland.

Melor was aghast. "That's not mine, I didn't create that, none of my people created that shit. This is a plot, a fit-up, you've got all that on another drive and you are trying to fabricate evidence against me."

Fastidiously, the Captain probed and delved, exactly as Pal had anticipated. With each revelation, Melor's protests grew louder and more indignant, more infuriated. Vassiliev remained strangely calm, he had already accepted his fate, whether it be bullet, poison, window, roof or ocean.

By the time the Captain discovered the social media messages Agron and Jo had so joyfully created, Melor knew he had lost everything. Surreptitiously, he sent his last text, 'Close down now, tell everyone.' One of the guards noticed the action and seized his phone.

"Your contacts list and text records will be interesting," he said tersely.

"I have seen enough," said the Captain.

"It is all a set-up," cried Melor. "None of that trash is real, it's a fucking fairy story."

"It's a game of hangman Melor. I'm the man and you'll hang, or worse. You've played Russian roulette with a full chamber; you see it's your ego…"

"What's my fucking ego got to do with anything?"

"I was about to give up earlier, and then I saw your smile. You thought you'd beaten us and that spurred me on. You might have got away with it, but for that smile, it will be the death of you. Hubris, Melor, hubris. It's a sin you know."

40

Anna and Adam hugged for several minutes. She felt past sobbing, past shock, she just revelled in relief and the kindness of another human being.

"I don't know if it was awful or thrilling," she admitted with an embarrassed laugh. "But when the gun fired, I thought that nice Mexican man had shot Mick and then I saw the other guy with a bigger gun, like a small rifle, the sort you get at a funfair."

"No so funny though eh?"

"No, I was properly scared then. I had ducked down behind a parked car and this sniper fellow was getting away on his toes. I could see the other Mexican man was too far away to, well you know, certainly not rugby tackle…"

"You mean shoot?"

"Yes, I suppose so. Isn't that terrible? Anyway, then I felt a real crossness and wanted to slow him down so they could catch him. I jumped out from behind the car and simply screamed my head off, must have sounded like an old witch!"

"But it did the trick."

"Yeah, but, oh Adam, the look that rifleman gave me, he stared at me with such malice. I hope he gets put away for a long time, I'd worry if he were still on the streets, he won't forget me, will he?"

She sounded genuinely worried, winding herself up, so Adam said, in his best Popeye imitation, "Don't worry Olive, I'll saves ya."

She smiled again and looked happier, "Mah heroo," she lisped.

"Before we celebrate your bravery and safe return to the fold, we should take that Land Rover back to your new friends," said Adam. "You drive it and I'll follow, ok? You know where they live?"

"Yes, Amanda told me. Odd that, isn't it, the police working with those two men, lovely though they are, they are obviously what you might call gangsters."

"I think there's a lot of history there. Perhaps we'll find out but I'm not going to pry."

Feeling emboldened by her adventure, Anna enjoyed giving the Land Rover a good high-speed workout, amusing Adam who pressed his accelerator to keep up.

She broadsided the big vehicle to a stop on the verge outside the brothers' drive and leapt out with a massive grin. "Now that was fun," she declared. "I feel invincible, let's buy a racing car!"

"Don't drive away yet ma'am," said Jesus, with mock sexiness. "Why don't you stay a while and have a real good, long look at my wound? I mean, it might be going green by now."

Anna, in the highest of spirits, laughed and brushed her hand along his shin with a flirtatious smile, "but I'm no nurse in comparison with your brother, I can see he's done a great job."

"Yes ma'am, he'd make someone a wonderful wife."

"And less of the ma'am if you don't mind, I'm not that old. I'm Anna and this is my dearest friend, Adam.

"Friend?"

Anna blushed.

"Adam, sir, this is one feisty lady you got here. You look after her right, or me and Angel will be on your tail and that's a promise."

Adam was about to say that he would when a car horn sounded followed by a short burst of a siren.

"Oh, it's the feds," said Jesus, "come for our new guests, I guess."

Two patrol cars and a secure prison minibus rolled up to the outbuilding where Pugh, Preston and Handly, along with Terry from Rushian, sat safely accommodated, ready to be bundled off to official remand.

The brothers greeted Amanda like a sister, and she smiled when she saw Anna again. "We do meet in the most unusual circumstances," she said, "and Adam too. How lovely to see you, Adam, a lot has happened since we first met and you had a vague suspicion, remember?"

"Oh, believe me, I remember."

As the prisoner transport drove away Angel said, "Look guys, let's have a fiesta. Man, you know, all of us, get Max; you can stay, can't you Amanda? Get Duggie and everyone. Go on, it'll be real neat."

Out of nowhere, Jesus and Angel provided beers, cocktails, nachos, quesadillas, chicken wings and an array of salads. They were busy preparing their party spread when Max and Duggie arrived, intending only to see their detainees safely off the premises and in police custody.

"Expecting us, were you?" enquired Max jokingly.

"Miracles of the microwave and good housekeeping," grinned Jesus. "We're always ready for a fiesta man, and that's what we are going to have, big time, man, big time."

Max struggled with the mental picture of the two deadly brothers in their pinnies running up a few delicate rellenos.

"Shall I get Dan to come over? The girls too, do you think?" asked Duggie to anyone who was listening.

"Oh, for sure man," replied a buoyant Angel, "the whole fucking gang, man, they all should come here and party!"

Although sharing a sense of relief at successfully beating a challenging foe, both Max and Duggie harboured a continuing disquiet.

"You know," said Duggie looking very unparty-like, "I don't like it, it doesn't add up. I've got a feeling, Max, a bad feeling. This isn't the end, it's just the beginning of another chapter. It can't all just die down and go back to normal. The drug dealers, none of them will be happy, they'll want retribution, payback, you know. I've really got a bad feeling, mate."

Max nodded, "I agree. So does Amanda and the rest of the rozzer crew. That bastard sniper is in the operating theatre today having some metal taken out of his back. Bloody lucky, it missed his spine and hit mainly fat and muscle just below his lung. We'll see, but I know Amanda and her drugs unit specialists are planning to add to his pain in the morning with an interrogation and I'm hoping to listen in to the bedside questioning. I know the medics don't usually allow this but in our sniper's case, there isn't a single person in Olderbury Hospital who would lift a finger to protect him from the law."

"Ok, I suppose there's nothing more to do tonight than enjoy all this," said Duggie, his eyes sweeping the party preparations, now including garden lights and a couple of mini but loud Bluetooth speakers.

As a rousing mariachi medley gave way to the more lilting tones of 'The Girl from Ipanema', another unexpected siren wailed above the music. In seconds, Amanda was running towards a fast patrol car, shouting over her shoulder, "It's all kicking off again, more street stabbings in Hounslow, Hayes and Southall. Similar attacks in Dudley, I'll call you…" and she was gone.

"Dudley?" Max asked the space where Amanda had been standing, "Why Dudley?"

The interruption sucked the zing out of the happy fiesta as everyone wondered exactly what was going on and what Amanda's dramatic departure meant.

Dan, who had only just arrived said loudly enough for everyone to hear, "I think I can shed some light on all this. I heard, just before I left the office, that rival drug gangs, each believing they had been stitched up by the other, are back out again, fighting each other on the streets. Current intel says that it isn't the leaders who are out to fight, it is the street kids, the direct sales runners if you like, who are beyond fury at the ruinous effect fake drugs have had on their income and customer bases. The police are out in force of course, trying to keep the violence to a minimum and, I expect, there is a major concern that we will have copycat fights and stabbings here on Olderbury's street very soon. I imagine Amanda and all the local officers are putting their emergency plans into action to keep the town as safe as possible. I don't think there is anything any of us can do, or should do, really," he added with a sideways glance at Angel and Jesus who, he knew, couldn't resist a good street fight.

Adam's good mood vanished. His immediate reaction was one of concern for Anna. Although there was no way any local street rabble could know about how the sniper got caught, he couldn't help but worry that her Rushian connection may put her in real danger. He phoned John to share his worry.

John's response was immediate, "You must come here, both of you. You'll be safe here. Nobody will know where you are or suspect you'd come here for safety."

Angel had overheard Adam. He looked excited and earnest at the same time. "Hey man, those drug-running pieces of shit will know for sure that their shooter was sent to Rushian's warehouse, and they'll be mighty pissed that he got hit and locked up. These scum ain't stupid you know, man, they'll know who worked at that place and they'll know who was involved in putting Rushian on the line. See what I mean? I mean to say, you might need babysitting for a while man, and, well, if Max thinks it's ok, we'll try to keep you nice and alive, yeah?"

Jesus joined in, "When my bro is right, he's for sure right and this time, well he's more than right 'cos I reckon the shooter's compadres will have been out on the street watching and listening, catching anything that would give them a clue about who they could blame for, well, anything really, they like to blame."

Angel nodded, "Bro, we might have a bigger babysitting job than I thought 'cos so many people here could easily be a target."

"Hold on there," said Max, "let's not run away with ourselves. "There's no way even you two with your magical, mystical powers can protect so many people in so many diverse locations. Anyway, some of them won't be on the radar enough for any spotter to identify them as a target. Adam and Anna certainly, and possibly me and Duggie, but I don't believe anyone else will have been seen by even the most observant gang spotter to be in any danger. Agreed everyone?"

"I suppose so," said Jo. "But I still feel a bit exposed."

"I understand that," agreed Max, "but you've only been involved from the offices. You haven't physically been in contact with anyone who might implicate you, other than Ben perhaps, but that was in the office anyway. So, I'm sure you can rest easy, and Dan will be by your side, who'd argue with Dan, eh?"

"That's a point though, Max," replied Jo, "I know you're right about me, just being a bit paranoid I suppose, but what about Ben? I mean, he's got to be high on the list for a bit of drug gang retribution."

"Yeah, I'll call him now."

"This is Ben Barrington; I can't take your call as I'm out of the country. Leave a message."

"Ben, it's Max, I was calling to say you might be in danger from the local, rather miffed, drug runners, but as you've gone away, I won't bother. Call me when you can, and I'll update you. Ok, mate. Take care."

"That's it then," said Adam. "I mean with Ben away it's just us who need to be careful. I'll take Anna to the farm where I don't think any townie gang yobbo would think of looking or even care to tread."

"I'm sure you're right," said Max, "but remember these people had enough nouse to firebomb the Rushian warehouse and then send a sharpshooter at a time when they could expect the Rushian folk to be wandering about the site. See? No fools, are they? Even if the foot soldiers are thugs, whoever tells them what to do is a whole lot brighter."

41

Away from the fizzled fiesta and back in Olderbury police station's holding and interview wing, Amanda and her colleague had set to work, teasing out, cajoling, probing and pressurising information from their 'perps'. As her interview partner, Amanda requested the young sergeant who had assisted her when she had been Gold Command in an anti-terrorist operation involving an Arab assassin and Iranian activist. The sergeant, Jack Grader, was impressed and a little star-struck by Amanda and thrilled to be selected to work with her again. He trained in interrogation whilst working his way up in S015 Counter Terrorism Command and relished the opportunity to flex his inquisitorial muscles against undoubted traitors.

His first assignment on revisiting Olderbury had been to accompany Amanda and, unusually, her civilian husband Max, about which Jack was initially a little unhappy, to the hospital and an injured suspect called Mick Turvey. He watched and enjoyed the short-lived interview; it was easy as Mick Turvey had mentally capitulated the moment that bullet caught his knee.

"It started after the warehouse was busted by you lot about ten years ago. The bossman did a runner, dunno where but nobody saw him again after the raid and some bloke, foreign he was, told me that the warehouse would start up again slowly after the raid and that I'd be in charge."

Jack watched as Amanda encouraged the injured man to talk. And talk he did, for over an hour. He explained that he didn't know who owned or directed the Rushian business, that it had all restarted in a well-funded and legal way with new business coming in regularly, so it made a good, honest profit. It became an expert in small-volume, high-value goods movement and built a good reputation for what it did.

"Well, after about a year, I'd got Bear and Tel working with me and it was all ok until I got a call telling me, the other depots and I would be getting new instructions and that we'd all bloody well do exactly what we were told or else, or else what it didn't say but I wasn't about to argue."

"And what instructions did you get Mick?" asked Amanda.

"Huh, you may well ask…"

"I did."

"They always came in sealed boxes, like diplomatic stuff you know? It was always fully detailed and it was clear as day as bent as a priest's knee. Well, me Bear and Tel had a conflab and we knew we had no choice and anyway, in the sealed boxes there was always a bloody big bonus, like a bank draft, for us so we didn't ask as much as we might have or should have, I suppose."

"Good, that's very good Mick, thank you. Now let's move on to more recent times. If I said to you, we believe you've been involved in handling stolen and fake drugs, what would you say?"

"Yeah, well lady, you see often as not we haven't got a scooby about what's in any of the crates, boxes and packages we handle. We just take stuff in and send stuff out. Anna, we had Anna by then of course, well, she asked what we were shipping more than what we did. She thought that 'cos of the temperature controls on some stuff, it must be perishable and probably drugs, given the hushty and mystery about it all. And then, well, when the NHS cartons started rushing in and out, we kinda knew what was going on."

"You didn't feel perhaps, you should report your suspicions to the authorities then?"

"Look lady, you're a fed, we ain't. We have to live in the real world, know what I mean?"

Amanda nodded.

"We kept shtum and did our jobs. Devil's own job to keep Anna from digging any deeper I can tell you. Right up till some smoothy git comes along and turns her head, then she started being all fucking Midsomer Murders about it and, oddly, that was just before all this shit happened, see what I'm saying?"

"Yes, Mick, I do see. Now tell me, if I were to suggest that instead of stolen drugs being shipped outwards, we have evidence that fake drugs were being illegally imported into this country, if I asked you what you know about that, what would you say?"

"I'd say yeah, we reckoned dodgy gear was coming in by the truckload, to us and all the other depots. And you know what?"

"No, I don't know what…"

"Well Bear, you know Brian, he says that the phoney stuff was being pushed through distribution out to what you lot call county lines and he reckons he knows this 'cos his brother buys off a bloke who gets his gear from some bunch of foreign geezers, like Turkish or something and anyway, Bear's bruv told him that this foreign mob were getting pretty violent 'cos they thought another drug outfit was fitting them up with knock-off stuff, so they could, you know, steal their turf, nab their customers who would be bloody narked about spending lots of dosh on fucking washing powder or whatever it was."

"I see, did Bear's brother have any other theories or insights?"

"Yeah, as it goes, he did. He said to me that we was up to our necks and being fingered as the bad guys for importing the sham shit, if you see what I mean, like we manipulate which drugs outfit gets all the business in these parts and the others get fuck all, cos nobody trusts their gear, see."

"Again Mick, I do see. Would you have an opinion as to who the sniper that shot at you might be? Where he comes from and why he chose you and your colleagues to take potshots at?"

"Bleedin' obvious innit, it's what I've just been telling you, it's a fuckin turf war and that fucking idiot who shot at us if from either the yardie bunch or them that gets their dope from some other foreign lot, from Afghanistan according to Bear's bruv, who get their dope from some big dealer in Hounslow, or Southall, somewhere like that anyway."

"And you still maintain that you don't know who paid you and gave you your orders and directions? Is that the case or are you hiding this because you're frightened of them? If so, let me tell you, you should be more frightened of me than them right now."

Mick stared at the deceptively caring detective, saw the steel in her eyes and he knew she was serious. His gaze moved to the young man with her and saw an expression of cold scorn and, for a second, he felt intimidated. Then he thought of the barbarism that even small-scale drug outfits could dish out and he knew who he feared most.

42

Over the intense period of eavesdropping, monitoring and gathering intelligence against the not-so-mythical Melor and his organisation in Moscow and beyond, Indira and Pal had become unlikely virtual mates. In the post-crescendo denouement phase, in which Pal had a fierce and vengeful interest, he and Indira had been swapping information about gleaning news of Melor's circumstances.

Indira had started a chain of events by sending a secure message over their encrypted link, saying, "You know SORM?"

"Yes. Of course. It is Russia's System of Operational – Investigatory Measures. Some FSB hardware that all carriers have to install so that the state can monitor users' communications metadata and content. We're talking about all their phone calls, email traffic, and web browsing activity. There's nowhere to hide, all the carriers are involved so even your cheap SIM from the airport will not protect you from the eyes and ears of the state."

"Exactly, so what about we get into the SORM system and monitor traffic from Melor, Vassiliev, Komorov and anyone who texts or contacts them? I'm trying but I just thought you might know a way in, or someone who does?"

"I'll ask the onion!"

Good heavens thought Indira, I've just had an almost joke from Pal.

"Ha! Brought tears to my eyes," she replied.

Unseen by Indira, Pal laughed too. He liked this person, and that was an unusual feeling for him.

It didn't take long for Pal to look around the dark web, initially via Tor Onion and then deeper until he found what he was looking for. On a Russian-speaking mobile industry hacker chatroom, he posted a high-value challenge offering a lot of money to anyone who could hack, to specific parameters, into SORM.

A reply from 'Agora's Ex' came in very quickly with a response suggesting that Pal access an invitation-only, Onion messaging service. Pal followed instructions and avoided the traps that Agora's Ex had skilfully deployed to catch any unwary, unwanted interlopers. After a day and a first instalment payment of ten thousand dollars' worth of Bitcoin, all three cell phones and most of the contacts on each account were effectively online to Pal's exclusive Agora's Ex message site.

"Cheap as your fried potatoes, I'm told," commented Pal as he announced his coup to Indira.

Like her, though he did, Pal had decided to keep the feeds to himself and share with Indira only what was important and relevant. Any titbits which might offer a hacking or profit-making opportunity he would hold back. In three days, the two new playmates had pieced together a surprisingly good picture of events as they had unfolded in Moscow after the in-depth investigation of Melorworld.

Indira told Max of the progress she and Pal had made, and Max suggested she arrange a meeting so everyone involved could hear what had been discovered. She had experience in addressing meetings but this time, in the imposing, impressive Onetelcall boardroom, she felt a little nervous. Sitting in the designated presenter's station with its high, ergonomic chair and spacecraft-like controls and screens, required a little time for composure. From her seat, she could reveal a video link to Mattinata and Graham and his crew in the Deepmatters unit. Although the room offered much technical trickery, like selectable mood lighting and high resolution, invisibly embedded wall screens with the ability to display any video feed, Indira opted for the stark 'news' approach and had prepared headlines and ticker-tape style rolling news for her revelations.

The headlines were alarming: 'Putin's judgement of Melorland two'; 'Komarov caught in his own trap'; 'FSB Captain awarded high honour'; 'Vassiliev under home arrest'; 'Who is Melor?'; 'Where is Bogdan Belov?'

For the second time, Pal whooped in delight. "Try to be me would he, ha, revenge is a good feeling."

"Ok," said Indira, "I shall run transcripts of the most relevant text and voice interactions we have traced, for you to read while I give you the latest gen. We know, as you can see that Major Vasily Vassiliev is under house arrest and is awaiting trial for a whole array of charges, including the Russian equivalent of treason which is, and I quote, 'Article 275 of the Criminal Code of Russia, as updated in April 2023, it defines treason as 'espionage, disclosure of state secrets, or any other assistance rendered to a foreign State, a foreign organisation, or their representatives in hostile activities to the detriment of the external security of the Russian Federation'."

"What's that mean do you think Indi?" asked Jo.

"I looked it up and the official tariff is twelve to life, and I can tell you that a sentence of twenty-five years was handed down to a man who committed the crime of being an investigative journalist, so heaven knows what will happen to Vassiliev, assuming he lives long enough to face trial."

"That's true," said Dan. "We, that is the Alliance, know of several instances where the offences have been such an embarrassment to the regime, they've never seen the light of day in court. Information may leak out and upset the carefully managed 'news' and propaganda flow, fed to the Russian people daily."

"No need to ask what happened to those who were charged, I suppose?" said Max cynically.

"That's right Max, no need at all. Car accidents, heart attacks, food poisoning and sudden falls… the usual murderous lies and, to be candid, I don't think our Vasily is very long for this world."

"Ha, good, very good," came the delighted tones of Pal across the video link.

"What's just as interesting," continued Indira, "is what's happened to General Savva Komarov, especially as this investigation was started at his instigation. You'd think he'd be hailed as a hero but no, far from it. Listen to this."

"Minister, I am Captain Arkadi Kozlov, senior aide to General Savva Komarov who I believe you know well."

"Yes, what of it?"

"I must request an urgent meeting with you, sir. I believe General Komarov to be complicit in crimes against the Federation, despite his accusations about Major Vasily Vassiliev. I can offer you compelling evidence as soon as you grant me an interview."

"Interesting," said Max, "is our young Captain playing a dangerous double-dealing game then?"

"Seems so," replied Indira. "From what we know, and you can see some of the conversations on your screen, it looks like the Captain had it sussed from the start. Listen."

She cued another voice capture: "Look, my friend, you and I both know that what we saw today is brilliant fakery; somebody has tied Vassiliev and Belov up so tightly they will never escape, guilty or not. But look, after working with that half-mad drunk and putting up with all his abuse, I am going to present a selection of the fakery to the Minister as being absolute fact, we'll catch Komarov in the same trap. What do you say?" The intercepted conversation ended.

"Ok," said Indira, "we know this was a conversation with a junior lieutenant called Polina Petrov, one of the small minority of women in the Russian forces. We don't have her reply, at least we couldn't hear enough to be sure, but we can assume she agreed with a plan to take Komorov down. What's more, they're using the stuff Pal and the rest of you created against Melor and

Vassiliev. Clever, cunning and duplicitous, eh? That Captain will go far in the Russian hierarchy."

"So that's what those headlines are all about?" asked Duggie.

"Yep, that's it Duggie. Our latest intel is a call from Putin's office to Captain Koslov informing him that he is to be awarded a fourth-class Order of St George for his successful defeat of three enemies of the Federation. We don't yet know if that promise will be fulfilled or when, if at all."

"Amazing," grinned Max, "what a country, the more of a liar you are the more the Kremlin lauds you. Drop your boss in the shit and get a medal, great eh. What do you say, er, boss?"

Dan chuckled, "I think you'll find, Max, that we have a pretty equal amount of ammo against each other for a truce to be called, should you ever consider a similar move."

Everyone in the room smiled, pleased to have a moment of humour.

"So, the Captain's mudslinging and use of our creative version of Melorland worked; General Komarov really is getting his comeuppance?" asked Duggie.

"Quite right, Duggie," replied Indira. "Pal has got an intercept on Komarov's mobile phone and from what he's heard, the General is in a state beyond fury."

"That's correct, I listened to some," confirmed Pal. "The man is raving and shouting and drunk all the time. Mostly he makes no sense and when he does speak sensibly, it is only to say how he will kill Vassiliev and Belov who he calls the lackey. Good eh, a lackey who thinks he is me? Me, Pal of all people, me, I mean I'd kill them both if I could."

"Komarov's sudden fall from power has been the subject of what we believe is a controlled leak," said Dan. "The Alliance knows of his house arrest and most of us, especially the foreign security members, believe that the leak will be a precursor to a show trial, manipulated to show the Russian people just how tough the regime can be, especially on those who act against its best interests. Komarov is perfect for this, oddly, because he is sort of completely innocent, so there is no risk of his trial revealing anything the regime doesn't want to be revealed. Whereas, if the state prosecuted Vassiliev, he might spill the beans about all sorts of nasties, like the Russian leaders' coffers swelling from the illegal sale of drugs, stolen, with their knowledge and approval from hospitals in the west. Not a good look; wouldn't go down too well with the average Igors and Olgas who still believe in Putin's honour."

"May I speak?" said Pal.

"How can we stop you?" replied Max.

Pal laughed, "You can't, no-one can, not even Agron but then he just speaks over me most of the time."

"What's happening Pal?" asked Max. "You are getting to be quite a happy, funny man, you're losing your grip mate, in danger of becoming a nice guy!"

"I ignore you, again, and I say instead that we think Dan is correct. I have heard incoming calls telling the mad drunkard that he is to be charged with embezzlement, misappropriation, corruption, abuse of power and fraud, at least I think I have understood what I heard correctly."

"Well done, Pal, yes, that sounds about right for a show trial," said Dan. "There is a safe cushion of obfuscation in so many charges, it will make reporting the trial over the popular media, the state-managed newspapers and TV, suitably complex so nobody spots the stage management of it all. He'll most probably get thirty years which, as everyone knows, he'll never see out."

"Actually Dan, if you hear him, you will know that he can't last more than two hours without a drink. He'll be lucky if his heart and liver last long enough to get to the courtroom," said Pal sounding singularly unsympathetic.

Kathy could contain herself no longer, "But what of Melor? Belov, Bogdan, whatever, what of him? Pal's great imitator, what is happening to him? All I see is a headline asking where he is. Has he done a runner, gone to ground, what?"

A short silence followed from Pal and Indira.

"Allow me to answer you, Kathy," offered Agron. "You see as far as we know, you know, we don't know…"

Jo chuckled, always delighting in Agron's inability to resist any form of wordplay.

"Thanks Jo," he quipped. "But that's the truth, he has hit the silent button and every trace we have on him, his devices, his mobile phones, his networks, his email accounts, the whole range of communication options available to him, that we know of anyway, come up silent. It's like he's disappeared but we don't know how."

"Thanks, Agron," replied Kathy, "but that's not much of an answer. I thought we had all the players comprehensively tracked and monitored."

"We do Kathy, we do," replied Indira with a hint of sensitivity, "but we cannot eavesdrop on a man who isn't speaking, now can we?"

"Sorry Indi, I didn't mean that you are not performing with your customary genius. I am just amazed that a man who should be in prison at least, can simply turn into vapour. Maybe he is mythological after all."

"Myth my arse," quipped Pal, "the little swine is somewhere, and I'll find him if I have to go to Moscow myself and dig him out of whatever gutter he's crawling in."

43

Jack and Amanda had finished with all the prisoners, except for the sniper who had been less than forthcoming when first interviewed soon after his bullet-removal operation. This time, in his small private room, guarded by a young constable, he appeared upright and more alert but no more communicative. He confirmed that he was known as Mehdi Turkic but would say no more about his past, where he had come from, how long he had been in the UK or how he got to be in Olderbury. Much as Jack had searched, he could find no records for the man which suggested he was using a false name or was in the country illegally.

Amanda harboured more interest in his colleagues in the drugs business. He opened up remarkably quickly on her threat to send him off for deep interrogation by anti-terrorist officers. Mehdi Turkic had heard how they extracted their information. He confirmed his 'sales organisation' had sent him to eliminate Rushian's building and the people they believed had sold them fake goods, imported by Rushian as part of a conspiracy against them. He gave Amanda some information about the drugs sold by his group, where they operated, where the competitors operated, how the area was divided up between gangs and which streets, pubs, offices, shops, taxi drivers and blocks of flats proved the most profitable.

He refused to give names but did confirm that his gang had based itself in Olderbury and planned to attack competitive groups, making a killing as his street pushers suffered a massive fall in sales because of the fake gear. Beyond their expectations and under clever and consistent quizzing from Amanda and Jack, he did let slip when and where the attack might take place.

Once they had squeezed all the information possible from the shooter, Jack stood up and made a show of the interview ending.

Amanda, too, got ready to leave, then in a casual, almost throw-away manner mentioned the shooting at Rushian and the woman who had screamed.

"Ah her," growled Turkic menacingly, "I shall remember her, she is why I am here."

Jack made sure Mehdi had not spoken to any of his group since the shooting and with no access to mobile phones, as long as he was in custody and subsequently prison, they knew Anna would be safe. Leaving the unrepentant marksman in his secure hospital room, Jack made plans to deal with the alleged inter-gang ruckus whilst Amanda put in a quick call to Anna.

"Hello, Amanda, is everything alright? Do you have any news? Are you ok…?" Anna answered in a nervous, garbled rush.

"Yes, Anna, everything is very ok. We have every reason to reassure you now, having questioned the man you screamed at, that you are safe. He wasn't able to tell anyone about you after he was shot and, although he remembers you, only to look at, not, we think, by name, he will be in no position to do anything now, or for many years to come. Attempted multiple murders and successful arson carry heavy penalties. He'll be banged up for a very long time, I can assure you."

"Oh, thanks so much Amanda, that's a relief. Me and Adam had planned to hide away at John's farm, he's Adam's mate, but I still felt like I was in danger, so we've arrived at the airport and will board the plane in half an hour. After that, nobody can find us."

"Good for you, good for you both. Give Adam my best and have a wonderful time wherever you go. I won't even ask."

Amanda called Max, "Anna and Adam are flying away, literally, as we speak and going into hiding, somewhere a long way from here…"

"Yep, I just heard. I called the boys to see what was happening. They're back at their country seat, bored and highly pissed off that they won't get to pop-pop anyone with their on-guard duties no longer needed," he replied, happily.

Amanda went on to tell Max about her interviews, "There's nothing much to say about Pugh, Handley and Preston; they admitted their roles almost before I asked and are willing to turn Queens if we find any of the rest of the organisation but, honestly Max, I'm not optimistic about that. They knew sweet fanny about the set-up other than Pugh being recruited by a Russian agent whilst he was at uni and that he has answered their call ever since, for what sounds like quite a lot of money which we shall attempt to recover. Again, I'm not optimistic, we just don't have the resources. Anyway, he gets all his instructions by phone or from Handley."

"Really, so Handley is a sort of go-between as we thought, yeah?"

"Kind of, Max, it seems he's less exciting than we hoped. They recruited him in a similar way to Pugh. He was an extreme left-wing and Marxist activist at college and got picked up as a minion of the Federation. Our Neil, well, he puts the foot into foot soldier. His job was to collect whatever, money, goods, instructions, all sorts, from the Kensington Place embassy and deliver it all to Pugh in Tavistock Square. Also, to others in the network, mainly in hospitals or other unions involved with people who work in hospitals and associated civil service jobs."

"Ah, I see, not as intriguing as I'd hoped. Still, do you think you'll pick up the others that Handley dealt with? I mean, I assume they would all be up to the same antics and therefore highly nickable."

"Of course, it's all gone to the Met now and they'll deal with it thank God, we've got enough to do. So let me tell you about the shooter, he's only dobbed up his druggy mates about a spot of gang warfare, he's even told us when it will all kick off and probably where. Jack is on it now and we are going to put a team together to join in, know what I mean?"

"I do, I do Amanda, and that's why I worry about you. Get that Jack to keep a protective eye on you - won't be too much of an ask, he can barely keep his eyes off you, a bit of a schoolboy crush I'd say. Still, as long as it's just his eyes."

"Ha, bloody ha."

"Before you go, when is this great confrontation, this battle of the dopeheads?"

"Now, I'm off in a few minutes to organise the team. Should all happen around ten-ish tonight out past the old riverside factory estate."

"Take care, do you want me to…"

"No Max, I don't. I know what you are thinking and this time I won't be able to get way with a few bodies having non-police slugs in them, so you and the boys keep well away. Please Max, I mean it, we'll be fine."

"Oki-Doki, you are the boss, just come back in one piece without additional ventilation, yeah?"

Max tapped in a fresh number, "Angel, fancy a bit of a night out?"

44

A firm believer in 'what ifs' and benefitting from the shrewd and predictive mind of a clever programmer, Melor had taken precautions. He had hoped this day wouldn't come but long ago when he first started his Melor initiative, he accepted that it might. He watched as Captain Kozlov ordered two of his armed guards to take Vassiliev to his home and keep him under their supervision. It surprised him that the Captain felt comfortable with such a small detachment and concluded that the arrogant officer did not consider either of his detainees to be a flight risk.

Whilst Vassiliev offered a spirited but futile resistance, Melor used the kerfuffle to sidle to the door and run like he had the devil after him, which in a way he had. He managed to weave his way through the maze of corridors to the rear entrance where Luka had first dropped him off. Amazed that no one had stopped him and with no sign or sound of a chasing pack, Melor, followed the wall, out of sight of most windows to the car park area and the rear vehicle entrance, thinking what a disaster the Captain would be in real combat.

Daydreaming at the wheel of his parked Moskvich, Luka spotted Melor scurrying in the shadows and knew immediately that something had gone very wrong. He turned his key and idled quietly and slowly towards Melor, pulled alongside and opened the front passenger door. With Melor three-quarters of his way in, Luka hit the throttle and shot out of the Lubyanka confines, hitting the main thoroughfare in seconds. He checked his mirrors, nothing, a clean escape.

"It's all lost, Luka, they captured your boss and put him under house arrest. I'm on the run from everyone. It's all gone, we are marked men Luka, I'll be lucky if I'm still alive by tonight."

"What do you want me to do, young sir, my friend? Where shall I drive you?"

"Do you mind Luka? I mean, if they stop us, not great for you…"

Luka smiled, "Where to young sir?"

"Ok, thank you, Luka, thank you. Can you take the third Ring Road and stop when I say?"

Keeping the Moskvitch to the designated, satisfyingly rapid 100kph along the wide arterial road and crossing the winding Moskva River twice, Luka drove carefully, despite his urge to go faster.

"Here, Luka, stop here," said Melor.

"I can't really, I'll take the next slip and drop you off somewhere less public, out of sight of the traffic cameras, ok?"

Luka found a small side road, under the cover of a line of Linden trees. "Here you are then, is this ok? Do you know that if you were wishing the ground would open up and swallow you, we are right over where the hidden underground city is supposed to start?"

Melor smiled wryly, "I don't know how to thank you, Luka. You have improved my chances of seeing tomorrow by a big margin. I owe you my life."

Melor walked about half a mile to the large ventilation grill he had found all that time ago when first exploring the area hoping to uncover the underground development, Luka had so vividly described. He heaved the grill open and descended the old iron footholds, to what would have been the reception level before the final descent to the underground city. He was sweating as he manoeuvred the heavy grill back into position.

With his usual foresight, Melor had found the entrance and underground passages and rooms soon after he moved into the flat Vasily provided for him and only days after Luka had romanticised about the hidden city. He had created a bolthole just-in-case and equipped it with batteries, supplies of food and water and all the necessities he could imagine for life in hiding, never believing he would one day need it.

He had enjoyed prowling the corridors of the subterranean complex, but it stretched so far, he could only explore small parts of it. His room had been some sort of storage area, with floor-to-ceiling racking on two walls and the security of a reinforced door. An airflow coursed through the room, presumably to stop perishable goods from rotting too quickly. He noticed that it had stayed fresher than the musty and damp inner reaches of the areas he recced. A washroom stood next door, no longer with running water but to Melor's delight, the drainage worked. At least he could live hygienically, a relief in more ways than one he thought, grinning to himself.

From halfway up the iron footholds to the grill, he could receive a MegaFon mobile phone signal and was able to check all the news channels and his multiple message accounts regularly and anonymously, on a mobile acquired on the closed market. He didn't know whether to be pleased or worried that there was no mention of him or Vassiliev in any news programmes and that he had no messages, anywhere from anyone after his imperative to shut down the operation.

During the first night in hiding, Melor ventured above ground and staying in as much cover as he could, walked towards his old flat to see if it was being guarded. It was. Two men, dressed in civilian clothes that only undercover FSB officers would wear, patrolled nonchalantly up and down the road past Melor's old front door. Now he knew the score. He returned to his burrow, ate several sweet cheese pirozhkis, made some instant coffee and slept more soundly than he had for a long time.

He spent the next day making plans and preparations and on the following afternoon, after another snack meal and good sleep, he emerged into the fresh air. He and his ID now looked very different from the old Melor or Bogdan Belov. His passport, complete with a genuine-looking China visa stamp, showed a picture of a man with a stubbly chin, blond to greying hair, gappy teeth and tinted spectacles. He was now Borys Adamov. As well as his passport, Borys had debit and credit cards, cash for all eventualities, including dollars, a new, powerful connectable laptop, clothes and all the essentials. Most importantly, he held a letter and his honorary fellowship from the Academy of Artificial Intelligence in Beijing. The letter was an invitation to share his skills and techniques with a strategic development arm of the infamous APT hacking group.

He couldn't help himself, he walked slowly, deliberately and in full view, directly past the FSB patrol outside his former home. Relishing the risk, he knew that if he remained unrecognised by these professional agents on high alert then he could pass anonymously anywhere he liked. From the corner of his street, he waited for the taxi he ordered over his app.

"Adamov?"

"Yes, me. Yaroslavsky Station please."

"You know the Mongolian Express isn't running anymore don't you sir?"

"I do, thank you."

Borys had bought a ticket from Moscow to Irkutsk and another for an onward journey from Irkutsk to Ulaanbaatar and, for the final leg, from Ulaanbaatar to Beijing. He could have flown, but this way he would be subject to less scrutiny at easy, inattentive border crossings. Besides, he looked forward to the journey. After the confines of Moscow, much as he loved that beautiful city, he longed for the sights and sounds of new places – and the Gobi, what wonders, he thought with excitement. It would take about a week, but what a week before allowing reality to creep back in.

45

"Max? Jesus. Just wondering what's the gig, man?"

"Not too sure really," replied Max.

"C'mon Max, we gotta know what we might be facing, just so we can heat up right, know what I'm saying."

"Yeah, all I can tell you is that Amanda and her best team of riot handlers are preparing to head for the old factory estate, where word has it they'll find a right old hoo-ha between two drug gangs who don't like each other very much."

"Ok, and we are going why?"

"Because I will move heaven and earth to keep Amanda safe and I don't like leaving that to some baton-waving police blokes behind shields. I want us there, you and Angel, to keep an eye on her and more than likely mop up any overly excited, drugged-up dickheads."

"Got ya man, that's all cool. Got a great idea already. What you say, see you there like on that little link road over the bridge into the estate, yeah?"

"Good idea, I'll be with Duggie in his car, it's a white iX1 Beemer."

"Yep, seen it."

"And Jesus?"

"Yeah?"

"It's just a watching job unless or until anything goes wrong, and it will be on my go signal, is that clear, understood, all ok?"

"Yeah, man be easy, you know us, we won't do nothing unless it's needed."

From the link bridge, out of sight of the police and the two slowly gathering groups of gang members, Max, Duggie, Angel and Jesus had a panoramic view. Somebody played a drumbeat, and the two gangs slowly formed into their fighting positions. As one group started to move forward, Max heard his wife's voice over a loudspeaker,

"This is the police! We are here to stop any violence and prevent any injuries, is that clear? You will now disperse. You will now turn round and go back home. If you don't, we will take action and use reasonable force to turn you around and clear this area. Turn around all of you, do it now, do it now."

Max stifled a grin and Angel laughed out loud. As soon as Amanda stopped speaking, an enormous yell erupted from both groups, and they lunged forward.

"Man, she might as well have said on your marks, set, go!"

It was quickly evident that members of both gangs were neither as fit nor as brave as they needed to be. Others, fuelled and overly antagonistic wanted to fight, fight anyone and fight until they could fight no more. The groups soon diminished to maybe only a dozen per side, the rest, some thirty or so young men, had vapourised in the night air.

The riot police moved in. Amanda positioned on higher ground, directed the manoeuvres by radio while Jack, at the head of the lead team, identified the group leaders and targeted them as fast as possible. The sight of the police moving in galvanised the young gang members who had drifted away and they came back with a vengeance, throwing stones and rocks, brandishing iron bars and railings taken from fences; they had paint sprays which they used when close enough to any police officer's visor and threw burning bottles and fireworks into the advancing force.

Amanda, seeing this rapid escalation quickly deployed her second team, positioned at what was now the rear of the fighting arena. They took most of the gangs by surprise and many ran away again, only to be caught, cuffed and secured in the waiting police vans.

As Jack stalked the stronger gang's leader, a thug dressed in black and sporting the traditional Taqiyah, Angel spotted the danger immediately. Even in the dark of the night, he saw the gleam of the man's blade. Two men separated from the core of the fight and walked slowly up behind Jack. Angel knew their intention; grab Jack from behind and the man with the blade would slash from the front. He'd seen it so many times.

He glanced at Max and nodded. Max's eyes said OK and as the leader's blade moved up into the air ready to strike, Angel sent a nine-millimetre bullet into the knifeman's hand as it hovered in the air. The two flank men decided to attack despite the sudden howl of pain from their gang boss and quickly discovered the cause of his agony as Angel followed his first shot with one each for the two attackers, both in the shoulder, not life-threatening but shatteringly painful and powerful enough to fell them where they stood. Max signalled his thanks and appreciation.

Amanda, also seeing Jack's jeopardy, had instinctively leapt forward to his defence, her police baton swirling wildly above her head at anyone within striking distance. She caught three men, also running towards Jack, with direct hits to their heads in one circular sweep. Max, only metres away by then couldn't help but laugh as he ran to protect his wife.

Now Angel and Jesus primed themselves to strike big time. The police valiantly held the centre of the battle but Jack, Amanda and now Max had fallen into inescapable danger. Duggie ran to the opposite side of the area, ready to leap onto anyone about to attack his friends. Angel and Jesus feared they had lost control. Too many individuals, at too much risk for them to manage. Jesus sprinted back to the Discovery and seized his surprise weapon, his 'great idea'. In seconds, he was back beside Angel who immediately saw his intention and grinned in approval.

It was old and less than accurate but for sheer drama nothing could beat the brothers' point fifty calibre, Browning machine gun, reputedly one of the loudest guns in the world. Jesus flicked out its ground-level tripod and took aim at a point about three metres above head height, designed to hit the decaying hulks of the factory units left to rot along the riverside. The Browning could hurl its big cartridges about two thousand meters at a rate of four hundred rounds per minute and sounded like the booming thunderclaps from hell itself; it was truly terrifying.

Laughing to himself, Jesus took a firm grasp of the two handgrips and let rip. The old factory buildings lit up like they had been possessed by the legions of Lucifer, sparks from cartridges hitting the metal framework danced in the sky like lightning and the thunderous, fulminating noise echoed around the estate, multiplying the deafening, unworldly effect.

"I tell ya, man, to quote your Churchill, never have so many shit themselves so quickly over something so goddam petrifying. It was beyond wonderful. Man, some of them would have won a gold in the Olympic sprint race. Oh, man, so good." As he shared his observation with Max, Angel was beside himself with pleasure; he leant against the Discovery watching the smoke dissipate as the smell of cordite wafted away.

The gangs had totally disappeared. The police filled their vans, capturing the leaders and the most violent fighters whilst the others fled, screaming and crying into the night. Jack dealt with the injured gang leader and questioned him before sending him off in an ambulance. He had also captured the opposing leader and simply put him in a police van ready for later questioning.

Soon the war zone calmed, the gangs had gone, the police left and Max, Duggie, Angel and Jesus drove back to Max's place where generous self-congratulatory drinks promoted laughter and ever more lurid tales of daring derring-do. Duggie, who had developed a liking for zero alcohol stout and had promised to drive the brothers back home later, watched with amusement as the stories got taller as the drinks got shorter.

46

Olderbury police station was inundated. The police vans disgorged their apprehended rioters, and a team of custody sergeants processed them as quickly as they could before squeezing them into all the cells, they had available. While Jack wrote up his notes from the brief interview with the injured gang leader at the scene, Amanda set about questioning the opposing head man. Although his English was limited, Amanda managed to extract details of his gang, where the drugs he sold came from and why he and the competitive gang were at war. She found no surprises, merely confirmations.

She ended her interview; it would be the first of several until she got some names she could act on and went to Jack's desk.

"Come on Jack, let's call it a day, I'm flagging now, and I still have to create some way of explaining what happened tonight. God, Jack, how on earth am I going to write this up?"

It was two hours before Amanda got home, bringing Jack with her for a well-earned nightcap.

"Ok, ok, so what were my last words to you, Max? Something about not interfering, not involving Butch and Sundance here, leaving it to the police, you know, those sorts of words? And how much notice did you take? None, that's how much, bloody none. You came steaming in with enough artillery to fight World War Three, you lot. You shot a member of the public and then you fired some contraption from Hades and turned an area of Olderbury into some B movie explosives fest. How the hell do you think I'm going to explain all that to my superiors, eh? Just what do you think I should say?"

Jesus and Angel looked down and shuffled like naughty schoolboys, Max and Duggie attempted to look aggrieved.

Jack summoned up his courage and said, "I say, ma'am, I mean Amanda, you know I do see your point, it is difficult to explain what some sort of battle cannon was doing at one of our crime scenes, but, well, you know, they did save our lives, at least that's how I see it. I don't know how it would all have ended if, well, if that amazing weapon hadn't panicked the gangs into running. I mean it was looking nasty and getting even nastier up 'til then…"

"When I want an opinion from you, I'll tell you what it is…"

"And your husband and Duggie showed a level of bravery which we can only dream about in the force, none of our riot guys could have taken such massive risks. I do think, ma'am, we might also say thank you, at least I'd like to thank you all, what you did was amazing."

Jack stopped and seeing Amanda's expression, looked distinctly uncomfortable.

Duggie, sensitive as always, led the applause and the other men joined in, "Thanks Jack," he said, "thank you very much, those words are as brave as our actions, and we appreciate what you said very much," he finished with a sideways glace at Amanda.

"It's all very well for you cowboys, you don't have to answer to my senior officers. They don't understand anything that isn't in the police training manual and, oddly enough, the tactical use of a weapon which can destroy an entire city in about a minute doesn't appear in the book. I mean, what am I going to say? I'm serious, this could be my job up the spout."

Max guessed what Jack would say next and he was right, "Ma'am…"

"Oh, for fuck's sake quit with the ma'am!"

"As you say, ma'am, Amanda, may I offer a thought?"

"Will it save our skins?"

"If I read young Jack here right," interrupted Max, "it will save your skins and make you real Marvel-type heroes, right Jack?"

"I think so, I mean, what if that damn great gun was, in fact, a weapon used by one of the gangs? What if we seized it, you know, valiantly disarmed a murderous thug and saved the day, what then Amanda?"

"Hold on a goddam minute you goddam limey fed," shouted Jesus. "You want to take my Browning off of me and Angel, it's our baby, and we love it, you can't take it just like that, I won't let you, so now what do you say?"

"I say I fully understand your attachment to such a prized possession," replied Jack, "but I would point out that owning it and firing it public breaks so many laws, I don't know where to start. So, you see, I'd say we take your gun into custody, or we take you in instead, which would you prefer?"

"I'd prefer to rip you goddam fuckin head off…"

"Yes sir, I can understand that but I'm afraid that's not an available option."

Jesus burst into laughter, "That's the last fuckin time, I tell you, the last time, next time you call with your promise of action and fun, Angel and me, we'll tell you to stick it."

"Sorry," said Max also smiling, "but our young officer here is quite right and there's nothing I can do about it."

Amanda looked guilty, "Look, I know I was out of order, bollocking you all when I know you saved the day and almost certainly our lives or, at least, limbs and I should be thanking you, which I do, really and sincerely I do. But I'm not joking about the seriousness of a heavy-duty, outrageously illegal machine gun being used in a police operation. If I don't come up with something, I'm toast, so is Jack, boom, no career. So, Angel, Jesus, thank you as I do, love you both as you know I do, I can't see any alternative to Jack's plan. What do you say?"

Max and Duggie, both knowing that the brothers had more money and a larger arsenal than many small countries, chortled at the guys' affected glum and angry expressions.

"Ah, what the fuck, anything to help a weak, helpless dame in her time of need," sighed Angel.

Jesus joined in the laughter as Amanda flew at his brother, "Weak, am I? Helpless, am I?" she cried, pummelling his chest in mock fury before planting a big, sloppy kiss on his cheek.

"Aw, come on now Amanda," he said. "You know we'd never let you down, 'course you can take the goddam old gun. We've got more of 'em anyway, we took a whole bunch of them off some Colombian coke baron who thought he'd start his own army."

"Right, enough of all this," said Max, "tell us, what did the guys you arrested have to say for themselves?"

"Exactly what you'd expect. They were certain that Rushian, who they believed to be a distributor to both gangs, had worked with the other gang to tuck them up with fake gear. Both sides thought the same and now they know differently which may help Anna in the long run; I hope so anyway. So, they have nothing new to say and we'll just charge them with everything we can think of and hope we get a judge who deals with them appropriately, although that's becoming a vain hope these days."

Jack, looking for approval from Amanda, added, "You haven't asked us about Adrian Simson. You know Pugh's stooge and Ben Barrington's understudy."

"No, I haven't," said Max. "To be honest, he'd slipped down my list of people to worry about."

"I didn't tell you, Max, sorry, so much happening," said Amanda. "It's a sad story. We had him in custody ready for questioning when- there's no easy way of saying this, he lost the plot completely and disappeared into a world of his own. You'd have mistaken him for a drunk. We had to pack him off to a specialist unit, half-rehab, half-psychiatric facility and hope for the best."

"Christ, that's terrible," said Max. "He seemed a nice chap, just fell or got pushed off the rails I suppose, and that arch shit Pugh wouldn't have helped, bastard."

"One positive outcome, Hetherington, the doctor who shopped him, came to the rescue. He helps gambling addicts and even though Simson caused the hacking of the doctor's practice with awful consequences, the old boy, a real grump by all accounts, offered him specialist counselling."

47

Graham Carter felt immensely proud of Onetelcall's Deepmatters AI facility, and how it added to the company's security services portfolio and effectiveness exponentially. Combined with the in-house specialist services, such as Kathy's team and their work in analysing new technologies and the 'eavesdropping' teams such as that run by Sue and Indira, Onetelcall had become a global leader in digital investigation and protection for its clients.

Dan, as CEO, felt equally proud. His contribution to the Alliance, an exclusive and highly secure, international cyber intelligence organisation, continued to impress his powerful peers from across the world, from leading IT agencies to government monitoring and policy-making bodies. If something untoward flagged up, Onetelcall invariably got there first.

The great resource of Deepmatters enabled Graham and his specialists to analyse an incredible amount of activity and electronic traffic, this included new areas of interest as well as all the previous targets from past investigations. Max had secured a lucrative contract from a collection of private investment companies with interests in NHS services, to maintain a close watch on any threats, hacks, trojan horses, bots, spyware and ransomware that may be inflicted yet again on the war-weary NHS. With all the power at his fingertips, Graham expected to be the first to any cybercrime but, this time, it was a phone call to Max which started a new and worrying subject of scrutiny.

"Max? It's Ben."

"Hey Ben, grand to hear from you, how are you? How was your, er, holiday?"

"Gosh, a distant memory. Four months ago now when I decided to go into temporary hiding."

"It was a good idea, Ben. No doubt you heard about all the shenanigans after you discovered the hacking and drug theft?"

"Indeed I did, chapter and verse, terrible stories really, and poor Adrian…"

"Yes, I know. He's making some progress; Amanda expects to talk to him in a few weeks."

"Really? Good. But look, Max, don't think I'm getting paranoid or whatever the computer version of hypochondria is, but I think we are being hacked, or something like that again. We're much more aware of IT security now and Perry, remember him? Yes, well, he spotted something he called an anomaly and asked me to call you."

"Thanks, Ben, I'll get our guys to call him. We'll be on it immediately; I can assure you."

"Graham? Max. Are we still sweeping Olderbury Hospital?"

"Funny you should say that Max, we are, and we've just had a flash. Can I call you back? I'll check it out now."

Max called Pal in Mattinata, "Hello my friend, how are you both?"

"Max, hello, we are good, what is it that you want from us?"

"Have you noticed anything odd recently? Any anomalies happening anywhere, or dark chat going on about a new attack on the UK's NHS?"

"Tell truth, Max," said Pal, who obviously hadn't been speaking in English for some time, "I am not looking much, me and Agron. We've been on holiday, yes, strange yes, but we hire Italian car, a Ferrari, and we drive round lakes in north, very lovely, we enjoy, it is a bit like mountains in Albania, we miss sometimes know, never done such a thing before."

"Oh? Good for you. I never thought of you as tourists, except into other peoples' computer systems of course."

"Ha, funny man, I will look for you if you like and call back, ok?"

Next, he spoke to Sue, "Any traffic come to the surface about another attack on the NHS?"

"No nothing, Max, nothing that we have seen anyway. It can't be the old Russian Team, your man Melor disappeared months ago, and we haven't heard a dickie about the others. We'll do a deeper search if you like?"

"Yes please."

Had it really been nearly six months since the combined fake Melorland effort had shut down the drug thefts, the fake drug imports and the ensuing inter-gang wars of the dealers? Max found it hard to believe that anyone could have rebuilt the Russian operation so quickly, ready to infiltrate the UK's crucial health systems again. Was that Melor character still active? If so how, where and for whom?

He didn't have long to wait for an answer; several answers and they all came at once. Sue and Graham both confirmed activity against the UK NHS and that it looked like a new exploratory foray. They also confirmed that whatever was going on didn't emanate from Russia. Sue said it was almost certainly from China and Onetelcall's systems had tracked back from a bot in an Olderbury Hospital peripheral system to a source in Beijing.

Oh God, thought Max, first the Russians, now the Chinese. Graham called him urgently.

"Max, this is very odd. Remember the previous attacks were all about denial of service for ransom, about theft and monetary gain with as much disruption as possible?"

"That about sums it up."

"OK, well, if my suspicions are correct, the intel that Deepmatters has compiled leads to a very different conclusion. This time it doesn't look like money, theft or nuisance, they want information."

"What sort of information?"

"Any information, patients' details, hospital details, treatment details, medical regimes and surgery details, anything and everything. From what we can see, the incursions are planting spotters and recorders, like vacuum cleaners, there to suck up all the info they can get. Weird. What are they up to? And who are they?"

48

One man had the answers. Bogdan, previously Melor, and now known as Borys. Over a spectacular journey of nearly eight thousand kilometres over six days, he had used his time purposefully. Gazing out of the train window and marvelling at the scenery, from the sands of the Gobi Desert to the snowy tundra, Borys felt inspired. Like many Russian students, Borys, back when he was Bogdan, had learned Chinese, first basic and then some advanced modern standard, as well as Chinese culture and current politics. He knew that the Chinese government, under President Xi Jinping, had cracked down hard on corruption and although it still existed, it didn't rise to the levels of the present venal and avaricious Russian regime.

He also knew that President Xi believed knowledge equalled power and would do everything necessary to expand his power base. To Borys, that meant an increasing hunger for strategically useful information. He knew that his invitation to join the Academy of Artificial Intelligence was predicated on his success in the UK and now he wondered how he could manipulate his knowledge and success to make him as indispensable to China as he had been to Russia, albeit more briefly than he'd hoped.

On his journey, he used the train's intermittent wi-fi to read all he could about developments and innovations in medical disciplines and treatments in the NHS, as well as associated universities and research centres. He noticed China's most prevalent killer disease was lung cancer along with cardiovascular disease and COPD. He read that the Chinese Thoracic Oncology Group had been conducting some clinical trials into lung cancer treatments and that much of its research was done in association with universities and research centres in the UK and the West, including the Early Lung Cancer Action Programme Centre in the USA.

By the time his final train from Mongolia's capital came to a halt in Beijing Central Station, Borys felt he knew sufficient to blag his way into a position of some authority. He would apply his mythical abilities to infiltrate the most secret and sensitive data relating to advances in lung cancer prevention, diagnosis and treatments, especially the fascinating advances in robotic navigation and surgery he found being developed in London's St Barts hospital.

Weighed down with his numerous bags, he stepped off the train and headed for the taxi area. His journey to the Wudaokou district gave him a glimpse of the famous, infamous, Tiananmen Square. The image from 1989 of one man facing down a tank remained strong in his mind, stirring a strand of democracy in his undemocratic mind. He travelled past the Silver Technical Tower, Peking University and out towards the University of Science and Technology, following a loop around the one-way system from the N4th Ring Road to the Academy's reception area.

They greeted him warmly and courteously, as expected, and showed him to a visitors' room where he had coffee. A man formally welcomed him and bowed effusively but did not give his name. This struck Borys as unusual. The man then escorted him firmly by the elbow to a door at the rear of the reception area and then to a black Tesla, with dark tinted windows, waiting silently with its nearside rear door open. They encouraged him to get in the car which drove off, faster than Borys would have liked, into the Beijing traffic. He could neither see nor recall the route, but he did know that the journey took some twenty minutes before the car halted outside a nondescript office block in a commercial part of the city.

He was shown out of the car and into another office where he was met by another man, this time a fellow Russian.

"Shall I call you Borys, or Melor or Bogdan?"

Borys's bowels turned to jelly, his stomach cramped and his mouth dried.

"I see I have you at a disadvantage," said the Russian. "Allow me to introduce myself, "I am Grigoriy Antonov, attached to the FSB. I think you know all about the FSB don't you, and I liaise between my superiors and the officials of the cyber intelligence branch of China's MSS, Ministry of State Security. It is I who arranged for your Honorary fellowship and implied invitation to share your undoubted expertise with the organisation known as Advanced Persistent Threat or APT as you will know them."

Borys felt confused and dismayed. "But I mean, how did you know I would come here? How did you know if and when I'd arrive, how did you know I had changed my name, my appearance?"

"Like many of your technically minded brethren, you dismiss the power of old-fashioned police work. We have had you in our sights from the moment you got into Vassiliev's car at Lubyanka; every hour, every day, every move you made, police work you see."

"No, it can't be so. I checked, I watched, I saw your spies and dodged them."

"Really? Come now, Borys, do you think we are so amateur? Did you think you could just wander out of Lubyanka and stroll off free as a bird? Naivety or too much belief in your abilities, either way, you are a fool. You have never escaped, and you never will."

"I don't understand, if you want me so much, what am I doing here?"

"As opposed to being dead, or, worse, in Penal Colony Number 6?"

"I came to China to offer them my services."

"And that's just what you'll do. You see Borys, you have become a token of goodwill, of cooperation, of joint development against the West; one government giving a small gift to another. In effect, Borys you have been given away. You will now serve China and by serving your new masters, you will continue to serve your home country, understand?"

Borys understood everything very quickly. He tried to settle into his new, constantly watched, flat on the edge of Beijing's Haidan District, home to many of the country's IT companies. From his flat he could see the roof-mounted identity letters of the professionally respected Beijing Computing Centre where, he was surprised to learn, he had been allocated a small, secure workroom equipped with everything that he could have asked for and more. They gave him a fluent, bi-lingual assistant, named Ah Cy who ensured that Borys could navigate his way around all the Chinese systems, networks and cloud services without any confusion.

Free but held in an open prison, he had no choice but to go to work, determined to find another opportunity to show the world that he was the best hacker ever. Borys would be the new Melor and in just days, he succeeded in presenting details of the thoracic robot tests and results from St Barts, Papworth and University College London hospitals to his new bosses. They may have been impressed, if so, they didn't express any approval. Instead of plaudits, they pushed Borys to go further, to achieve more, to find information that the Chinese specialists and consultants in the field of lung cancer didn't already know via the professional media and their agents in the UK's hospitals and universities.

As he had done so many times before, Borys wondered what his hero, Pal, would do to dig ever deeper.

49

In the months following the cessation of NHS hacking, theft and ransoms and the subsequent multiple arrests, life in Mattinata grew tranquil and enjoyable. Agron went all analogue with an old typewriter, sheaves of paper and Arthur Miller glasses as he embarked on his great opus, a novel based on his Albanian childhood. This went on to describe his first successes in writing and the realisation that communication could be weaponised, his time with a psychotic drugs lord and how it felt to be wealthy but still want to achieve more.

Pal, although still harbouring a deep resentment for 'that Russian plagiarist shithead' had become less misanthropic. He nearly agreed to accompany Sue, with Indira for company, on the holiday to Florida that he had given her but baulked at the thought of leaving his remote home. As an academic exercise, he continued to monitor, search and experiment with new techniques for his cyber crusade and he kept in contact with the Onetelcall experts who had become close, if distant, friends. At around the time Ben had called Max, Pal, too, had noticed unusual activity, a digital footprint from China stomping all over the familiar old ground of systems associated with the UK's NHS.

After developing and deploying the now infamous chatbot bug, which turned many of the world's robotic customer service voice systems into babbling junk, Pal had continued to train his bespoke AI-enhanced LLM facility in every aspect of cyber criminality. The brain had become refined and accurate in predicting patterns, processes and purposes. Now, in conjunction with Deepmatters, Pal and Graham could track and assess every captured activity from the new China-located interloper.

As Agron tapped away in Mattinata and Graham studied a client's network security vulnerabilities in Olderbury, Pal's high-pitched scream shattered their concentration,

"It's him, it's fucking him, that shithead bastard fucking copycat arsehole, it's him I tell ya!" he yelled from the always-on comms link.

"Who, what… what's happening…?" shouted Agron over Pal's rising hysteria.

"Pal, you ok?" ventured Graham.

"I tell ya. Listen, it's him, it's that *kacke* Melor or whatever he's calling himself now and he isn't in Russia, no, not at all, and I'll bet he thinks he's anonymous again, but I'd recognise his work anywhere 'cos it's a rip off of my work and I'm telling you it's him."

His fury fed his determination to destroy the person who would pretend to be him, "There is only one Pal!" he roared.

Without respite, he watched as various hacks appeared across the range of systems and networks, all linked to the NHS, that were being monitored by him and by the specialist teams in Onetelcall. As time progressed, the cyber incursions increased, all with one notable feature, none of them seemed dangerously malicious, none of them left bugs, bots or any spy or ransomware and all of them seemed to be veering in one direction.

Pal's video link with Onetelcall flashed into life as Sue announced, "Pal, my dear colleague, you may well owe me another exotic holiday…"

"Oh yes, Sue? Why would I want to provide you with another gift of appreciation?" he replied stiffly.

"Because you can keep your Deepmatters, your AIs, your LLMs, your quantum and supercomputers or whatever, because here in the good old listening-in station, we have discovered something that you don't know and I do, so…"

Pal, realising that Sue was teasing, allowed himself to smile, much to Agron's astonishment. "Then tell me, Sue, tell me what your listening has achieved."

"One word, Pal, one word, Xiaomi."

"Ah, I think I understand already, the cell phone with inbuilt vulnerability?"

"On the head Pal, that's exactly it. Indira and I, even Jo, have been searching and searching and we believe we've hit gold. If we're right, this Melor character, now calling himself Borys, has an assistant, probably from the government official watchdog, and we believe it is a female called Ah Cy."

"Tell me more," said Pal urgently, feeling he could be another step nearer to nailing his nemesis.

"It seems that Melor or Borys or whatever isn't the only player in this game with a super-sized ego, his new workmate appears to be pretty up herself too. We caught a post she made on her phone to the social media site Zhihu, a sort of Quora-like platform and news aggregator for those who fancy themselves as big thinkers, and in her post which we traced, she said, "Lung cancer affects over a million people every year in China. I can now reveal that our great leaders have authorised a new research campaign which will gather the best new medical techniques from around the world, to add to our own brilliant expertise and ensure those people who get the disease will have the best opportunity of survival. I will post more as this campaign develops."

"Shit, what kind of complete asshole would post such a stupid comment? This Ah Cy is almost boasting about the theft of other countries' research and advances in medicine. I mean, surely even the Chinese must think this is not good."

"You'd think so wouldn't you, but there's been no comeback yet that we can see. Perhaps there is a general acceptance that China has a right to all available information because it pays for most of it," replied Sue sourly.

"Look, we are not here to talk about politics or ethics," joined in Agron, "we are all after the same thing, the end of this excessive hacking and intellectual theft from your health service systems. Oh, and the total destruction of the dickhead who would dare to copy Pal. It seems to me this could be a heaven-sent opportunity for us to do all that."

"What do you mean?" asked Sue.

"I have an idea forming," he replied, looking knowingly at Pal. "But it isn't there yet, give me a little while and I'll get back to you. And hey, get Max involved, will you? If my idea is workable, we'll need him in on it."

As Pal looked questioningly at his friend, Agron said, "My, my Ah Cy, how pretty you look today."

50

Borys felt delighted with his progress. He now knew where to find the most valuable seams of information for him to mine. His greatest success was finding a backdoor, via a phished email account, into the records filing function of one of the independent companies; one that had designed and built the latest and best portable, modular robotic surgery unit. He had been given access to WuDao, the multi-model AI, developed by the Beijing Academy of Artificial Intelligence, and reckoned to be the largest pre-trained example in the world with an estimated 1.75 trillion parameters.

As he planted an infection of bugs, spiders and bots that spread virally from the phished and hacked company's network, Borys used his new immensely powerful asset to assess the enormous quantities of data and files as they were discovered. WuDao dispensed with non-critical information and captured essential intelligence. It then compiled all of it into a complete dossier on every aspect of the UK's world-leading developments in cardio-thoracic and lung cancer surgery advancements and treatments. He knew that, combined with China's existing and impressive advancements in these fields, he would enable the CCP to become the undoubted centre of excellence and world-dominant authority on such lifesaving techniques and procedures.

He felt less happy having to tolerate an assistant whom he didn't like, trust or understand, even though his basic Chinese usually proved more than adequate. It was mutual. Ah Cy had not wanted the assignment of shadowing this Russian and having to spy on him, but as time progressed and her dislike of Borys grew, she found her natural duplicity fired by an increasing desire to, somehow, feed him to the wolves. She decided on a slow death; it would be too easy to manufacture evidence against him in the workplace and report the fabricated wrongdoing to her section head. Not nearly satisfying or vindictive enough for Ah Cy. No, she had a better plan.

Knowing his reputation for hubris and for self-promotion, Ah Cy would drip feed, slowly at first, indiscreet social media posts in her own name but with a trail which, when followed as it eventually would be, would lead to Borys as the originator. She also knew that Borys didn't use any of the Chinese social media platforms except WeChat and her choice of the more intellectual Zhihu service would ensure he stayed ignorant of her activities until the authorities came to call.

The timing was important, Ah Cy had no intention of compromising the full potential of Bory's unparalleled success in finding and accessing any system he wanted. She sowed her seeds according to the speed of Borys's progress, hoping that she would reach her peak of treachery as his campaign of hacking and theft had yielded its maximum amount of powerful knowledge. At first, she barely bothered to check on her social media posts. When she did check it was only to ensure that her posts had appeared as they should; she didn't bother to explore further or read any reaction that the posts may have generated.

It must have been some seven or eight weeks after she had posted her first Zhizu message, just as Borys was stealing the results of a recent Cardiothoracic Interdisciplinary Research Network surgery trial, that she noticed her last post was significantly longer than she had originally written. She read with some horror that her post had been immediately followed by a second in such a way that it purported to be part of the same communication. Ah Cy saw that what she had written, again saying how China would be enabled to be the world leader and implying this would be achieved by espionage, had been embellished with a footnote saying, 'China is already the world leader in hacking and theft of information and so it is no surprise that this is how it will become similarly dominant in any field it wants.'

She looked back and saw that her last three posts had been either added to or rewritten. She noticed, too, that there had been no interference with her work before that. Three weeks ago? What had happened three weeks ago? Nothing. Four weeks ago? Yes, four weeks ago, the time when she had been given her new mobile phone, the best, latest, highly secure Extreme XLT version. It couldn't be that, surely it couldn't be her new phone.

Who better to ask, she thought.

"Borys, how do I know if my mobile phone has been illegally accessed?" she asked innocently.

"Let me see. Hmmm, nice phone."

He looked at the phone, its screen, its battery usage history, and its app activity and announced in minutes that the phone had most certainly been hacked and its texts and messages most probably read and tracked.

"Have you used this phone to text me? Oh, shit, you have, haven't you? You sent me a text only a few days ago to say you'd be late for work."

Borys examined his phone, it didn't seem to have been violated in any way and he breathed a sigh of relief until he had another thought. "Ah Cy, have you used your phone to email me?"

"Yes, Borys, you know I have. I forwarded some URLs I found while I was working at home, remember?"

"I do remember. I am very afraid I remember all too well, and now I suppose you know what that means…"

Borys and Ah Cy both looked panic-stricken but for quite different reasons. Within seconds, he had activated all his fail-safe procedures. His systems were shut down and all, or his outward-facing links closed. Next, he initiated a security check; this sweeper was his own design and looked for the tiniest of telltales that others would miss, telltales on even the smallest evidence of any nosiness, any unexpected attempts to enter or search for system properties.

After fifteen minutes of intense scanning, his report showed nothing, just a couple of innocent-looking international server hits without entry or digital enquiry. Anomalies? Borys was unsure, acknowledging subconsciously that it would be possible, just possible that someone like Pal could get that close or even closer without being spotted by his security scanners. He pondered. International servers? He looked again. They seemed random but then they would, wouldn't they if a hacker like him, like Pal, was hiding his identity by bouncing around the globe, server to server.

No matter what he called himself, the paranoia that Belov felt as a boy and Melor as a myth was just the same, just as strong. Borys sensed all was not well and contemplated another escape. He realised as he plotted that he hadn't achieved a first escape. Was a second attempt at freedom equally doomed?

51

The thrill of the chase took hold in both Olderbury and Mattinata. The old team of Agron and Jo reformed to create the most damaging and pernicious of posts possible for Ay Cy's new Zhihu endeavours and Pal, supported as ever in such matters, by Kathy even though he vehemently denied needing any help from anyone, designed the most delicious of all fakes.

They called Ben Barrington and persuaded him to beg a few favours from the pre-eminent clinicians and consultants he knew in CIRN; especially those who had taken part in any of the surgical trials to which, they now knew, Borys had gained access. Agron advised Pal that it would take too long for him to dig his way into Borys's systems, find the reports, lift them, alter them and replace them. Better to create entirely new, false and erroneous reports and trial results and place those on the CIRN system where Borys and his AI trawlers would not be able to resist thieving them.

Ben and his colleagues obliged with speed and no little relish. Within hours, the hacked section of the CIRN network had been fed new, high-level papers on pre-surgical, post-surgical, minimally invasive robotic methods, trial results, assessments and recommendations for the next series of surgical procedures. The contents were vital and too high grade to be ignored. They were also liberally spiced with a multitude of hidden malevolent spy and destruct codes which would multiply faster than Roger the rabbit in whatever machine eventually became their home.

To be sure, Max and Dan also authorised his task force to enter machines which would usually be too politically sensitive to consider for covert activity. Dan had consulted with the Alliance and all the countries represented by its members and received unanimous approval, apart from a Chinese delegate who, whilst despising the methods being used by Borys, could not bring himself to approve his government's systems being so openly abused. The Alliance thanked the Chinese delegate for his forbearance and Dan had taken some added precautions to ensure there would be no seepage to Beijing.

Pal and Graham identified, from Borys's servers, the programmed distribution destinations and the destructive, erroneous reports, amended from the versions shown to the Alliance as a precaution. These soon started to proliferate throughout the CCP's highest-level thoracic academic and research networks.

"As long as he doesn't shut down in the next couple of hours, we've stuffed him," declared an almost euphoric Graham.

Pal smiled, "That Graham, he's usually more serious than me and now even he makes funny."

Graham didn't know it, but he had beaten Borys to shut down by at least two days.

Agron and Jo, pumped with excitement, had fed Zhuhi with as much as they could and, like naughty children, turned their attention to some of the other Chinese social media platforms where they had seen from her phone that Ah Cy had accounts. As well as WeChat, Ah Cy had a profile with Baidu Teipa and Sina Weibo. For added puckishness, they opened accounts as Borys Melor and created conversations between the two. They knew that under expert scrutiny all their postings would be seen to be imposters but, what the heck, they gave it a good go anyway.

"It sticks, you know," said Jo coyly.

"You mean mud?"

"No Agron, not quite."

Agron sniggered.

For the second time in the battle against Bogdan Belov, Pal wanted to be in for the kill. "If I can't be there, at least I want to know exactly what happens," he said.

"Not so easy this time, old friend," said Agron, "but you and the girls can monitor all the comms traffic coming from phones and over the networks we are watching, so I'm sure you'll get a good idea of what goes down."

"As long as he goes down for good this time, I'll be happy. Copy me, would he? Ha!"

52

The Russian man appeared at the front door of Borys's flat at dawn. He was accompanied by two officers from The People's Armed Police. Only half-dressed, he was dragged to a waiting car and driven the short journey to the Central Military Commission's interrogation suite, just a stone's throw from the beautiful Summer Palace, temples and lakes in the north of the Haidian district. Borys yelled his innocence of whatever he was being arrested for, but nobody spoke to him. The Russian man looked at him with disgust but would not be drawn into a comment and the Chinese PAP officers wouldn't even look at him. This would be no Vassiliev manoeuvre, he knew, and Borys resigned himself to a tough time, although he was still unaware of any misdemeanour that he may have committed.

Ah Cy had to beg to put some clothes on when the PAP called at her flat in the Qianmen district. She had draped a towel around her to answer the urgent banging on her first-floor studio apartment and, after much pleading, the officers relented, having had a furtive sight of her naked form, and allowed her to dress before driving her to the interrogation suite where she was bundled into the same room as Borys.

The inquisitor didn't waste time, there was no need, innocent or guilty, the damage had been done in their names and they were the people closest to the fake stolen intelligence and the anti-state social media posts. They were both charged with offences against the state without appeal. An immediate summary court hearing followed and Borys was sentenced to be deported back to Russia for punishment.

Ah Cy was told that the death penalty had been considered but, given some doubt about her complicity in the planting of fake information on the China Medical Resources Network, she would be found guilty of the social media offences and her attempts to pass the blame to another. For this, she would be sent to Beijing Women's Prison where she would undergo a programme of no less than five years of physical and mental retraining.

The next morning, Ah Cy woke up in prison. Borys had become Melor again and found himself aboard a Russian military flight for the journey to Oral airport in Kazakhstan where a helicopter would transfer him to Russia's infamous Black Dolphin prison. He wanted nothing more than to be able to jump from the helicopter and bring his living nightmare to an end. He knew all about the Black Dolphin, the electrocution, the beatings, the forced positions of agony, and the brutality of the guards and the inmates, he preferred death, he wanted to die.

On arrival, he was amazed to hear that Kozlov, now a lieutenant colonel, had intervened on his behalf and instead of being in the maximum security 'lifers' wing, he was to be imprisoned in a lower security zone where, eventually, he would be allowed to work outside the facility. As his heart soared, he was told that despite Kozlov's clemency bid, he would still serve five years in the medium security section but would at least avoid the harshest the Black Dolphin had to offer. Melor was under no illusion that his life would be terrible, but he would survive.

53

Belov Bogdan, Melor the Myth or Boris, whatever his name, the man survived only three months. It wasn't the prison regime that killed him, ironically, but a severe thoracic infection which turned into pneumonia and with only limited medicines available in the prison, he succumbed. Out of unusual courtesy, the prison officials sent an email to Kozlov telling him of Melor's death. Kozlov, more out of duty than courtesy, forwarded the email to Komarov who, still under house arrest, was himself suffering from cirrhosis and pancreatic cancer.

In Mattinata, an old intercept alarm pinged on Pal's system.

Meanwhile, Perry and Dug met up in The Carpenters Arms, for a convivial catch-up.

"You know, Perry," said Duggie, presenting his friend with a large craft gin and tonic, "I don't suppose anyone has said a proper thank-you for all you did to help us with the Russian invaders."

"Well, that's not totally true," replied a smiling Perry. "Ben, you know Barrington, he thanked me so many times it was getting embarrassing, and the hospital trust number crunchers diverted some funds from, I don't know, an inclusivity programme somewhere, to give to me to spend as I thought fit on security measures and the like. Ben suggested I spent it on a contract with your lot in the hackers' playground you call work, but now I understand that your man Max is tucking up everyone even remotely connected to the NHS with Onetelcall contracts. So, Dug, it seems to me that I got some thanks, and you've all got a major payday."

Duggie laughed, "Man's gotta live, Perry. I wanted to talk to you about that. Max and me and the team, thought you'd like to do a spot of consultancy with us. Ben approves before you ask and it's not a huge thing, just your insight into NHS systems and protocols development and the like."

"A sort of Onetelcall spy you mean?"

"That's the ticket, Perry. You tell us, we pay you, good, eh?"

"Yeah, good it is, thanks, Duggie, I know what you are doing, and I appreciate it, I really do, it's kind and unusually thoughtful and decent. Not that there's much to tell at the moment to earn my new stipend, we've got it all back under control and our drugs systems are tighter than a wax-sealed duck's arse, but that doesn't stop us from being vigilant. Mind you, effecting changes is an uphill struggle, so much perishing bureaucracy for such simple activities, you need a risk assessment and diversity statement to go to the fucking toilet. But enough of what we all already know, Duggie, you still haven't told me about these mysterious allies you've got in the hackersphere. I've heard they're criminals on the run and hiding out somewhere in Italy but that can't be right, I mean, can it?"

In Mattinata, a jubilant Pal celebrated the incarceration of his invidious imitator and in all honesty, secretly revelled in the news of his premature death.

"I would have killed him myself, so why should I feel any sympathy for him 'cos a bug, a virus – ha-ha, bug and virus, ha-ha, got him first!"

His euphoria at returning to the role of undisputed world hacker supremo prompted Pal to an act of unexpected generosity.

"Pal and Agron invite you - all floors of best hotel in Mattinata booked for you – many as can come! We celebrate Albanian way but no guns."

Agron said they ought to create a more stylish, or at least grammatically correct invitation, but Pal insisted on sending it himself to everyone he knew in Onetelcall. As an afterthought, he added, "Bring those murdering Mexican bastards too if they are brave enough."

In Olderbury, Indira was a bit of a quiver. "You know Sue, I've become quite fascinated by Pal. I think he likes me. Is he, you know, good-looking do you think…?"

"It was me he bought tickets to the Keys for Indi," replied Sue, packing her case with hastily bought ensnaring summer party and beach wear.

"Yeah, but he wanted me to go too," said Indira, wondering if she dared to wear her new high-cut bottom, low-cut top swimsuit, thinking that 'suit' was something of a misnomer.

Angel and Jesus leapt at the idea. "Hey, Max man, how many, like on the trip, you know, how many?"

Max counted them off on his fingers, "Dan, Jo, Sue, Indira, Duggie, Kathy, me and Amanda, possibly Graham and his wife the very wonderful Jodie, you two natch and er, well, that's all, I think. Adam and Anna came home and buggered off somewhere else on some buying trip in East Asia. So, Angel, I'd say it will be twelve in all, why?"

Jesus chuckled, "I tell you why. Angel, see he has wings, he flies, he's Angel the pilot and is planning on hiring some fancy aircraft for us all, ain't that right bro?"

"For sure, bro, you know me, have wings… Fly me to the moon, let me play amongst the stars…"

While Angel crooned, Max wrestled with his conscience. He had planned on chartering an executive jet for the journey, it was something he'd always wanted to do but now, he just didn't have the heart to dampen his friend's soaring spirits.

Angel immediately put in the necessary flying hours and hired a twin-engine Beechcraft. By the day of departure, he knew the aircraft intimately and, forsaking his usual sunglasses for a pair of Ray-Ban Aviators, he welcomed his passengers aboard like a professional pilot. This amused some but made the more nervous others only a little more comfortable about being flown fifteen hundred miles by a Mexican mobster.

Once airborne, the sisterhood of Amanda, Kathy and Jo talked at great length about the challenges women faced in an increasingly misogynistic woke society, while Dan and Max relaxed in the deep, luxurious leather seats for the duration of the flight. Twiddling the stem of his faux flute filled with fine champagne, Dan looked at his friend and said,

"This is quite special you know, Max. Who'd have thought that we'd be flying away to party with two men from a gang who wanted to kill us, destroy us and blow your bollocks off? I mean, it does sound odd you'd agree."

"Sure thing, boss," grinned the irrepressible Max, "I'd trust these two hoods with Duggie's life." He nodded towards Angel and Jesus at the aircraft's controls. "They think the absolute world of him, me, you and the rest of us. We're like surrogate family now they've turned their backs on their old lives for good."

"Yeah, they are amazing. By the way, I didn't tell you in all the recent activity, I heard from the guys' old boss, Jimmy Lopez. He says he's cool with the brothers staying here in the UK and, for what it's worth, he's always on our team."

"So, let's hope old chum, we have seen the last of our battling days."

"You have always been skilled in self-delusion, Max. With the fight against cybercrime still in its infancy; everywhere you look, cyber-attacks on us in the UK and the rest of the world, ramp up on an hourly basis. They are all at it. The Chinese are using cyber tactics to control the world's car industry, they limit exports of vital components, pushing up prices and reducing production so they can flood the markets with vehicles they equip with all manner of data gathering spyware."

"What's brought all this on, your sudden interest in the automobile industry? You usually have headier matters on your mind," asked Max.

"Yes, normally I do but this is a little different and I'm ashamed to say a little narrow-minded of me…"

"What's that, boss?"

"Well, Jo and I went to a business dinner in Paris recently, one of those achievement celebration gigs, not my style but, you know, good for the Onetelcall international profile."

"Of course, boss, no need to explain to me."

"Arse," growled Dan. "Anyway, on our table was a fella who is one of those unknown big noises in the car-making world, with interests in vehicle production, oil, and unusually, eco-fuels and electric or alternative energy motors."

"Sounds interesting, so what's the problem with him?"

"I can hardly describe it, Max, without sounding like an envious, moaning loser. He just exuded power, you know, one of those guys who treads on everything and everyone and always gets what he wants. Legal, illegal, moral, immoral, it doesn't matter, he just gets it, and does whatever he wants with no limits, no sanction, no questions, no checks or balances. He's a human free radical with the wealth and power to back it up and I really, really didn't trust him, like some sort of James Bond villain."

"So, he tried to pull Jo then, did he?"

"Now you come to mention it, he did. But you know Jo, she put him down with her rapier wit and he didn't like that at all. But it's not that, it's just that I've got a feeling, a premonition if you like."

"Uh-oh, so that's what you mean when you say our battles might not be over?"

"Max, what do you know about a man called…"

The intercom crackled and Angel announced their descent to Foggia Airport, destination Mattinata.

Raucous cheers and loud singing drowned out Dan's holiday-busting proposal.

"Called?" persisted Max.

About the Author

Anthony (Tony) Silman has been writing for most of his life, as a newspaper columnist and editor as well as script, copy and speech writing for global company programmes, conferences, press and product launches and major events.

Tony lives in Wiltshire with his beloved wife, Sarah.

Acknowledgements

from Anthony Silman

"I must thank Caroline, as always, for her brilliant editing and wise words of guidance and advice.

I thank Karolina for yet another outstanding cover design and I thank Keith and Michael Terence Publishing (MTP) for continued and much appreciated support.

And I owe my wonderful wife, Sarah, the most gratitude for her encouragement and tolerance of my frequent disappearances into the fictional world of Max, Olderbury and Onetelcall.

Finally, may I thank you for reading my words, I hope they give you pleasure."

Printed in Great Britain
by Amazon

54874130R00162